AVERAGE JONES

SAMUEL HOPKINS ADAMS

Edited, with an introduction and notes,
by Leslie S. Klinger

LIBRARY LIBRARY OF CONGRESS

Poisoned Pen PRESS

Published by Poisoned Pen Press, an imprint of Sourcebooks,
in association with the Library of Congress
P.O. Box 4410, Naperville, Illinois 60567-4410
(630) 961-3900
sourcebooks.com

This edition of *Average Jones* is based on the first edition in the Library
of Congress's collection, originally published in 1911 by the Bobbs-Merrill
Company. The illustrations by M. Leone Bracker are original to the book.

Library of Congress Cataloging-in-Publication Data

Names: Adams, Samuel Hopkins, author. | Klinger, Leslie S., editor.
Title: Average Jones / Samuel Hopkins Adams ; Edited, with an introduction
    and notes, by Leslie S. Klinger.
Description: Naperville, Illinois : Library of Congress/Poisoned Pen Press,
    [2022] | Series: Library of Congress Crime Classics | Includes
    bibliographical references.
Identifiers: LCCN 2021056037 (print) | LCCN 2021056038
(ebook) | (trade paperback) | (epub)
Classification: LCC PS3501.D317 A94 2022 (print) | LCC PS3501.D317
    (ebook) | DDC 813/.52--dc23/eng/20220118
LC record available at https://lccn.loc.gov/2021056037
LC ebook record available at https://lccn.loc.gov/2021056038

Printed and bound in the United States of America.
SB 10 9 8 7 6 5 4 3 2 1

CONTENTS

FOREWORD

Crime writing as we know it first appeared in 1841, with the publication of "The Murders in the Rue Morgue." Written by American author Edgar Allan Poe, the short story introduced C. Auguste Dupin, the world's first wholly fictional detective. Other American and British authors had begun working in the genre by the 1860s, and by the 1920s we had officially entered the golden age of detective fiction.

Throughout this short history, many authors who paved the way have been lost or forgotten. Library of Congress Crime Classics bring back into print some of the finest American crime writing from the 1860s to the 1960s, showcasing rare and lesser-known titles that represent a range of genres, from cozies to police procedurals. With cover designs inspired by images from the Library's collections, each book in this series includes the original text, reproduced faithfully from an early edition in the Library's collections and complete with strange spellings and unorthodox punctuation. Also included are a contextual introduction, a brief biography of the author, notes, recommendations for further reading, and suggested discussion questions. Our hope is for these books to start conversations, inspire further research, and bring obscure works to a new generation of readers.

Early American crime fiction is not only entertaining to read, but it also sheds light on the culture of its time. While many of the titles in this series include outmoded language and stereotypes now considered offensive, these books give readers the opportunity to reflect on how our society's perceptions of race, gender, ethnicity, and social standing have evolved over more than a century.

More dark secrets and bloody deeds lurk in the massive collections of the Library of Congress. I encourage you to explore these works for yourself, here in Washington, DC, or online at www.loc.gov.

—Carla D. Hayden, Librarian of Congress

INTRODUCTION

The enormous success of Arthur Conan Doyle's Sherlock Holmes stories led to dozens of English and American writers seeking to create imitations of the Great Detective, with Holmes's reported death in 1893[*] encouraging many to fill the vacuum. Most, however, lacked originality or skill,[†] and few of the Holmes copies are remembered today. In America, however, a different kind of detective was also developing—a detective immersed in social and political issues of the day. This was perhaps the natural result of the growing list of journalists who began writing fiction, including Willa Cather, Stephen Crane, Richard Harding Davis, Theodore Dreiser, William Dean Howells, Jack London, and, of course, Mark Twain. An unexpected addition to that corps was Samuel Hopkins Adams (1871–1958). In the first few years of the

---

[*] Arthur Conan Doyle, "The Final Problem," *The Memoirs of Sherlock Holmes* (London: George Newnes, 1894), 256–79.

[†] One notable exception was fictional criminologist Craig Kennedy, "the American Sherlock Holmes," who first appeared in Arthur B. Reeve's *The Silent Bullet* and who was highly popular for a few decades. However, as discussed in the introduction to the Library of Congress Crime Classics edition of *The Silent Bullet*, Kennedy is virtually forgotten today.

twentieth century, Adams distinguished himself as a "muck-raking" journalist, taking on the patent medicine industry in a series of articles. He was also critical of the government's failure to enforce the newly enacted Pure Food and Drug Act and wrote extensively about medicine, public health, and false advertising. By the middle of the decade, however, Adams began to write short stories, many of which had a crusading element.

Adams was already an experienced crime writer—he wrote thirty-eight bylined stories on the sensational 1907 trial of playboy Harry Kendall Thaw for the murder of the prominent architect Stanford White—and decided to try his hand at detective fiction.* He chose as his protagonist an American version of a British aristocrat (in some ways, an early Lord Peter Wimsey, the detective created by Dorothy Sayers in 1923 in her novel *Whose Body?*), a very wealthy young man named Adrian Van Reypen Egerton Jones, known wittily as "Average" Jones. Jones decides on detection as a hobby—he has no need of income—because everyone else in his favorite club, the Cosmic Club, has a unique pastime. He chooses a specialized form of detection, finding his investigative leads among the "agony columns"—the romantic, often bizarre personal and commercial advertisements that populated the pages of many American newspapers. These ranged from the despairing† to the tantalizing‡ to the

---

* Adams had actually written a few undistinguished mystery short stories previously, but none featured a detective, and his novels, *The Mystery* (1907, cowritten with Stewart Edward Wright) and *The Flying Death* (1908), were more adventure stories than mysteries.

---

† "GOOD HOME wanted for two sisters: aged 11 and 6, in an influential family. Address SISTERS, Box 14, Eagle office." *Brooklyn Daily Eagle*, February 2, 1910.

---

‡ "Wanted: Men in every town and city to sell our latest specialty; no talking needed; sells on sight. For full particulars, address The North Shore Specialty Co., Salem, Mass." *New York Tribune*, February 1, 1910.

ridiculous.* Of course, for Adams, this was a natural tie-in with his intense interest in false advertising.

With his lead character in mind, Adams looked for a market for a series of stories. Having written previously for *McClure's*, *Collier's*, *Everybody's*, and *American* magazines, he approached his former *Collier's* colleague Sam Merwin, who had begun publishing fiction in *Success* magazine. *Success*, founded by Orison Swett Marden† in 1891, was originally subtitled "A monthly journal of inspiration, progress, and self-help" and was devoted to articles about successful men. By the end of the first decade of the twentieth century, however, Marden sought to expand the readership by publishing commentary on public affairs as well as fiction. Zane Grey was one of the first authors to contribute fiction, with several stories appearing in late 1910.

The result was the publication of ten stories by Adams between April 1910 and April 1911 featuring Jones.‡ The stories were regarded well enough for Adams to take them to a book publisher. The publisher of his first two novels, McClure, had gone out of business, but he managed to interest the venerable Indiana-based

---

* "Run Down Nervous System. Mr. H. F. Corcoran When on the Verge of Collapse Took Duffy's Pure Malt Whiskey and Now He Feels Like a New Man… It is recognized as a family medicine everywhere. It is invaluable for overworked men, delicate women and sickly children." This "infomercial" appeared in *The Sun*, where Adams launched his journalistic career in New York, on February 1, 1910.

---

† Marden, a vital member of the New Thought Movement—which itself dates to the teachings of mesmerist and healer Phineas Quimby (1802–1866)—is regarded as the father of the American self-help movement.

---

‡ One of the ten, "The Million Dollar Dog," was originally written featuring a different detective, Everett King (not so coincidentally, also a member of the Cosmic Club), and appeared in the *Red Book Magazine* in March 1911. Perhaps Adams thought its semi-romantic tale was unsuited for *Success*, where the Jones stories had all appeared. But when he sold the collection of Jones stories to a book publisher, Adams included this story, changing the detective's name and a few other small points and converting it to a coda to Jones's career. He also slightly edited the other stories to add cross-references and arranged them in an order different from the magazine publications to form more of an arc.

Bobbs-Merrill Company. Bobbs-Merrill had already achieved success with crime fiction, publishing many of the later novels of Anna Katharine Green (hailed as the "mother of American crime fiction") as well as Mary Roberts Rinehart (the first American mystery writer to achieve lasting fame after Green). *Average Jones* appeared in 1911, a year that Ellery Queen later dubbed the beginning of the second golden era of crime fiction.[*]

According to the anonymous author of the dust jacket on the first edition, Average Jones was "the cleverest detective since Sherlock Holmes. Everything about the book is refreshingly original. Humor is as strong as mystery. Adventure is emphasized above sensation. Instead of the ghastly and the grewsome, here is an entertainment always gay, brisk, and fascinating." "The blurb-writer was over-enthusiastic," remarked Ellery Queen, "yet more accurate than most of his craft."[+] The book did well commercially too. While it did not make the *Bookman*'s monthly list of the top six books in sales, it sold more than five thousand copies.[‡]

In fact, Adams's stories combine elements never before seen in detective fiction. The dialogue is topical and clever, the conundrums zany (a falling asteroid, a man who speaks only Latin, a strolling trombone player), the diction facetious. Jones, who styles himself an "Ad-Visor," deceptively appears to be a young

---

[*] Howard Haycraft also called 1911 one of the "mile-posts in the history of detective literature," noting that it was the beginning of the decade that saw the creation of both G. K. Chesterton's Father Brown (*The Innocence of Father Brown*, 1911) and Melville Davisson Post's Uncle Abner (*Uncle Abner, Master of Mysteries*, 1918). Howard Haycraft, *Murder for Pleasure: The Life and Times of the Detective Story* (London: Peter Davies, 1942), 93.

[+] *Queen's Quorum: A History of the Detective-Crime Short Story as Revealed by the 106 Most Important Books Published in this Field since 1845* (Boston: Little, Brown, 1951), 61.

[‡] According to Samuel V. Kennedy III, however, the book failed to earn Adams more than his $1,500 advance. *Samuel Hopkins Adams and the Business of Writing* (Syracuse, NY: Syracuse University Press, 1999), 74.

man bored with life. There are numerous allusions to college life, and a clubby atmosphere prevails. The brilliant Jones is contrasted with his occasional sidekick, a semicomical idler, Robert Bertram, who is far from the model of the redoubtable Dr. Watson.[*] These features would appear soon enough in the writings of P. G. Wodehouse, and a decade later they would populate the crime fiction of Margery Allingham and Dorothy Sayers. While some of Adams's tales involve serious muckraking, with corrupt politicians, quack patent medicine, and the meatpacking industry, most are concerned with personal issues, which do not have serious consequences. Murder is actually committed in only one of the ten stories.[†]

The Jones tales are remarkable forerunners of the golden age that was to follow. LeRoy Lad Panek observed, in *Probable Cause: Crime Fiction in America*: "Almost ten years before they appeared in England, Adams assembled the parts of the Golden Age story: witty dialogue, disparate facts, the truly sophisticated amateur, the emphasis on thinking without a lot of mumbo jumbo, all focused on a case that has few mortal consequences. It may be, then, that the Golden Age detective formula is yet another product that can be labeled Made in America."[‡]

The stories are also delightful. Howard Haycraft, one of the great historians of the mystery field, lamented in 1942, "The tales [are] well above the level of their era, both in conception and style, and it is a source of perennial regret that this excellent storyteller has shown no inclination to revive his attractive hero."[§]

---

[*] Curiously, the Basil Rathbone/Nigel Bruce portrayals of Holmes and Watson on film are closer to Adams's mold than to the original Doyle stories.

[†] Three, if canine homicide is included.

[‡] LeRoy Lad Panek, *Probable Cause: Crime Fiction in America* (Bowling Green, OH: Bowling Green State University Popular Press, 1990), 83.

[§] Haycraft, *Murder for Pleasure*, 101–2.

Adams wrote for many more years (his last work appearing in 1959),* but sadly, Average Jones was not to return.

—Leslie S. Klinger

---

* *Tenderloin* (New York: Random House) was published posthumously in 1959.

CHAPTER I
THE B-FLAT TROMBONE

Three men sat in the Cosmic Club* discussing the question: "What's the matter with Jones?" Waldemar, the oldest of the conferees, was the owner, and at times the operator, of an important and decent newspaper. His heavy face wore the expression of good-humored power, characteristic of the experienced and successful journalist. Beside him sat Robert Bertram, the club idler, slender and languidly elegant. The third member of the conference was Jones himself.

Average Jones had come by his nickname inevitably. His parents had foredoomed him to it when they furnished him with the initials A. V. R. E. as preface to his birthright of J for Jones. His character apparently justified the chance concomitance. He was, so to speak, a composite photograph of any thousand well-conditioned, clean-living Americans between the ages of twenty-five and thirty. Happily, his otherwise commonplace face was relieved by the one unfailing characteristic of composite

---

* The name may well have been intended as a joke. There was a Cosmos Club formed in New York in 1909, for governesses; it changed its name to the Women's Cosmopolitan Club in 1910 and broadened its membership to all women interested in the liberal arts or professions. In 1915, the club dropped "Women's" from its name, and it continues to thrive today (with a membership still restricted to women).

photographs, large, deep-set and thoughtful eyes. Otherwise he would have passed in any crowd, and nobody would have noticed him pass. Now, at twenty-seven, he looked back over the five years since his graduation from college and wondered what he had done with them; and at the four previous years of undergraduate life and wondered how he had done so well with those and why he had not in some manner justified the parting words of his favorite professor.

"You have one rare faculty, Jones. You can, when you choose, sharpen the pencil of your mind to a very fine point. Specialize, my boy, specialize."

If the recipient of this admonition had specialized in anything, it was in life. Having twenty-five thousand a year of his own* he might have continued in that path indefinitely, but for two influences. One was an irruptive craving within him to take some part in the dynamic activities of the surrounding world. The other was the "freak" will of his late and little-lamented uncle, from whom he had his present income, and his future expectations of some ten millions. Adrian Van Reypen Egerton had, as Waldemar once put it, "gone into the mayor's chair with a good name and come out with a block of ice stock." In a will whose cynical humor was the topic of its day, Mr. Egerton jeered posthumously at the public which he had despoiled, and promised restitution, of a sort, through his heir.

"Therefore," he had written, "I give and bequeath to the said Adrian Van Reypen Egerton Jones, the residue of my property, the principal to be taken over by him at such time as he shall have completed five years of continuous residence in New York

---

* In terms of relative income comparisons, this is well over $3.5 million per year in 2021 dollars. Samuel H. Williamson, "Seven Ways to Compute the Relative Value of a U.S. Dollar Amount, 1790 to present," Measuring Worth, 2021, http://www .measuringworth.com.

City. After such time the virus of the metropolis will have worked through his entire being. He will squander his unearned and undeserved fortune, thus completing the vicious circle, and returning the millions acquired by my political activities, in a poisoned shower upon the city, for which, having bossed, bullied and looted it, I feel no sentiment other than contempt."

"And now," remarked Waldemar in his heavy, rumbling voice, "you aspire to disappoint that good old man."

"It's only human nature, you know," said Average Jones. "When a man puts a ten-million-dollar curse on you and suggests that you haven't the backbone of a shrimp, you—you—"

"—naturally yearn to prove him a liar," supplied Bertram.

"Exactly. Anyway, I've no taste for dissipation, either moral or financial. I want action; something to do. I'm bored, in this infernal city."

"The wail of the unslaked romanticist," commented Bertram.

"Romanticist nothing!" protested the other. "My ambitions are practical enough if I could only get 'em stirred up."

"Exactly. Boredom is simply romanticism with a morning-after thirst. You're panting for romance, for something bizarre. Egypt and St. Petersburg and Buenos Ayres and Samoa have all become commonplace to you. You've overdone them. That's why you're back here in New York waiting with stretched nerves for the Adventure of Life to cat-creep up from behind and toss the lariat of rainbow dreams over your shoulders."

Waldemar laughed. "Not a bad diagnosis. Why don't you take up a hobby, Mr. Jones?"

"What kind of a hobby?"

"Any kind. The club is full of hobby-riders. Of all people that I know, they have the keenest appetite for life. Look at old Denechaud; he was a misanthrope until he took to gathering scarabs. Fenton, over there, has the finest collection of circus posters in the world. Bellerding's house is a museum of obsolete musical instruments. De Gay collects venomous insects from all over the world; no harmless ones need apply. Terriberry has a mania for old railroad tickets. Some are really very curious. I've often wished I had the time to be a crank. It's a happy life."

"What line would you choose?" asked Bertram languidly.

"Nobody has gone in for queer advertisements yet, I believe," replied the older man. "If one could take the time to follow them up—but it would mean all one's leisure."

"Would it be so demanding a career?" said Average Jones, smiling.

"Decidedly. I once knew a man who gave away twenty dollars daily on clues from the day's news. *He* wasn't bored for lack of occupation."

"But the ordinary run of advertising is nothing more than an effort to sell something by yelling in print," objected Average Jones.

"Is it? Well perhaps you don't look in the right place."

Waldemar reached for the morning's copy of the *Universal* and ran his eye down the columns of "classified" matter. "Hark to this," he said, and read:

"Is there any work on God's green earth for a man who has just *got* to have it?"

"Or this:

"WANTED—A venerable looking man with white beard and medical degree. Good pay to right applicant."

"What's that?" asked Average Jones with awakened interest.

"Only a quack medical concern looking for a 'stall' to impress their 'come-ons,'" explained Waldemar.

Average Jones leaned over to scan the paper in his turn.

"Here's one," said he, and read:

"WANTED—Performer on B-flat trombone.* Can use at once. Apply with instrument, after 1 p.m. 300 East 100th Street."

"That seems ordinary enough," said Waldemar.

"What's it doing in a daily paper? There must be—er—technical publications—er—journals, you know, for this sort of demand."

"When Average's words come slow, you've got him interested," commented Bertram. "Sure sign."

"Nevertheless, he's right," said Waldemar. "It is rather misplaced."

"How is this for one that says what it means?" said Bertram.

"WANTED—At once, a brass howitzer† and a man who isn't afraid to handle it. Mrs. Anne Cullen, Pier 49½ East River."

---

* Properly the contrabass trombone, a musical wind instrument dating back to the Renaissance. In the early nineteenth century, it was pitched in the scale of F-flat, but with the introduction of the double-slide at the end of the nineteenth century, B-flat became the preferred mode. In 1921, a new model was developed with two rotary valves, pitched in F, and that instrument predominates today. There are a few operatic compositions still in the common repertory that require a B-flat trombone.

---

† A short-barreled, muzzle-loading cannon-like weapon.

"The woman who is fighting the barge combine,"* explained Waldemar. "Not so good as it looks. She's bluffing."

"Anyway, I'd like a shy† at this business," declared Average Jones with sudden conviction. "It looks to me like something to do."

"Make it a business, then," advised Waldemar. "If you care really to go in for it, my newspaper would be glad to pay for information such as you might collect. We haven't time, for example, to trace down fraudulent advertisers. If you could start an enterprise of that sort, you'd certainly find it amusing, and, at times, perhaps, even adventurous."

"I wouldn't know how to establish it," objected Average Jones.

The newspaper owner drew a rough diagram on a sheet of paper and filled it in with writing, crossing out and revising liberally. Divided, upon his pattern, into lines, the final draft read:

---

* A combination of persons or businesses protecting their own common commercial interests. In 1890, Congress passed the Sherman Act, prohibiting "every contract, combination in the form of trust or otherwise, or conspiracy in restraint of trade." Soon thereafter, the Supreme Court decided that the Sherman Act did not prohibit *every* restraint of trade, only those that are *unreasonable*. A "combine" was not illegal per se, unless it engaged in illegal acts such as price fixing or bid rigging to force competitors out of the marketplace.

---

† According to J. S. Farmer and W. E. Henley's *Historical Dictionary of Slang* (first published in 1890 as *Slang and Its Analogues*), "a piece of the action: as a throw, a chance, an attempt." The phrase is found as early as 1824 in Pierce Egan's *Boxiana*.

Have You Been Stung?

Thousands have.
Thousands will be.
They're Laying for You.
Who?
The Advertising Crooks.

A. Jones
Ad-Visor

Can Protect You Against Them.

Before Spending Your Money Call on Him. Advice on all Subjects Connected with Newspaper, Magazine or Display Advertising. Free Consultation to Persons Unable to Pay. Call or Write, Enclosing Postage. *This Is On The Level.*

Jones, Ad-Visor.

"Ad-Visor! Do you expect me to blight my budding career by a poisonous pun like that?" demanded Average Jones with a wry face.

"It may be a poisonous pun, but it's an arresting catch-word," said Waldemar, unmoved. "Single column, about fifty lines will do it in nice, open style. Caps and lower case, and black-faced type for the name and title. Insert twice a week in every New York and Brooklyn paper."

"Isn't it—er—a little blatant?" suggested Bertram, with lifted eyebrows.

"Blatant?" repeated its inventor. "It's more than that. It's howlingly vulgar. It's a riot of glaring yellow.* How else would you expect to catch the public?"

"Suppose, then, I do burst into flame to this effect?" queried the prospective "Ad-Visor." "*Et après?*† as we proudly say after spending a week in Paris."

"*Aprés?* Oh, plenty of things. You hire an office, a clerk, two stenographers and a clipping expert, and prepare to take care of the work that comes in. You'll be flooded," promised Waldemar.

"And between times I'm to go skipping about, chasing long white whiskers and brass howitzers and B-flat trombones, I suppose."

"Until you get your work systematized you'll have no time for skipping. Within six months, if you're not sandbagged or jailed on fake libel suits, you'll have a unique bibliography of swindles. Then I'll begin to come and buy your knowledge to keep my own columns clean."

The speaker looked up to meet the gaze of an iron-gray man with a harsh, sallow face.

---

* "Yellow journalism" indulged in lurid or highly speculative sensationalism.

---

† Literally, "and after?" meaning "what next?"

"Excuse my interrupting," said the new-comer. "Just one question, Waldemar. Who's going to be the nominee?"*

"Linder."

"Linder? Surely not! Why, his name hasn't been heard."

"It will be."

"His Federal job?"

"He resigns in two weeks."

"His record will kill him."

"What record? You and I know he's a grafter. But can we prove anything? His clerk has always handled all the money."

"Wasn't there an old scandal—a woman case?" asked the questioner vaguely.

"That Washington man's wife? Too old. Linder would deny it flatly, and there would be no witnesses. The woman is dead— killed by his brutal treatment of her, they say. But the whole thing was hushed up at the time by Linder's pull, and when the husband threatened to kill him Linder quietly set a commissioner of insanity† on the case and had the man put away. He's never appeared since. No, that wouldn't be politically effective."

The gray man nodded, and walked away, musing.

"Egbert, the traction boss,"‡ explained Waldemar. "We're generally on opposite sides, but this time we're both against Linder. Egbert wants a cheaper man for mayor. I want a straighter one.

---

* In 1909, corruption was indirectly an issue on the ballot. Tammany Hall (the group of power brokers who ran New York politics) backed William J. Gaynor for mayor of New York City, expecting to continue the reign of dirty dealings that had epitomized city politics for decades. However, Gaynor was a great disappointment to them, backing reforms and refusing to make appointments of unqualified but politically connected individuals. Before running for mayor, he was a strong-minded judge, serving for sixteen years on the bench. Gaynor defeated William Randolph Hearst, the prominent publisher and businessman, who had run previously in 1905.

† A judicial officer appointed to determine a person's legal competency or sanity.

‡ That is, the head of the "traction" combine—traction referring to the companies that operated streetcars.

And I could get him this year if Linder wasn't so well fortified. However, to get back to our project, Mr. Jones—"

Get back to it they did with such absorption that when the group broke up, several hours later, Average Jones was committed, by plan and rote, to the new and hopeful Adventure of Life.

In the great human hunt which ever has been and ever shall be till "the last bird flies into the last light"—some call it business, some call it art, some call it love, and a very few know it for what it is, the very mainspring of existence—the path of the pursuer and the prey often run obscurely parallel. What time the Honorable William Linder matured his designs on the mayoralty, Average Jones sat in a suite of offices in Astor Court,[*] a location which Waldemar had advised as being central, expensive, and inspirational of confidence, and considered, with a whirling brain, the minor woes of humanity. Other people's troubles had swarmed down upon him in answer to his advertised offer of help, as sparrows flock to scattered bread crumbs. Mostly these were of the lesser order of difficulties; but for what he gave in advice and help the Ad-Visor took payment in experience and knowledge of human nature. Still it was the hard, honest study, and the helpful toil which held him to his task, rather than the romance and adventure which he had hoped for and Waldemar had foretold—until, in a quiet street in Brooklyn, of which he had never so much as heard, there befell that which, first of many events, justified the prophetic Waldemar and gave Average Jones a part in the greater drama of the metropolis. The party of the second part was the Honorable William Linder.

Mr. Linder sat at five P. M., of an early summer day, behind lock and bolt. The third floor front room of his ornate mansion

---

[*] A building on Broadway between Eighty-Ninth and Ninetieth Streets, on the Upper West Side of Manhattan. The Astor Court Building opened in 1916, constructed for developer Vincent Astor. However, it is an apartment building, not mixed use.

on Brooklyn's Park Slope* was dedicated to peaceful thought. Sprawled in a huge and softly upholstered chair at the window, he took his ease in his house. The chair had been a recent gift from an anonymous admirer whose political necessities, the Honorable Mr. Linder idly surmised, had not yet driven him to reveal his identity. Its occupant stretched his shoeless feet, as was his custom, upon the broad window-sill, flooded by the seasonable warmth of sunshine, the while he considered the ripening mayoralty situation. He found it highly satisfactory. In the language of his inner man, it was a cinch.

Below, in Kennard Street,† a solitary musician plodded. His pretzel-shaped brass rested against his shoulder. He appeared to be the "scout" of one of those prevalent and melancholious German bands,‡ which, under Brooklyn's easy ordinances, are privileged to draw echoes of the past writhing from their forgotten recesses. The man looked slowly about him as if apprising potential returns. His gravid glance encountered the prominent feet in the third-story window of the Linder mansion, and rested. He moved forward. Opposite the window he paused. He raised the mouthpiece to his lips and embarked on a perilous sea of notes from which the tutored ear might have inferred that once popular ditty, *Egypt*.

Love of music was not one of the Honorable William Linder's attributes. An irascible temper was. Of all instruments the B-flat

---

* Located on the western slope of Prospect Park, this northwestern neighborhood of Brooklyn, in the area once known as South Brooklyn, was upscale, with large Victorian mansions built in the 1880s and 1890s. It remains a desirable neighborhood in Brooklyn.

---

† A fictional street.

---

‡ According to the *Encyclopedia of New York City* (New Haven, CT: Yale University Press, 1995), the German population of New York peaked in 1900 at almost 750,000 people, more than 20 percent of the city's residents. Beer halls, and the brass bands that played there, were plentiful.

trombone possesses the most nerve-jarring tone. The master of the mansion leaped from his restful chair. Where his feet had ornamented the coping his face now appeared. Far out he leaned, and roared at the musician below. The brass throat blared back at him, while the soloist, his eyes closed in the ecstasy of art, brought the "verse" part of his selection to an excruciating conclusion, half a tone below pitch. Before the chorus there was a brief pause for effect. In this pause, from Mr. Linder's open face a voice fell like a falling star. Although it did not cry "Excelsior," its output of vocables might have been mistaken, by a casual ear, for that clarion call. What the Honorable Mr. Linder actually shouted was:

"Gettahelloutothere!"

The performer upturned a mild and vacant face.

"Vhat you say?" he inquired in a softly Teutonic accent.

The Honorable William Linder made urgent gestures, like a brakeman.

"Go away! Move on!"

The musician smiled reassuringly.

"I got already paid for this," he explained.

Up went the brass to his lips again. The tonal stairway which leads up to the chorus of *Egypt* rose in rasping wailfulness. It culminated in an excessive, unendurable, brazen shriek—and the Honorable William Linder experienced upon the undefended rear of his person the most violent kick of a lifetime not always devoted to the arts of peace. It projected him clear of the window-sill. His last sensible vision was the face of the musician, the mouth absurdly hollow and pursed above the suddenly removed mouthpiece. Then an awning intercepted the politician's flight. He passed through this, penetrated a second and similar stretch of canvas shading the next window below, and lay placid on his own front steps with three ribs caved in and a variegated fracture of the collar-bone. By the time the descent was ended the German musician had tucked his brass under his arm and was hurrying, in panic, down the street, his ears still ringing with the concussion which had blown the angry householder from his own front window. He was intercepted by a running policeman.

"Where was the explosion?" demanded the officer.

"Explosion? I hear a noise in the larch house on the corner," replied the musician dully.

The policeman grabbed his arm. "Come along back. You fer a witness! Come on; you an' yer horn."

"It iss not a horn," explained the German patiently, "it iss a B-flat trombone."

Along with several million other readers, Average Jones followed the Linder "bomb outrage" through the scandalized head-lines of the local press. The perpetrator, declared the excited journals, had been skillful. No clue was left. The explosion had taken care of that. The police (with the characteristic stupidity of a corps of former truck-drivers and bartenders, decorated with brass buttons and shields and without further qualification dubbed "detectives")* vacillated from theory to theory. Their putty-and-pasteboard fantasies did not long survive the Honorable William Linder's return to consciousness and coherence. An "inside job," they had said. The door was locked and bolted, Mr. Linder declared, and there was no possible place for an intruder to conceal himself. Clock-work, then.

"How would any human being guess what time to set it for," demanded the politician in disgust, "when I never know, myself, where I'm going to be at any given hour of any given day?"

---

* New York City was one of the first cities in America to create a professional police force. However, officers of the NYPD, including its detectives, often had lucrative arrangements with the business elite as well as the purveyors of vice. In 1895, Theodore Roosevelt became president of the NYPD Police Commission, and while he instituted many reforms aimed at professionalization, change was slow.

"Then that Dutch horn-player threw the bomb," propounded the head of the "Detective Bureau" ponderously.

"Of course; tossed it right up, three stories, and kept playing his infernal trombone with the other hand all the time. You ought to be carrying a hod!"[*]

Nevertheless, the police hung tenaciously to the theory that the musician was involved, chiefly because they had nothing else to hang to. The explosion had been very localized, the room not generally wrecked; but the chair which seemed to be the center of disturbance, and from which the Honorable William Linder had risen just in time to save his life, was blown to pieces, and a portion of the floor beneath it was much shattered. The force of the explosion had been from above the floor downward; not up through the flooring. As to murderously inclined foes, Mr. Linder disclaimed knowledge of any. The notion that the trombonist had given a signal he derided as an "Old Sleuth pipe-dream."[+]

As time went on and "clues" came to nothing, the police had no greater concern than quietly to forget, according to custom, a problem beyond their limited powers. With the release of the German musician, who was found to be simple-minded to the verge of half-wittedness, public interest waned, and the case faded out of current print.

Average Jones, who was much occupied with a pair of blackmailers operating through faked photographs, about that time, had almost forgotten the Linder case, when, one day, a month after the explosion, Waldemar dropped in at the Astor Court offices. He found a changed Jones; much thinner and "finer" than when, eight weeks before, he had embarked on his new career, at the newspaper owner's instance. The young man's color was

---

[*] A hod carrier carried bricks and mortar on worksites, a task that required no intellect.

[+] "Old Sleuth" was the popular detective of dozens of dime novels, primarily written by Harlan Halsey but credited as the actual accounts of Old Sleuth himself.

less pronounced, and his eyes, though alert and eager, showed rings under them.

"You have found the work interesting, I take it," remarked the visitor.

"Ra-ather," drawled Average Jones appreciatively.

"That was a good initial effort, running down the opium pill mail-order enterprise."

"It was simple enough as soon as I saw the catch-word in the 'Wanted' line."

"Anything is easy to a man who sees," returned the older man sententiously. "The open eye of the open mind—that has more to do with real detective work than all the deduction and induction and analysis ever devised."

"It is the detective part that interests me most in the game, but I haven't had much of it, yet. You haven't run across any promising ads lately, have you?"

Waldemar's wide, florid brow wrinkled.

"I haven't thought or dreamed of anything for a month but this infernal bomb explosion."

"Oh, the Linder case. You're personally interested?"

"Politically. It makes Linder's nomination certain. Persecution. Attempted assassination. He becomes a near-martyr. I'm almost ready to believe that he planted a fake bomb himself."

"And fell out of a third-story window to carry out the idea? That's pushing realism rather far, isn't it?"

Waldemar laughed. "There's the weakness. Unless we suppose that he under-reckoned the charge of explosive."

"They let the musician go, didn't they?"

"Yes. There was absolutely no proof against him, except that he was in the street below. Besides, he seemed quite lacking mentally."

"Mightn't that have been a sham?"

"Alienists* of good standing examined him. They reported him just a shade better than half-witted. He was like a one-ideaed child, his whole being comprised in his ability and ambition to play his B-flat trombone."

"Well, if I needed an accomplice," said Average Jones thoughtfully, "I wouldn't want any better one than a half-witted man. Did he play well?"

"Atrociously. And if you know what a soul-shattering blare exudes from a B-flat trombone—" Mr. Waldemar lifted expressive hands.

Within Average Jones' overstocked mind something stirred at the repetition of the words "B-flat trombone." Somewhere they had attracted his notice in print; and somehow they were connected with Waldemar. Then from amidst the hundreds of advertisements with which, in the past weeks, he had crowded his brain, one stood out clear. It voiced the desire of an unknown gentleman on the near border of Harlem for the services of a performer upon that semi-exotic instrument. One among several, it had been cut from the columns of the *Universal*, on the evening which had launched him upon his new enterprise. Average Jones made two steps to a bookcase, took down a huge scrapbook from an alphabeticized row, and turned the leaves rapidly.

"Three Hundred East One Hundredth Street," said he, slamming the book shut again. "Three Hundred East One Hundredth. You won't mind, will you"—to Waldemar—"if I leave you unceremoniously?"

"Recalled a forgotten engagement?" asked the other, rising.

"Yes. No. I mean I'm going to Harlem to hear some music. Thirty-fourth's the nearest station, isn't it? Thanks. So long."

---

* A psychiatrist; initially, a person whose responsibility it was to determine legal sanity. The term was first used by the French in the mid-nineteenth century.

Waldemar rubbed his head thoughtfully as the door slammed behind the speeding Ad-Visor.

"Now, what kind of a tune is he on the track of, I wonder?" he mused. "I wish it hadn't struck him until I'd had time to go over the Linder business with him."

But while Waldemar rubbed his head in cogitatation and the Honorable William Linder, in his Brooklyn headquarters, breathed charily, out of respect to his creaking rib, Average Jones was following fate northward.

Three Hundred East One Hundredth Street is a house decrepit with a disease of the aged. Its windowed eyes are rheumy. It sags backward on gnarled joints. All its poor old bones creak when the winds shake it. To Average Jones' inquiring gaze on this summer day it opposed the secrecy of a senile indifference. He hesitated to pull at its bell-knob, lest by that act he should exert a disruptive force which might bring all the frail structure rattling down in ruin. When, at length, he forced himself to the summons, the merest ghost of a tinkle complained petulantly from within against his violence.

An old lady came to the door. She was sleek and placid, round and comfortable. She did not seem to belong in that house at all. Average Jones felt as if he had cracked open one of the grisly locust shells which cling lifelessly to tree trunks, and had found within a plump and prosperous beetle.

"Was an advertisement for a trombone player inserted from this house, ma'am?" he inquired.

"Long ago," said she.

"Am I too late, then?"

"Much. It was answered nearly two months since. I have never," said the old lady with conviction, "seen such a frazzled lot of folks as B-flat trombone players."

"The person who inserted the advertisement—"

"Has left. A month since."

"Could you tell where he went?"

"Left no address."

"His name was Telford, wasn't it?" said Average Jones strategically.

"Might be," said the old lady, who had evidently formed no favorable impression of her ex-lodger. "But he *called* himself Ransom."

"He had a furnished room?"

"The whole third floor, furnished."

"Is it let now?"

"Part of it. The rear."

"I'll take the front room."

"Without even looking at it?"

"Yes."

"You're a queer young man. As to price?"

"Whatever you choose."

"You're a *very* queer young man. Are you a B-flat trombone player?"

"I collect 'em," said Average Jones.

"References?" said the old lady abruptly and with suspicion.

"All varieties," replied her prospective lodger cheerfully. "I will bring 'em to-morrow with my grip."

For five successive evenings thereafter Average Jones sat in the senile house, awaiting personal response to the following advertisement which he had inserted in the *Universal:*

WANTED—B-flat trombonist. Must have had
experience as street player. Apply between 8 and
10 P. M. R—, 300 East 100th Street.

Between the ebb and flow of applicant musicians he read exhaustively upon the unallied subjects of trombones and high explosives, or talked with his landlady, who proved to be a sociable person, not disinclined to discuss the departed guest. "Ransom," his supplanter learned, had come light and gone light. Two dress-suit cases had sufficed to bring in all his belongings. He went out but little, and then, she opined with a disgustful sniff, for purposes strictly alcoholic. Parcels came for him occasionally. These were usually labeled "Glass. Handle with care." Oh! there was one other thing. A huge, easy arm-chair from Carruthers and Company, mighty luxurious for an eight-dollar lodger.

"Did he take that with him?" asked Average Jones.

"No. After he had been here a while he had a man come in and box it up. He must have sent it away, but I never saw it go."

"Was this before or after the trombone players came?"

"Long after. It was after he had picked out his man and had him up here practising."

"Did—er—you ever—er—see this musician?" drawled Average Jones in the slow tones of his peculiar excitement.

"Bless you, yes! Talked with him."

"What was he like?"

"He was a stupid old German. I always thought he was a sort of a natural."*

"Yes?" Average Jones peered out of the window. "Is this the man, coming up the street?"

"It surely is," said the old lady. "Now, *Mister* Jones, if he commences his blaring and blatting and—"

"There'll be no more music, ma'am," promised the young man, laughing, as she went out to answer the door-bell.

The musician, ushered in, looked about him, an expression of bewildered and childish surprise on his rabbit-like face.

---

* In this context, a person of low intelligence or learning ability.

"I am Schlichting," he murmured; "I come to play the B-flat trombone."

"Glad to see you, Mr. Schlichting," said Average Jones, leading the way up-stairs. "Sit down."

The visitor put his trombone down and shook his head with conviction.

"It iss the same room, yes," he observed. "But it iss not the same gent, no."

"You expected to find Mr. Ransom here?"

"I don't know Mr. Ransom. I know only to play the B-flat trombone."

"Mr. Ransom, the gentleman who employed you to play in the street in Brooklyn."

Mr. Schlichting made large and expansive gestures. "It iss a pleasure to play for such a gent," he said warmly. "Two dollars a day."

"You have played often in Kennard Street?"

"I don't know Kennard Street. I know only to play the B-flat trombone."

"Kennard Street. In Brooklyn. Where the fat gentleman told you to stop, and fell out of the window."

A look of fear overspread the worn and innocent face.

"I don't go there no more. The po-lice, they take me."

"But you had gone there before?"

"Not to play; no."

"Not to play? Are you sure?"

The German considered painfully. "There vass no feet in the window," he explained, brightening.

Upon that surprising phrase Average Jones pondered. "You were not to play unless there were feet in the window," he said at length. "Was that it?"

The musician assented.

"It *does* look like a signal to show that Linder was in," mused the interrogator. "Do you know Mr. Linder?"

"I don't know nothing only to play the B-flat trombone," repeated the other patiently.

"Now, Schlichting," said Average Jones, "here is a dollar. Every evening you must come here. Whether I am here or not, there will be a dollar for you. Do you understand?"

By way of answer the German reached down and lifted his instrument to his lips.

"No, not that," forbade Average Jones. "Put it down."

"Not to play my B-flat trombone?" asked the other, innocently hurt. "The other gent he make me play here always."

"Did he?" drawled Average Jones. "And he—er—listened?"

"He listened from out there." The musician pointed to the other room.

"How long?"

"Different times," was the placid reply.

"But he was always in the other room?"

"Always. And I play *Egypt*. Like this."

"No!" said Average Jones, as the other stretched out a hopeful hand.

"He liked it—*Egypt*," said the German wistfully. "He said: 'Bravo! *Encore! Bis!*' Sometimes nine, sometimes ten times over I play it, the chorus."

"And then he sent you home?"

"Then sometimes something goes 'spring-g-g-g-g!' like that in the back room. Then he comes out and I may go home."

"Um—m," muttered Average Jones discontentedly. "When did you begin to play in the street?"

"After a long time. He take me away to Brooklyn and tell me, 'When you see the feet iss in the window you play hard!'"

There was a long pause. Then Average Jones asked casually:

"Did you ever notice a big easy chair here?"

"I do not notice nothing. I play my B-flat trombone."

And there his limitations were established. But the old lady had something to add.

"It's all true that he said," she confirmed. "I could hear his racket in the front room and Mr. Ransom working in the back and then, after the old man was gone, Mr. Ransom sweeping up something by himself."

"Sweeping? What—er—was he—er—sweeping?"

"Glass, I think. The girl used to find little slivers of it first in one part of the room, then in another. I raised the rent for that and for the racket."

"The next thing," said Average Jones, "is to find out where that big easy chair went from here. Can you help me there?"

The old lady shook her head. "All I can do is to tell you the near-by truckmen."

Canvass of the local trucking industry brought to light the conveyor of that elegant article of furniture. It had gone, Average Jones learned, not to the mansion of the Honorable William Linder, as he had fondly hoped, but to an obscure address not far from the Navy Yard in Brooklyn. To this address, having looked up and gathered in the B-flat trombonist, Average Jones led the way. The pair lurked in the neighborhood of the ramshackle house watching the entrance, until toward evening, as the door opened to let out a tremulous wreck of a man, palsied with debauch, Schlichting observed:

"That iss him. He hass been drinking again once."

Average Jones hurried the musician around the corner into concealment. "You have been here before to meet Mr. Ransom?"

"No."

"Where did he meet you to pay you your wages?"

"On some corner," said the other vaguely.

"Then he took you to the big house and left you there," urged Jones.

"No; he left me on the street corner. 'When the feet iss in the window,' he says, 'you play.'"

"It comes to this," drawled Average Jones intently, looking the employee between his vacuous eyes. "Ransom shipped the chair to Plymouth Street and from there to Linder's house. He figured out that Linder would put it in his study and do his sitting at the window in it. And you were to know when he was there by seeing his feet in the window, and give the signal when you saw him. It must have been a signal to somebody pretty far off, or he wouldn't have chosen so loud an instrument as a B-flat trombone."

"I can play the B-flat trombone louder as any man in the business," asserted Schlichting with proud conviction.

"But what gets me," pursued Average Jones, "is the purpose of the signal. Whom was it for?"

"I don't know nothing," said the other complacently. "I only know to play the B-flat trombone louder as any man in the world."

Average Jones paid him a lump sum, dismissed him and returned to the Cosmic Club, there to ponder the problem, What next? To accuse Ransom, the mysterious hirer of a B-flat trombone virtuosity, without sufficient proof upon which to base even a claim of cross-examination, would be to block his own game then and there, for Ransom could, and very likely would, go away, leaving no trace. Who was Ransom, anyway? And what relation, if any, did he bear to Linder?

Absorbed in these considerations, he failed to notice that the club was filling up beyond its wont. A hand fell on his shoulder.

"Hello, Average. Haven't seen you at a Saturday special night since you started your hobby."

It was Bertram. "What's on?" Average Jones asked him, shaking hands.

"Freak concert. Bellerding has trotted out part of his collection of mediæval musical instruments, and some professionals are going to play them. Waldemar is at our table. Come and join us."

Conversation at the round-table was general and lively that evening, and not until the port came on—the prideful club port, served only on special occasions and in wonderful, delicate glasses—did Average Jones get an opportunity to speak to Waldemar aside.

"I've been looking into that Linder matter a little."

"Indeed. I've about given up hope."

"You spoke of an old scandal in Linder's career. What was the husband's name?"

"Arbuthnot, I believe."

"Do you know what sort of looking man he was?"

"No. I could find out from Washington."

"What was his business?"

"Government employment, I think."

"In the—er—scientific line, perhaps?" drawled Jones.

"Why, yes, I believe it was."

"Um—m. Suppose, now, Linder should drop out of the combination. Who would be the most likely nominee?"

"Marsden—the man I've been grooming for the place. A first-class, honorable, fearless man."

"Well, it's only a chance; but if I can get one dark point cleared up—"

He paused as a curious, tingling note came from the platform where the musicians were tuning up.

"One of Bellerding's sweet dulcets," observed Bertram.

The performer nearest them was running a slow bass scale on a sort of two-stringed horse-fiddle of a strange shape. Average Jones' still untouched glass, almost full of the precious port, trembled and sang a little tentative response. Up—up—up mounted the thrilling notes, in crescendo force.

"What a racking sort of tone, for all its sweetness!" said Average Jones. His delicate and fragile port glass evidently shared the opinion, for, without further warning, it split and shivered.

"They used to show that experiment in the laboratory," said Bertram. "You must have had just the accurate amount of liquid in the glass, Average. Move back, you lunatic, it's dripping all over you."

But Average Jones sat unheeding. The liquor dribbled down into his lap. He kept his fascinated gaze fixed on the shattered glass. Bertram dabbed at him with a napkin.

"Tha—a—anks, Bertram," drawled the beneficiary of this attention. "Doesn't matter. Excuse me. Good night."

Leaving his surprised companions, he took hat and cane and caught a Third Avenue car. By the time he had reached Brooklyn Bridge he had his campaign mapped out. It all depended upon the opening question. Average Jones decided to hit out and hit quick.

At the house near the Navy Yard he learned that his man was out. So he sat upon the front steps while one of the highest-priced wines in New York dried into his knees. Shortly before eleven a shuffling figure paused at the steps, feeling for a key.

"Mr. Arbuthnot, otherwise Ransom?" said Average Jones blandly.

The man's chin jerked back. His jaw dropped.

"Would you like to hire another B-flat trombonist?" pursued the young man.

"Who are you?" gasped the other. "What do you want?"

"I want to know," drawled Average Jones, "how—er—you planted the glass bulb—er—the sulphuric acid bulb, you know—in the chair that you sent—er—to the Honorable William

Linder, so that—er—it wouldn't be shattered by anything but the middle C note of a B-flat trombone?"

The man sat down weakly and bowed his face in his hands. Presently he looked up.

"I don't care," he said. "Come inside."

At the end of an hour's talk Arbuthnot, alias Ransom, agreed to everything that Average Jones proposed.

"Mind you," he said, "I don't promise I won't kill him later. But meantime it'll be some satisfaction to put him down and out politically. You can find me here any time you want me. You say you'll see Linder to-morrow?"

"To-morrow," said Average Jones. "Look in the next day's papers for the result."

Setting his telephone receiver down the Honorable William Linder lost himself in conjecture. He had just given an appointment to his tried and true, but quite impersonal enemy, Mr. Horace Waldemar.

"What can Waldemar want of me?" ran his thoughts. "And who is this friend, Jones, that he's bringing? Jones? Jones! Jones?!" He tried it in three different accents, without extracting any particular meaning therefrom. "Nothing much in the political game," he decided.

It was with a mingling of gruffness and dignity that he greeted Mr. Waldemar an hour later. The introduction to Average Jones he acknowledged with a curt nod.

"Want a job for this young man, Waldemar?" he grunted.

"Not at present, thank you," returned the newspaper owner. "Mr. Jones has a few arguments to present to you—"

"Arguments," repeated the Honorable William Linder contemptuously. "What kind of arguments?"

"Political arguments. Mayoralty, to be specific. To be more specific still, arguments showing why you should drop out of the race."

"A pin-feather reformer, eh?"

The politician turned to meet Average Jones' steady gaze and mildly inquiring smile.

"Do you—er—know anything of submarine mines, Mr. Linder?" drawled the visitor.

"Huh?" returned the Honorable William Linder, startled.

"Submarine mines," explained the other. "Mines—in—the—sea, if you wish words of one syllable."

The lids of the Honorable Linder contracted.

"You're in the wrong joint," he said, "this ain't the Naval College."

"Thank you. A submarine mine is a very ingenious affair. I've recently been reading somewhat extensively on the subject. The main charge is some high explosive, usually of the dynamite type. Above it is a small jar of sulphuric acid. Teeth, working on levers, surround this jar. The levers project outside the mine. When a ship strikes the mine, one or more of the levers are pressed in. The teeth crush the jar. The sulphuric acid drops upon the main charge and explodes it.* Do you follow me?"

"I'll follow you as far as the front door," said the politician balefully. He rose.

"If the charge were in a chair, in the cushion of an easy chair, we'll say, on the third floor of a house in Brooklyn—"

The Honorable William Linder sat down again. He sat heavily.

"—the problem would be somewhat different. Of course, it would be easy to arrange that the first person to sit down in the chair, would, by his own weight, blow himself up. But the first

---

* In early submarine or naval mines, the acid either energized a lead-acid battery (that had no acid) or ignited a mixture of potassium perchlorate and sugar.

person might not be the right person, you know. Do you still follow me?"

The Honorable William Linder made a remark like a fish.

"Now, we have, if you will forgive my professorial method," continued Average Jones, "a chair sent to a gentleman of prominence from an anonymous source. In this chair is a charge of high explosive and above it a glass bulb containing sulphuric acid. The bulb, we will assume, is so safeguarded as to resist any ordinary shock of moving. But when this gentleman, sitting at ease in his chair, is noticed by a trombonist, placed for that purpose in the street, below—"

"The Dutch horn-player!" cried the politician. "Then it was him; and I'll—"

"Only an innocent tool," interrupted Average Jones, in his turn. "He had no comprehension of what he was doing. He didn't understand that the vibration from his trombone on one particular note of the slide up the scale—as in the chorus of *Egypt*—would shiver that glass and set off the charge. All that he knew was to play the B-flat trombone and take his pay."

"His pay?" The question leaped to the politician's lips. "Who paid him?"

"A—man—named—er—Arbuthnot," drawled Average Jones.

Linder's eyes did not drop, but a film seemed to be drawn over them.

"You once knew—er—a Mrs. Arbuthnot?"

The thick shoulders quivered a little.

"Her husband—her widower—is in Brooklyn. Shall I push the argument any further to convince you that you'd better drop out of the mayoralty race?"

Linder recovered himself a little. "What kind of a game are you ringing in on me?" he demanded.

"Don't you think," suggested Average Jones sweetly, "that considered as news, this—"

Linder caught the word out of his mouth. "News!" he roared. "A fake story ten years old, news? That ain't news! It's spite work. Even your dirty paper, Waldemar, wouldn't rake that kind of muck up after ten years. It'd be a boomerang. You'll have to put up a stronger line of blackmail and bluff than that."

"Blackmail is perhaps the correct word technically," admitted the newspaper owner, "but bluff—there you go wrong. You've forgotten one thing; that Arbuthnot's arrest and confession would make the whole story news. We stand ready to arrest Arbuthnot, and he stands ready to confess."

There was a long, tense minute of silence. Then—

"What do you want?" The straight-to-the-point question was an admission of defeat.

"Your announcement of withdrawal. I'd rather print that than the Arbuthnot story."

There was a long silence. Finally the Honorable William Linder dropped his hand on the table, palm up.

"You win," he declared curtly. "But you'll give me the benefit, in the announcement, of bad health caused by the shock of the explosion, to explain my quitting, Waldemar?"

"It will certainly make it more plausible," assented the newspaper owner with a smile.

Linder turned on Average Jones.

"Did you dope this out, young fellow?" he demanded.

"Yes."

"Well, you've put me in the Down-and-Out-Club, all right. And I'm just curious enough to want to know how you did it."

"By abstaining," returned Average Jones cryptically, "from the best wine that ever came out of the Cosmic Club cellar."

CHAPTER II

RED DOT

From his inner sanctum, Average Jones stared obliquely out upon the whirl of Fifth Avenue, warming itself under a late March sun.

In the outer offices a line of anxious applicants was being disposed of by his trained assistants. To the advertising expert's offices had come that day but three cases difficult enough to be referred to the Ad-Visor himself. Two were rather intricate financial lures which Average Jones was able to dispose of by a mere "Don't." The third was a Spiritualist* announcement behind which lurked a shrewd plot to entrap a senile millionaire into a marriage with the medium. These having been settled, the expert was free to muse upon a paragraph which had appeared in all the important New York morning papers of the day before.

REWARD—$1,000 reward† for information as to slayer of Brindle Bulldog "Rags" killed in office

---

* Spiritualism developed in the mid-nineteenth century and gained in popularity through the early twentieth century. It essentially fostered the belief that incorporeal spirits (especially those of the dead) could communicate with the living, typically by means of a medium. Many prominent individuals adhered to its cause; Sir Arthur Conan Doyle became its international spokesperson.

† Almost $150,000 in 2021's money—a very large reward for information regarding a dog's death. Williamson, Measuring Worth, 2021.

of Malcolm Dorr, Stengel Building, Union Square,
March 29.

"That's too much money for a dog," decided Average Jones. "Particularly one that hasn't any bench record.* I'll just have a glance into the thing."

Slipping on his coat he walked briskly down the avenue, and crossing over to Union Square, entered the gloomy old building which is the sole survival of the days when the Stengel estate[†] foresaw the upward trend of business toward Fourteenth Street. Stepping from the elevator at the seventh floor, he paused underneath this sign:

MALCOLM DORR

ANALYTICAL AND CONSULTING CHEMIST

Hours 10 to 4

Entering, Average Jones found a fat young man, with mild blue eyes, sitting at a desk.

"Mr. Dorr?" he asked.

"Yes," replied the fat young man nervously, "but if you are a reporter, I must—"

"I am not," interrupted the other. "I am an expert on advertising, and—I want that one thousand dollars reward."

---

* A record, that is, of its victories and rankings in dog shows and trials.

---

† Union Square, at the intersection of Broadway and what is now Fourth Avenue, near Fourteenth Street, in Lower Manhattan, was largely developed by Samuel Ruggles in the first half of the nineteenth century. Flanked initially by mansions, it became a commercial center in the second half of the century, and by the early years of the twentieth century, it was a transportation hub. The subway's Union Square Station (at Fourteenth Street) opened in 1904. The Stengel Building is fictitious; the *Spingler* Building, however, is named after Henry Spingler, an early settler—the Spingler family owned property in Union Square until the 1950s. The Spingler Building burned in 1892, but was rebuilt in 1896.

The chemist pushed his chair back and rubbed his forehead. "You mean you have—have found out something?"

"Not yet. But I intend to."

Dorr stared at him in silence.

"You are very fond of dogs, Mr. Dorr?"

"Eh? Oh, yes. Yes, certainly," said the other mechanically.

Average Jones shot a sudden glance of surprise at him, then looked dreamily at his own finger-nails.

"I can sympathize with you. I have exhibited for some years. Your dog was perhaps a green-ribboner?"

"Er—oh—yes; I believe so."

"Ah! Several of mine have been. One in particular, took medal after medal; a beautiful glossy brown bulldog, with long silky ears, and the slender splayed out legs that are so highly prized but so seldom seen nowadays. His tail, too, had the truly Willoughby curve, from his dam, who was a famous courser."

Mr. Dorr looked puzzled. "I didn't know they used that kind of dog for coursing," he said vaguely.

Average Jones smiled with almost affectionate admiration at the crease along the knee of his carefully pressed trousers. His tone, when next he spoke, was that of a youth bored with life. Any of his intimates would have recognized in it, however, the characteristic evidence that his mind was ranging swift and far to a conclusion.

"Mr. Dorr," he drawled, "who—er—owned your—er—dog?"

"Why, I—I did," said the startled chemist.

"Who gave him to you?"

"A friend."

"Quite so. Was it that—er—friend who—er—offered the reward?"

"What makes you think that?"

"This, to be frank. A man who doesn't know a bulldog from a

bed-spring isn't likely to be offering a thousand dollars to avenge the death of one. And the minute you answered my question as to whether you cared for dogs, I knew you didn't. When you fell for a green ribbon, and a splay-legged, curly-tailed medal-winner in the brindle bull class (there's no such class, by the way), I knew you were bluffing. Mr. Dorr, who—er—has been—er—threatening your life?"

The chemist swung around in his chair.

"What do you know?" he demanded.

"Nothing. I'm guessing. It's a fair guess that a reasonably valuable brindle bull isn't presented to a man who cares nothing for dogs without some reason. The most likely reason is protection. Is it in your case?"

"Yes, it is," replied the other, after some hesitation.

"And now the protection is gone. Don't you think you'd better let me in on this?"

"Let me speak to my—my legal adviser first." He called up a down-town number on the telephone and asked to be connected with Judge Elverson. "I may have to ask you to leave the office for a moment," he said to his caller.

"Very well. But if that is United States District Attorney Roger Elverson,* tell him that it is A. V. R. Jones who wants to know, and remind him of the missing letter opium advertisement."

Almost immediately Average Jones was called back from the hallway, whither he had gone.

"Elverson says to tell you the whole thing," said the chemist—"in confidence, of course."

"Understood. Now, who is it that wants to get rid of you?"

---

* There is no "United States District Attorney." This probably refers to the US attorney for the Southern District of New York (which included Manhattan). The US attorney for that district from 1906 to 1909 was Henry L. Stimson, who later served as secretary of war for presidents William Taft, Franklin Roosevelt, and Harry Truman, and as secretary of state for President Herbert Hoover.

"The Paragon Pressed Meat Company."

Average Jones became vitally concerned in removing an infinitesimal speck from his left cuff. "Ah," he commented, "the Canned Meat Trust.* What have you been doing to them?"

"Sold them a preparation of my invention for deodorizing certain by-products used for manufacturing purposes. Several months ago I found they were using it on canned meats that had gone bad, and then selling the stuff."

"Would the meat so treated be poisonous?"

"Well—dangerous to any one eating it habitually. I wrote, warning them that they must stop."

"Did they reply?"

"A man came to see me and told me I was mistaken. He hinted that if I thought my invention was worth more than I'd received, his principals would be glad to take the matter up with me. Shortly after I heard that the Federal authorities were going after the Trust, so I called on Mr. Elverson."

"Mistake Number One. Elverson is straight, but his office is fuller of leaks than a sieve."

"That's probably why I found my private laboratory reeking of cyanide fumes a fortnight later," remarked Dorr dryly. "I got to the outer air alive, but not much more. A week later there was an explosion in the laboratory. I didn't happen to be there at the time. The odd feature of the explosion was that I hadn't any explosive drugs in the place."

"Where is this laboratory?"

"Over in Flatbush, where I live—or did live. Within a month

---

* A "trust" in this context means a group of companies or industries organized to reduce or eliminate competition or to control production and distribution for their common advantage, similar to a combine. In some instances, control of the companies might be concentrated in the hands of trustees. "Trust-busting" was a hot legal topic of the day, and the Sherman Act, enacted in 1890 (see note on page 6) was commonly known as the "Sherman Anti-Trust Act."

after that, a friendly neighbor took a pot-shot at a man who was sneaking up behind me as I was going home late one night. The man shot, too, but missed me. I reported it to the police, and they told me to be sure and not let the newspapers know. Then they forgot it."

Average Jones laughed. "Of course they did. Some day New York will find out that 'the finest police force in the world' is the biggest sham outside the dime museum business. Except in the case of crimes by the regular, advertised criminals, they're as helpless as babies. Didn't you take any other precautions?"

"Oh, yes. I reported the attempt to Judge Elverson. He sent a secret service man over to live with me.* Then I got a commission out in Denver. When I came back, about a month ago, Judge Elverson gave me the two dogs."

"Two?"

"Yes. Rags and Tatters."

"Where's Tatters?"

"Dead. By the same road as Rags."

"Killed at your place in Flatbush?"

"No. Right here in this room."

Average Jones became suddenly very much worried about the second button of his coat. Having satisfied himself of its stability, he drawled, "Er—both of—er—them?"

"Yes. Ten days apart."

"Where were you?"

"On the spot. That is, I was here when Tatters got his death. I had gone to the wash-room at the farther end of the hall when Rags was poisoned."

---

* The "Secret Service" was originally conceived as an arm of the Department of the Treasury to deal with financial crimes; protection of the president and other officials was not added to its mission until 1901. The FBI did not exist until 1908, when it was known as the "Bureau of Investigation."

"Why do you say poisoned?"

"What else could it have been? There was no wound on either of the dogs."

"Was there evidence of poison?"

"Pathological only. In Tatters' case it was very marked. He was dozing in a corner near the radiator when I heard him yelp and saw him snapping at his belly. He ran across the room, lay down and began licking himself. Within fifteen minutes he began to whine. Then he stiffened out in a sort of spasm. It was like strychnine poisoning. Before I could get a veterinary here he was dead."

"Did you make any examination?"

"I analyzed the contents of his stomach, but did not obtain positive results."

"What about the other dog?"

"Rags? That was the day before yesterday. We had just come over from Flatbush and Rags was nosing around in the corner—"

"Was it the same corner where Tatters was attacked?"

"Yes; near the radiator. He seemed to be interested in something there when I left the room. I was gone not more than two minutes."

"Lock the door after you?"

"It has a special spring lock which I had put on myself."

Average Jones crossed over and looked at the contrivance. Then his glance fell to a huge, old-fashioned keyhole below the new fastening.

"You didn't use that larger lock?"

"No. I haven't for months. The key is lost, I think."

Retracing his steps the investigator sighted the hole from the radiator, and shook his head.

"It's not in range," he said. "Go on."

"As I reached the door on my return, I heard Rags yelp. You may believe I got to him quickly. He was pawing wildly at his nose.

I called up the nearest veterinary. Within ten minutes the convulsions came on. The veterinary was here when Rags died, which was within fifteen minutes of the first spasm. He didn't believe it was strychnine. Said the attacks were different. Whatever it was, I couldn't find any trace of it in the stomach. The veterinary took the body away and made a complete autopsy."

"Did he discover anything?"

"Yes. The blood was coagulated and on the upper lip he found a circle of small pustules. He agreed that both dogs probably swallowed something that was left in my office, though I don't see how it could have got there."

"That won't do," returned Average Jones positively. "A dog doesn't cry out when he swallows poison, unless it's some corrosive."

"It was no corrosive. I examined the mouth."

"What about the radiator?" asked Average Jones, getting down on his knees beside that antiquated contrivance. "It seems to have been the center of disturbance."

"If you're thinking of fumes," replied the chemist, "I tested for that. It isn't possible."

"No; I suppose not. And yet, there's the curious feature that the fatal influence seems to have emanated from the corner which is the most remote from both windows and door. Are your windows or transom left open at night?"

"The windows, sometimes. The transom is kept double-bolted."

"Do they face any other windows near by?"

"You can see for yourself that they don't."

"There's no fire-escape and it's too far up for anything to come in from the street." Average Jones examined the walls with attention and returned to the big keyhole, through which he peeped.

"Do you ever chew gum?" he asked suddenly.

The chemist stared at him. "It isn't a habit of mine," he said.

"But you wouldn't have any objection to my sending for some, in satisfaction of a sudden irresistible craving?"

"Any particular brand? I'll 'phone the corner drug store."

"Any sort will suit, thank you."

When the gum arrived, Average Jones, after politely offering some to his host, chewed up a single stick thoroughly. This he rolled out to an extremely tenuous consistency and spread it deftly across the unused keyhole, which it completely though thinly veiled.

"Now, what's that for?" inquired the chemist, eying the improvised closure with some contempt.

"Don't know, exactly, yet," replied the deviser cheerfully. "But when queer and fatal things happen in a room and there's only one opening, it's just as well to keep your eye on that, no matter how small it is. Better still, perhaps, if you'd shift your office."

The fat young chemist pushed his hair back, looked out of the window, and then turned to Average Jones. The rather flabby lines of his face had abruptly hardened over the firm contour below.

"No. I'm hanged if I will," he said simply.

An amiable grin overspread Average Jones' face.

"You've got more nerve than prudence," he observed. "But I don't say you aren't right. Since you're going to stick to the ship, keep your eye on that gum. If it lets go its hold, wire me."

"All right," agreed young Mr. Dorr. "Whatever your little game is, I'll play it. Give me your address in case you leave town."

"As I may do. I am going to hire a press-clipping bureau on special order to dig through the files of the local and neighboring city newspapers for recent items concerning dog-poisoning cases. If our unknown has devised a new method of canicide, it's quite possible he may have worked it somewhere else, too. Good-by, and if you can't be wise, be careful."

Dog-poisoning seemed to Average Jones to have become a popular pastime in and around New York, judging from the succession of news items which poured in upon him from the clipping bureau. Several days were exhausted by false clues. Then one morning there arrived, among other data, an article from the Bridgeport *Morning Delineator* which caused the Ad-Visor to sit up with a jerk. It detailed the poisoning of several dogs under peculiar circumstances. Three hours later he was in the bustling Connecticut city. There he took carriage for the house of Mr. Curtis Fleming, whose valuable Great Dane dog had been the last victim.

Mr. Curtis Fleming revealed himself as an elderly gentleman all grown to a point: pointed white nose, eyes that were pin-points of irascible gleam, and a most pointed manner of speech.

"Who are you?" he demanded rancidly, as his visitor was ushered in.

Average Jones recognized the type. He knew of but one way to deal with it.

"Jones!" he retorted with such astounding emphasis that the monosyllable fairly exploded in the other's face.

"Well, well, well," said the elder man, his aspect suddenly mollified. "Don't bite me. What kind of a Jones are you, and what do you want of me?"

"Ordinary variety of Jones. I want to know about your dog."

"Reporter?"

"No"

"Glad of it. They're no good. Had my reporters on this case. Found nothing."

"Your reporters?"

"I own the Bridgeport *Delineator*."

"What about the dog?"

"Good boy!" approved the old martinet. "Sticks to his point. Dog was out walking with me day before yesterday. Crossing a vacant lot on next square. Chased a rat. Rat ran into a heap of old timber. Dog nosed around. Gave a yelp and came back to me. Had spasm. Died in fifteen minutes. And hang me, sir," cried the old man, bringing his fist down on Average Jones' knee, "if I see how the poison got him, for he was muzzled to the snout, sir!"

"Muzzled? Then—er—why do you—er—suggest poison?" drawled the young man.

"Fourth dog to go the same way in the last week."

"All in this locality?"

"Yes, all on Golden Hill."

"Any suspicions?"

"Suspicions? Certainly, young man, certainly. Look at this."

Average Jones took the smutted newspaper proof which his host extended, and read:

WARNING—Residents of the Golden Hill neighborhood are earnestly cautioned against unguarded
handling of timber about woodpiles or outbuildings
until further notice. Danger!"

"When was this published?"

"Wasn't published. *Delineator* refused it. Thought it was a case of insanity."

"Who offered it?"

"Professor Moseley. Tenant of mine. Frame house on the next corner with old-fashioned conservatory."

"How long ago?"

"About a week."

"All the dogs you speak of died since then?"

"Yes."

"Did he give any explanation of the advertisement?"

"No. Acted half-crazy when he brought it to the office, so the business manager said. Wouldn't sign his name to the thing. Wouldn't say anything about it. Begged the manager to let him have the weather reports in advance, every day. The manager put the advertisement in type, decided not to run it, and returned the money."

"Weather reports, eh?" Average Jones mused for a moment. "How long was the ad to run?"

"Until the first hard frost."

"Has there—er—been a—er—frost since?" drawled Average Jones.

"No."

"Who is this Moseley?"

"Don't know much about him. Scientific experimenter of some kind, I believe. Very exclusive," added Mr. Curtis Fleming, with a grin. "Never associated with any of us neighbors. Rent on the nail, though. Insane, too, I think. Writes letters to himself with nothing in them."

"How's that?" inquired Average Jones.

The other took an envelope from his pocket and handed it over. "It got enclosed by mistake with the copy for the advertisement. The handwriting on the envelope is his own. Look inside."

A glance had shown Average Jones that the letter had been mailed in New York on March twenty-fifth. He took out the enclosure. It was a small slip of paper. The date was stamped on with a rubber stamp. There was no writing of any kind. Near the center of the sheet were three dots. They seemed to have been made with red ink.

"You're sure the address is in Professor Moseley's writing?"

"I'd swear to it."

"It doesn't follow that he mailed it to himself. In fact, I should judge that it was sent by some one who was particularly anxious not to have any specimen of his handwriting lying about for identification."

"Perhaps. What's your interest in all this, anyway, my mysterious young friend?"

"Two dogs in New York poisoned in something the same way as yours."

"Well, I've got *my* man. He confessed."

"Confessed?" echoed Average Jones.

"Practically. I've kept the point of the story to the last. Professor Moseley committed suicide this morning."

If Mr. Curtis Fleming had designed to make an impression on his visitor, his ambition was fulfilled. Average Jones got to his feet slowly, walked over to the window, returned, picked up the strange proof with its message of suggested peril, studied it, returned to the window, and stared out into the gray day.

"Cut his throat about nine o'clock this morning," pursued the other. "Dead when they found him."

"Do you mind not talking to me for a minute?" said Average Jones curtly.

"Told to hold my tongue in my own house by an uninvited stripling," cackled the other. "You're a singular young man. Have it your own way."

After a five minutes' silence the visitor turned from the window and spoke. "There has been a deadly danger loose about here for which Professor Moseley felt himself responsible. He has killed himself. Why?"

"Because I was on his trail," declared Mr. Curtis Fleming. "Afraid to face me."

"Nonsense. I believe some human being has been killed by this thing, whatever it may be, and that the horror of it drove Moseley to suicide."

"Prove it."

"Give me a morning paper."

His host handed him the current issue of the *Delineator.*

Average Jones studied the local page.

"Where's Galvin's Alley?" he asked presently.

"Two short blocks from here."

"In the Golden Hill section?"

"Yes."

"Read that."

Mr. Curtis Fleming took the paper. His eyes were directed to a paragraph telling of the death of an Italian child living in Galvin's Alley. Cause, convulsions.

"By jove!" said he, somewhat awed. "You can reason, young man."

"I've got to reason a lot further, if I'm to get anywhere in this affair," said Average Jones with conviction. "Do you care to come to Galvin's Alley with me?"

Together they went down the hill to a poor little house, marked by white crêpe. The occupants were Italians who spoke some English. They said that four-year-old Pietro had been playing around a woodpile the afternoon before, when he was taken sick and came home, staggering. The doctor could do nothing. The little one passed from spasm into spasm, and died in an hour.

"Was there a mark like a ring anywhere on the hand or face?" asked Average Jones.

The dead child's father looked surprised. That, he said, was what the strange gentleman who had come that very morning asked; a queer, bent little gentleman, very bald and with big eyeglasses, who was kind, and wept with them and gave them money to bury the "bambino."

"Moseley, by the Lord Harry!" exclaimed Mr. Curtis Fleming. "But what was the death-agent?"

Average Jones shook his head. "Too early to do more than guess. Will you take me to Professor Moseley's place?"

The old house stood four-square, with a patched-up conservatory on one wing. In the front room they found the recluse's body decently disposed, with an undertaker's assistant in charge. From the greenhouse came a subdued hissing.

"What's that?" asked Jones.

"Fumigating the conservatory. There was a note found near the body insisting on its being done. 'For safety,' it said, so I ordered it looked to."

"You're in charge, then?"

"It's my house. And there are no relatives so far as I know. Come and look at his papers. You won't find much."

In the old-fashioned desk was a heap of undecipherable matter, interspersed with dates, apparently bearing upon scientific experiments; a package of letters from the Denny Research Laboratories of St. Louis, mentioning enclosure of checks; and three self-addressed envelopes bearing New York postmarks, of dates respectively, March 12, March 14 and March 20. Each contained a date-stamped sheet of paper, similar to that which Mr. Curtis Fleming had shown to Average Jones. The one of earliest date bore two red dots; the second, three red dots, and the third, two. All the envelopes were endorsed in Professor Moseley's handwriting; the first with the one word "Filled." The second writing was "Held for warmer weather." The last was inscribed "One in poor condition."

Of these Average Jones made careful note, as well as of the laboratory address. By this time the hissing of the fumigating apparatus had ceased. The two men went to the conservatory and gazed in upon a ruin of limp leaves and flaccid petals, killed by the powerful gases. Suddenly, with an exclamation of astonishment, the investigator stooped and lifted from the floor a marvel of ermine body and pale green wings. The moth, spreading nearly a foot, was quite dead.

"Here's the mate, sir," said the fumigating expert, handing him another specimen, a trifle smaller. "The place was crowded with all kinds of pretty ones. All gone where the good bugs go now."

Average Jones took the pair of moths to the desk, measured them and laid them carefully away in a drawer.

"The rest must wait," he said. "I have to send a telegram."

With the interested Mr. Curtis Fleming in attendance, he went to the telegraph office, where he wrote out a despatch.

"Mr. A. V. R. Jones?" said the operator. "There's a message here for you."

Average Jones took the leaflet and read:

"Found gum on floor this morning when I arrived.
MALCOLM DORR*."*

Then he recalled his own blank, tore it up, and substituted the following, which he ordered "rushed:"

*"*MALCOLM DORR, STENGEL BUILDING, NEW YORK CITY:
"Leave office immediately. Do not return until it has been fumigated thoroughly. Imperative.
*"*A. V. R. JONES*."*

"And now," said Average Jones to Mr. Fleming, "I'm going back to New York. If any collectors come chasing to you for luna moths, don't deal with them. Refer them to me, please. Here is my card."

"Your orders shall be obeyed," said the older man, his beady eyes twinkling. "But why, in the name of all that's unheard of, should collectors come bothering me about luna moths?"

"Because of an announcement to this effect which will appear in the next number of the *National Science Weekly,* and in coming issues of the New York *Evening Register.*"

He handed out a rough draft of this advertisement:

"FOR SALE—Two largest known specimens of *Tropaea luna*, unmounted; respectively 10 and 11½ inches spread. Also various other specimens from collection of late Gerald Moseley, of Bridgeport, Conn. Write for particulars. Jones, Room 222, Astor Court Temple, New York."

"What about further danger here?" inquired Mr. Fleming, as Average Jones bade him good-by. "Would we better run that warning of poor Moseley's, after all?"

For reply Jones pointed out the window. A late-season whirl of snow enveloped the streets.

"I see," said the old man. "The frost. Well, Mr. Mysterious Jones, I don't know what you're up to, but you've given me an interesting day. Let me know what comes of it."

On the train back to New York, Average Jones wrote two letters. One was to the Denny Research Laboratories in St. Louis, the other to the Department of Agriculture at Washington. On the following morning he went to Dorr's office. That young chemist was in a recalcitrant frame of mind.

"I've done about ten dollars' worth of fumigating and a hundred dollars' worth of damage," he said: "and now, I'd like to have a Missouri sign.* In other words, I want to be shown. What did some skunk want to kill my dogs for?"

"He didn't."

"But they're dead, aren't they?"

"Accident."

"What kind of an accident?"

"The kind in which the innocent bystander gets the worst of it. You're the one it was meant for."

"Me?"

"Certainly. You'd probably have got it if the dogs hadn't."

The speaker examined the keyhole, then walked over to the radiator and looked over, under and through it minutely. "Nothing there," he observed; and, after extending his examination to the windows, book-shelf and desk, added:

"I guess we might have spared the fumigation. However, the safest side is the best."

"What is it? Some new game in projective germs?" demanded the chemist.

"Oh, disinfectants will kill other things besides germs," returned Average Jones. "Luna moths, for instance. Wait a few days and I'll have some mail to show you on that subject. In the meantime, have a plumber solder up that keyhole so tight that nothing short of dynamite can get through it."

Collectors of *lepidoptera* rose in shoals to the printed offer of luna moths measuring ten and eleven inches across the wings. Letters came in by every mail, responding variously with fervor, suspicion, yearning eagerness, and bitter skepticism to Average Jones' advertisement. All of these he put aside, except such as bore a New York postmark. And each day he compared the new names

---

* The official Missouri state motto is now "The Show-Me State," though the origin of the phrase is a matter of dispute. Popularly, people from Missouri were hard to convince—they had to be shown things.

signed to the New York letters with the directory of occupants of the Stengel Building. Less than a week after the luna moth advertisement appeared, Average Jones walked into Malcolm Dorr's office with a twinkling eye.

"Do you know a man named Marcus L. Ross?" he asked the chemist.

"Never heard of him."

"Marcus L. Ross is interested, not only in luna moths, but in the rest of the Moseley collection. He writes from the Delamater Apartments, where he lives, to tell me so. Also he has an office in this building. Likewise he works frequently at night. Finally, he is one of the confidential lobbyists of the Paragon Pressed Meat Company. Do you see?"

"I begin," replied young Mr. Dorr.

"It would be very easy for Mr. Ross, whose office is on the floor above, to stop at this door on his way down-stairs after quitting work late at night when the elevator had stopped running and— let us say—peep through the keyhole."

Malcolm Dorr got up and stretched himself slowly. The sharp, clean lines of his face suddenly stood out again under the creasy flesh.

"I don't know what *you're* going to do to Mr. Ross," he said, "but I want to see him first."

"I'm not going to do anything to him," returned Average Jones, "because, in the first place, I suspect that he is far, far away, having noted, doubtless, the plugged keyhole and suffered a crisis of the nerves. It's strange how nervous your scientific murderer is. Anyway, Ross is only an agent. I'm going to aim higher."

"As how?"

"Well, I expect to do three things. First, I expect to scare a peaceful but murderous trust multimillionaire almost out of his senses; second, I expect to despatch a costly yacht to unknown seas; and third, I expect to raise the street selling price of the evening "yellow" journals, temporarily, about one thousand per cent. What's the answer? The answer is—'Buy to-night's papers.'"

New York, that afternoon, saw something new in advertising. That it really was advertising was shown by the "*Adv.*" sign, large and plain, in both the papers which carried it. The favored journals were the only two which indulged in "fudge" editions; that is, editions with glaring red-typed inserts of "special" news.[*] On the front page of each, stretching narrowly across three columns, was a device showing a tiny mapped outline in black marked Bridgeport, Conn., and a large skeleton draft of Manhattan Island showing the principal streets. From the Connecticut city downward ran a line of dots in red. The dots entered New York from the north, passed down Fourth Avenue to the south side of Union Square, turned west and terminated. Beneath this map was the legend, also in red:

WATCH THE LINE ADVANCE IN LATER EDITIONS

It was the first time in the records of journalism that the "fudge" device had been used in advertising.

Great was the rejoicing of the "newsies" when public curiosity made a "run" upon these papers. Greater it grew when the "afternoon edition" appeared, and with their keen business instinct, the urchins saw that they could run the price upward, which they promptly did, in some cases even to a nickel. This edition carried the same "fudge" advertisement, but now the red dots crossed over to Fifth Avenue and turned northward as far as Twenty-third Street. The inscription was:

---

[*] "Fudge" was a piece of late-breaking news inserted into a newspaper page already set in print.

UPWARD AND ONWARD
SEE NEXT EXTRA

For the "Night Extra" people paid five, ten, even fifteen cents. Rumor ran wild. Other papers, even, took the matter up as news, and commented upon the meaning of the extraordinary advertisement. This time, the red-dotted line went as far up Fifth Avenue as Fiftieth Street. And the legend was ominous:

WHEN I TURN, I STRIKE

That was all that evening. The dotted line did not turn.

Keen as newspaper conjecture is, it failed to connect the "red-line maps," with the fame of which the city was raging, with an item of shipping news printed in the evening papers of the following day:

CLEARED—For South American Ports, steam yacht *Electra*, New York. Owner John M. Colwell.

And not until the following morning did the papers announce that President Colwell, of the Canned Meat Trust, having been ordered by his physician on a long sea voyage to refurbish his depleted nerves, after closing his house on West Fifty-first Street, had sailed in his own yacht. The same issue carried a few lines about the "freak ads" which had so sensationally blazed and so suddenly waned from the "yellows." The opinion was offered that they represented the exploitation of some new brand of whisky which would announce itself later. But that announcement never came, and President Colwell sailed to far seas, and Mr. Curtis Fleming came to New York, keen for explanations, for he, too, had seen the "fudge" and marveled. Hence, Average Jones had him, together with young Mr. Dorr, at a private room luncheon at the Cosmic Club, where he offered an explanation and elucidation.

"The whole affair," he said, "was a problem in the connecting up of loose ends. At the New York terminus we had two deaths in the office of a man with powerful and subtle enemies, that office being practically sealed against intrusion except for a very large keyhole. Some deadly thing is introduced through that keyhole; so much is practically proven by the breaking out of the chewing gum with which I coated it. Probably the scheme was carried out in the evening when the building was nearly deserted. The killing influence reaches a corner far out of the direct line of the keyhole. Being near the radiator, that corner represents the attraction of warmth. Therefore, the invading force was some sentient creature."

Dorr shuddered. "Some kind of venomous snake," he surmised.

"Not a bad guess. But a snake, however small, would have been instantly noticed by the dogs. Now, let's look at the Bridgeport end. Here, again, we have a deadly influence loosed; this time by accident. A scientific experimentalist is the innocent cause of the disaster. Here, too, the peril is somewhat dependent upon warmth, since we know, from Professor Moseley's agonized eagerness for a frost, that cold weather would have put an end to it. The cold weather fails to come. Dogs are killed. Finally a child falls victim, and on that child is found a circular mark, similar to the mark on Mr. Dorr's dog's lip. You see the striking points of analogy?"

"Do you mean us to believe poor old Moseley a cold-blooded murderer?" demanded Mr. Curtis Fleming.

"Far from it. At worst an unhappy victim of his own carelessness in loosing a peril upon his neighborhood. You're forgetting a connecting link; the secretive red-dot communications from New York City addressed by Moseley to himself on behalf of some customer who ordered simply by a code of ink-dots. He was the man I had to find. The giant luna moths helped to do it."

"I don't see where they come in at all," declared Dorr bluntly. "A moth a foot wide couldn't crawl through a keyhole."

"No; nor do any damage if it did. The luna is as harmless as it is lovely. In this case the moths weren't active agents. They were important only as clues—and bait. Their enormous size showed Professor Moseley's line of work; the selective breeding of certain forms of life to two or three times the normal proportions. Very well; I had to ascertain some creature which, if magnified several times, would be deadly, and which would still be capable of entering a large keyhole. Having determined that—"

"You found what it was?" cried Dorr.

"One moment. Having determined that, I had still to get in touch with Professor Moseley's mysterious New York correspondent. I figured that he must be interested in Professor Moseley's particular branch of research or he never could have devised his murderous scheme. So I constructed the luna moth advertisement to draw him, and when I got a reply from Mr. Ross, who is a fellow-tenant of Mr. Dorr's, the chain was complete. Now, you see where the luna moths were useful. If I had advertised, instead of them, the *Lathrodectus*, he might have suspected and refrained from answering."

"What's the *Lathrodectus*?" demanded both the hearers at once.

For answer Average Jones took a letter from his pocket and read:

BUREAU OF ENTOMOLOGY,
U. S. DEPARTMENT OF AGRICULTURE,
WASHINGTON, D. C., APRIL 7.

Mr. A. V. R. Jones,
Astor Court Temple, New York City.
DEAR SIR—*Replying to your letter of inquiry, the only insect answering your specifications is a small spider* Lathrodectus

mactans,* *sometimes popularly called the red dot, from a bright red mark upon the back. Rare cases are known where death has been caused by the bite of this insect. Fortunately its fangs are so weak that they can penetrate only very tender skin, otherwise death from its bite would be more common, as the venom, drop for drop, is perhaps the most virulent known to science.*

This Bureau knows nothing of any experiments in breeding the Lathrodectus for size. Your surmise that specimens of two or three times the normal size would be dangerous to life is undoubtedly correct, and selected breeding to that end should be conducted only under adequate scientific safeguards. A Lathrodecins mactans with fangs large enough to penetrate the skin of the hand, and a double or triple supply of venom, would be, perhaps, more deadly than a cobra.

The symptoms of poisoning by this species are spasms, similar to those of trismus, and agonizing general pains. There are no local symptoms, except, in some cases, a circle of small pustules about the bitten spot.

Commercially, the Lathrodectus has value, in that the poison is used in certain affections of the heart. For details, I would refer you to the Denny Laboratories of St. Louis, Mo., which are purchasers of the venom.

The species is very susceptible to cold, and would hardly survive a severe frost. It frequents wood piles and outhouses.

Yours truly,
L. O. Howard,
Chief of Bureau.

---

* Known after the nineteenth century as *Latrodectus mactans*, the southern black widow spider, bearing a distinctive red hourglass shape on its back, is rarely fatal to healthy humans, and only mature females have large enough fangs to envenom a human being.

"Then Ross was sneaking down here at night and putting the spiders which he had got from Professor Moseley through my keyhole, in the hope that sooner or later one of them would get me," said Dorr.

"A very reasonable expectation, too. *Vide,* the dogs," returned Average Jones.

"And now," said Mr. Curtis Fleming, "will some one kindly explain to me what this Ross fiend had against our friend, Mr. Dorr?"

"Nothing," replied Average Jones.

"Nothing? Was he coursing with spiders merely for sport?"

"Oh, no. You see Mr. Dorr was interfering with the machinery of one of our ruling institutions, the Canned Meat Trust. He possessed information which would have indicted all the officials. Therefore it was desirable—even essential—that he should be removed from the pathway of progress."

"Nonsense! Socialistic nonsense!" snapped Mr. Curtis Fleming. "Trusts may be unprincipled, but they don't commit individual crimes."

"Don't they?" returned Average Jones, smiling amiably at his own boot-tip. "Did you ever hear of Mr. Adel Meyer's little corset steel which he invented to stick in the customs scales and rob the government for the profit of his Syrup Trust? Or of the individual oil refineries which mysteriously disappeared in fire and smoke at a time when they became annoying to the Combination Oil Trust?* Or of the Traction Trust's two plots to murder Prosecutor Henry in San Francisco? I'm just mentioning a few cases from memory. Why, when a criminal trust faces only loss it will commit forgery, theft or arson. When it faces jail, it will commit murder just as determinedly. Self-defense, you know. As for the case of

---

* That would be the Standard Oil Company and Trust, founded by John D. Rockefeller, which controlled the American oil industry until 1911.

Mr. Dorr—" and he proceeded to detail the various attempts on the young chemist's life.

"But why so roundabout a method?" asked Dorr skeptically.

"Well, they tried the ordinary methods of murder on you through agents. That didn't work. It was up to the Trust to put one of its own confidential men on it. Ross is an amateur entomologist. He devised a means that looked to be pretty safe and, in the long run, sure."

"And would have been but for your skill, young Jones," declared Mr. Curtis Fleming, with emphasis.

"Don't forget the fortunate coincidences," replied Average Jones modestly. "They're about half of it. In fact, detective work, for all that is said on the other side, is mostly the ability to recognize and connect coincidences. The coincidence of the escape of the red dots from Professor Moseley's breeding cages; the coincidence of the death of the dogs on Golden Hill, followed by the death of the child; the coincidence of poor Moseley's having left the red-dot letters on the desk instead of destroying them; the coincidence of Dorr's dogs being bitten, when it might easily have been himself had he gone to turn on the radiator and disturbed the savage little spider—"

"And the chief coincidence of your having become interested in the advertisement which Judge Elverson had me insert, really more to scare off further attempts than anything else," put in Dorr. "What became of the spiders that were slipped through my keyhole, anyway?"

"Two of them, as you know, were probably killed by the dogs. The others may well have died of cold at night when the heat was off and the windows open. The cleaning woman wouldn't have been likely to notice them when she swept the bodies out. And, sooner or later, if Ross had continued to insert red dots through the keyhole one of them would have bitten you,

Dorr, and the Canned Meat Trust would have gone on its way rejoicing."

"Well, you've certainly saved my life," declared Dorr, "and it's a case of sheer force of reasoning."

Average Jones shook his head. "You might give some of the credit to Providence," he said. "Just one little event would have meant the saving of the Italian child, and of Professor Moseley, and the death of yourself, instead of the other way around."

"And that event?" asked Mr. Curtis Fleming.

"Five degrees of frost in Bridgeport," replied Average Jones.

CHAPTER III

OPEN TRAIL

"Not good enough," said Average Jones, laying aside a sheet of paper upon which was pasted a newspaper clipping. "We can't afford luxuries, Simpson."

The confidential clerk rubbed his high, pale forehead indeterminately. "But five thousand dollars, Mr. Jones," he protested.

"Would pay a year's office rent, you're thinking. True. Nevertheless I can't see the missing Mr. Hoff as a sound professional proposition."

"So you think it would be impossible to find him?"

"Now, why should I think any such absurd thing? I think, if you choose, that he wouldn't be worth the amount, when found, to loser."

"The ad says different, sir." Simpson raised the paper and read:

"FIVE THOUSAND DOLLARS—The aforesaid sum will be paid without question to any one furnishing information which leads to the discovery of Roderick Hoff, twenty-four years old, who left his home in Toledo, O., on April 12. Communicate with Dr. Conrad Hoff, Toledo.

"Surely Doctor Hoff is good for the amount."

"Oh, he's good for millions, thanks to his much-advertised quack 'Catarrh-Killer.'* The point is, from what I can discover, Mr. Roderick Hoff isn't worth retrieving at any price above one dime."

"Was the information about him that you wished, in the telegram?" asked the confidential clerk.

"Yes; all I wanted. Thanks for looking after it. Have the Toledo reporter, who sent it, forward his bill. And if the old inventor who's been haunted by disembodied voices comes again, bring him to me."

"Yes, sir," said Simpson, going out.

Left to himself, Average Jones again ran over the despatches, conveying the information as to the lost Toledo youth. They had given a fairly complete sketch of young Hoff's life and character. At twenty-four, it appeared, Roderick Hoff had achieved a career. Emerging, by the propulsive method, from college, in the first term of his freshman year, he had taken a post-graduate course in the cigarette ward of a polite retreat for nervous wrecks. He had subsequently endured two breach-of-promise suits, had broken the state automobile record for number of speed violation arrests, had been buncoed, badgered, panelled, blackmailed and short-carded out of sums varying between one hundred and ten thousand dollars; and now, in the year of grace, 19—, was the horror of the pulpit and the delight of the press of the city which he called his home. For the rest, he was a large, mild, good-humored, pulpy individual, with a fixed delusion that the human organism can absorb a quart of alcoholic miscellany per day and be none the worse for it. The major premise of his proposition

---

* Catarrh is a buildup of mucus in the sinus membranes. It is a common symptom of colds, influenza of various types, and sinus infections. Certainly no single remedy could cure all of these ills. Catarrh is usually treated with warm water and saline solutions, drinking a lot of water, taking hot showers, and occasionally using an indoor humidifier.

was perfectly correct. He proved it daily. The minor premise was an error. Bets were even in the Toledo clubs as to whether delirium tremens or paresis would win the event around young Mr. Hoff's kite-shaped race-track of a brain.

With his tastes the income of twenty-five thousand dollars per annum which his father allowed him from the profits of "Dr. Hoff's Catarrh-Killer," proved sadly insufficient to his needs. He mentioned this fact to his father, so Average Jones' information ran, early in April, and suggested an increase, only to be refused with some acerbity.

"Oh, very well," said he, "I'll go and make it myself."

The amazement inspired in Doctor Hoff's mind by this pro-nunciamento was augmented in the next few days by the fact that Roderick was very busy about town in his motor-car, and was changed to vivid alarm immediately thereafter by the young man's disappearance. To all intents and appearances, Roderick Hoff had dropped off the earth on or about April twelfth. By April fifteenth New York, Pittsburg, Chicago, Washington and other clearing-houses for the distribution of the unspent increment were apprised of the elder Hoff's five-thousand-dollar anxiety through the medium of the daily press. This advertisement it was, upon the practical merits of which Average Jones and his confidential clerk had differed.

"If there were any chance of sport in it," mused Average Jones, "I'd go in. But to follow the trail of a spurious young sport from bar-room to brothel and from brothel to gambling hell—" He shook his head. "Not good enough," he repeated.

Simpson's face appeared at the door. His blond forehead was wrinkled with excitement.

"Doctor Hoff is here, Mr. Jones. I told him you couldn't see him, but he wouldn't take no. Says he was recommended to you by a former client."

Following the word, there burst into Average Jones' private sanctum a gross old man, silk-hatted and bediamonded, whose side-whiskers bristled whitely with perturbed self-importance. In his hand was a patchy bundle.

"They tried to stop me!" he sputtered. "Me! I'm worth ten million dollars, an' a ten-dollar-a-week office toad tries to hold me up when I come here myself person'ly, from Toledo to see you."

Analysis of advertising in all its forms had inspired Average Jones with a profound contempt and dislike for the crudest of all forms of swindling—medical quackery. And this swollen, smug-faced intruder looked a particularly offensive specimen of his kind. Therefore the Ad-Visor said curtly:

"I can't take your case. Good day."

"Not take it! Did you read the reward?"

"Yes. It is interesting as showing the patent medicine faker's touching confidence in the power of advertising. Otherwise it doesn't interest me. Get some one else to find your young hopeful."

"It ain't no case of findin' now. The boy's dead." His strident voice quavered and broke, but rose again to a snarl. "And, by God, I'll spend a million to get the dogs that murdered him."

At the word "murdered" Average Jones' clean-cut, agreeable, but rather stolidly neutral face underwent a subtle transformation. Another personality looked out from the deep-set, somnolent, gray eyes; a personality resolute, forceful and quietly alert. It was apparently belied by the hesitant drawl, which, as all who had ever seen the Ad-Visor at his chosen pursuits well knew, signified awakened or intensified interest in the matter in hand.

"Where—er—is—the—er—body?"

"I don't know. It ain't been found."

"Then how do you know he's dead?"

The other tore open the bundle he carried, and spread before Average Jones a white silk shirt stained with ominous brown splotches.

"It's his shirt. There's the initials. Mailed to my house and got there just after I left. My seccattery brought it on, with the note that come pinned to it. Here it is."

He produced a bit of coarse wrapping-paper upon which was this message in rough capital letters:

**TWO DAGOES SHOT HIM DASSENT SAY NO MORE
FROM A FRIEND IN CINCINNATI***

Average Jones examined the wrapper. It was postmarked Cincinnati. He next smoothed out the creased silk and studied minutely the blotches, which were heaviest about the left breast and shoulder.

To the surprise of Doctor Hoff, the young man's glance roved the big desk before him, settling with satisfaction upon a sponge-cup for moistening stamps. Applying this to one of the spots on the shirt, he rubbed the wetted portion vigorously on a sheet of paper which lay near at hand. His lips pursed. He whistled very softly and meditatively. He scratched his chin with a slow movement.

"Is that all?" he shot out suddenly at the older man.

"All! Ain't it enough? He's been murdered; murdered, I tell you, an' you set there an' whistle!"

Average Jones directed a dreamy smile toward a far corner of the room.

"I don't see anything so far," he observed, "to indicate that your son is not alive and well at this moment."

---

* The disparaging term "dago" for someone of Spanish descent was originally used in the Southwestern United States, supposedly a corruption of "Diego"; now it has been extended to apply to Hispanics, Portuguese, and Italians.

Doctor Hoff struck his fist down heavily on the desk. "What's this you're givin' me? Can't you read? Look at that note there, an' the blood on the shirt."

"Would you mind moderating your voice? My outside office is full of more or less excitable clients," said the Ad-Visor mildly. "Moreover, it's not blood anyway."

"What is it, then?"

"That's beside the question. Dried blood rubs off a faint buff color." He picked up the sheet of paper from his desk. A deep brownish streak showed where he had applied the moistened cloth. "It's the rawest kind of a blind. Why, the idiot who sent the shirt didn't even have the sense to fake bullet holes. Enough to make one lose all interest in the case," he added disgustedly.

Doctor Hoff began tugging at his side-whiskers. "Don't do nothing like that," he pleaded. "Come with me to Cincinnati. If he ain't dead they've kidnapped him for a ransom."

"Then Cincinnati is the last place on the map to look, because there's where they want you to think he is. But it doesn't look like a case of ransom to me. Let's see. Was he particularly drunk the day before he disappeared?"

"No. He was sober."

"Unusually sober, maybe?" suggested the other.

"Yes, he was. Been sober for a week. An' he was studyin', too."

"Ah! Studying what?"

"Spanish."

"Spanish, eh? Ever exhibit any interest in foreign tongues before?"

"Not enough to get him through one term in college," returned the other grimly.

"How did you know about his studying?"

"Seen the perfessor in the house."

"Some one you knew?"

"No. I asked him. Roddy was sore because I found out what he was up to."

Upon that point Average Jones meditated a moment.

"Did you see this Spanish professor again?" he inquired presently.

"Now that you speak of it, I didn't see him but the once."

"Can you leave for Toledo on to-night's train?"

"You're goin' to take the case, then?" the quack clawed nervously at his professional white whiskers. "What's your terms?" he demanded.

"That I'm to have full control and that you're to take orders and not give them."

Doctor Hoff swallowed that with a gulp. "You're on," he said finally.

On the train Doctor Hoff regaled his companion with a strictly paternal view of his son's character and pursuits as he knew them. This served, at least, to enlarge his auditor's ideas as to the average American father's vast and profound ignorance of the life, habits, manners and customs of that common but variable species, the Offspring. Beyond this it had little value. Average Jones gave its author a few specific instructions as to minor lines of home investigation, and retired to map out a tentative campaign.

His first call, on arriving at Toledo, was at the business office of the *Daily Saw*, in which he inserted the following paragraph on a repeat-until-stopped order:

WANTED—Instructor in Spanish. One with recent experience preferred. Apply between 9 and 10 A. M. Doctor Hoff, 360 Fairfield Avenue.

Thence he climbed the stairs to the den of the city editor, to whom he stated his errand openly, being too wise in his day and generation to attempt concealment or evasion with a newspaper man from whom he wanted information. The city editor obligingly furnished further details regarding "Rickey" Hoff, as he called the young man, which, while differing in important respects from Doctor Hoff's, bore the ear-marks of superior accuracy.

"The worst of it is," said the newspaper man, "that there are elements of decency about the young cub, if he'd keep sober. He won't go into the old boy's business, because he hates it. Says it's all rot and lies. He's dead right, of course. But there's nothing else for him to do, so he just fights booze. Better make a few inquiries at Silent Charley's."

"What's that?"

"Quiet little bar kept by a talkative Swede. 'Rickey' Hoff hung out there a lot. Charley even had a room fixed up for him to lay off in when he was too pickled to go home."

"Would—er—young Hoff—er—perhaps keep a few—er—extra clothes there?" asked Average Jones, seemingly struggling with a yawn.

The city editor stared. "Oh, I dare say. He used to end his sprees pretty much mussed up."

"That would perhaps explain where the shirt came from," murmured the Ad-Visor. "Much obliged for the suggestion. I'll just step around."

"Silent Charley" he found ready, even eager to talk. Yes; "Rickey" Hoff had been in his place right along. Drunk? No; not even drinking much lately. Two other gentlemen had met him there quite often. They sat in the back room and talked. No, neither of them was Spanish. One was big and clean-shaven and wore a silk hat. They called him "Colonel." A swell dresser. The other man drank gin, and a lot of it. His name was Fred. He was very tanned. One day there had been a hot discussion over a sheet of paper that lay on the table in front of the three men in the back room. "Rickey" had called a messenger boy and sent him out for a geography. "I told you there wasn't any such thing there," the saloonkeeper heard him say triumphantly, when the geography arrived. Then Fred replied: "To h—ll with you and your schoolbook! I tell you I've waded across it." The colonel smoothed things over and it ended in a magnum of champagne being ordered.

"For which the colonel paid?" asked Average Jones.

"Why, yes, he did," assented the saloon man. "He said, 'Well, it's a go, then. Here's luck to us.' He was a good spender, the colonel."

"And you haven't seen any of them since, I suppose?"

"Nary a one."

On his return to the Hoff mansion the investigator found the head thereof in a state of great excitement.

"Say, I've found out something," he cried. "Roddy's gone to Yurrup."

"Where did you find that out?" asked Average Jones with a smile.

"I been going through his papers like you told me. He's been outfitting for a trip. Bought lots of truck the last few days and I found the duplicate sale-checks that come in the packages. There's stubs for a steamer rug and for a dope for seasickness and for a compass," he concluded triumphantly.

"Compass, eh?" observed Average Jones thoughtfully. "Ship's compass is good enough for most of us going to Europe. Anything else?"

"Lot of clothes."

"What kind of clothes?"

"Cheap stuff mostly. Khaki riding-pants, negly-jee shirts and such-like."

"Not much suggestion of Europe there. What more?"

Doctor Hoff consulted a list. "Colored glasses."

"That looks like desert travel."

"Aneroid barometer."

"Mountain climbing."

"Permanganate of potash outfit."

"Snake country," commented the other.

"Patent water-still."

Average Jones leaned forward. "How big?"

"Don't know. Cost twenty dollars."

"Little one, then. That means about three people. Taken with the compass, it means a small-boat trip on salt water."

"Small boat nothin'!" retorted the other. "His doctor met me this morning an' told me Roddy had sent for him and ast him a lot of questions about eatin' aboard ship and which way to have his berth made up, and all that."

"A small-boat trip following a sea trip, then. What else have you found?"

"Nothin' much. Mosquito nettin', pills, surgeon's plaster and odds and ends of drugs."

"Let me see the drug list."

He ran his eye down the paper. Then he looked at Doctor Hoff with a half smile.

"You didn't notice anything peculiar about this list?"

"Don't know as I did."

"Not the—er—nitric acid, for instance?"

"Nope. What of it?"

"Mr. Hoff, your son has been caught by one of the oldest tricks in the whole bunco list—the lost Spanish mine swindle. That acid, together with the rest of the outfit, means a gold-hunt as plain as if it were spelled out. And the Spanish professor was sent for, not to give lessons, but to translate the fake letter. Where does your son bank?"

"Fifth National."

"Telephone there and find out how much he drew."

Doctor Hoff sat down at the 'phone. "Five hundred dollars," he said presently.

"Is that all?" asked the other, disappointed.

"Yes. Wait. He had six checks certified aggregating ten thousand dollars."

"Then it isn't South America or the West Indies. He'd want a letter of credit there. Must be some part of the United States, or just across the border. Well, we've done a good day's work, and I've got a hard evening's thinking before me. We might be able to head off the colonel's personally conducted expedition yet, if we could locate it."

The evening's thinking formulated itself into a telegram to Average Jones' club, the Cosmic. It was one among the many distinctions of the modest little club in Gramercy Park, * that its membership pretty well comprised the range of available information on any topic. Under the "favored applications clause," a person whose knowledge of any particular subject was unique and authoritative, whether the topic were Esperanto† or fistiana,‡ went to the head of the waiting-list automatically and had his initiation fee remitted. Hence, Average Jones was confident of a helpful reply to his message of inquiry, which summed up his conclusions and surmises thus far:

"COSMIC CLUB, NEW YORK CITY:

"*Refer following to geographical expert: Where is large,*

---

* The area between Third Avenue and Park Avenue, bounded by Eighteenth Street and Twenty-Second Street, in Manhattan, the neighborhood includes one of only two private parks in New York City. The National Arts Club and the Players Club are situated in Gramercy Park.

† An artificial language intended to promote universality, created in 1888 by Dr. Ludwik Lazarus Zamenhof, a Polish physician.

‡ A fancy term for boxing.

*shallow, unmapped body of salt water in United States, or
near border, surrounded by hot, snake-infested desert and
mountainous country, reputed to contain gold? Spanish
associations indicated. Wire details and name of best
guide, if obtainable.*

A. JONES."

The reply was disappointing:

"Cyrus C. Allen absent from town. Will forward your wire.
"COSMIC CLUB."

Well poised as Average Jones normally was, he chafed over
the ensuing delay of four days, each of which gave the colonel's
expedition just so much start upon its unknown course. The
only relief was a call from the Spanish instructor who answered
Jones' advertisement. He was the same who had served young
Hoff. As the Ad-Visor surmised, his former employment had
been merely the translation of a letter. The letter was in base
Spanish, he said. He didn't remember much of it, but there
was something about a lost gold mine. Yes; there was reference
to a map. No; no geographical names were mentioned, but
in several places the capital letters B. C. seemed to indicate a
locality. He hadn't noted the date or the signature. That was
all he could tell.

Doctor Hoff, who had been ramping with impatience over
the man's lack of definite memory, now rushed to the atlas and
began to study the maps.

"You needn't trouble," said Average Jones coolly. "You won't
find it there."

"I'll find that B. C. if I have to go over every map in the
geography."

"Then you'll have to get a Spanish edition. For a guess, B. C. is Baja California, the Mexican peninsula of California."

Jones sent a supplementary wire to this effect to Cyrus C. Allen, of the Cosmic Club, and within a few hours received a reply from that eminent cartographer, who had been located in a remote part of Connecticut:

"Probably Laguna Salada, not on map. Seventy miles long; four to eight wide. Between Cocopah and Sierra Gigantica* ranges. Country very wild and arid. Can be reached by water from Yuma, or pack train from Calexico. White, who has hunted there, says Captain Funcke, Calexico, best guide.

"ALLEN."

Average Jones tossed this over to the father.

"As I figure it," he said, "your son's two friends had this all mapped out beforehand for him. One went west direct. He was the imbecile who stopped in Cincinnati and mailed you the bloody shirt to throw you off the scent. Meantime the colonel took Roderick around by a sea route, probably New York and New Orleans."

"That'd explain the steamer rug and the seasickness," admitted Doctor Hoff; "but I don't know what he'd want to go that long way for."

"Simple enough, when you reckon with this colonel person as having brains in his head. He would foresee a hue and cry as soon as the young man disappeared. So he cooks up this trip to keep his prey out of touch with the newspapers for the few days when the news of the disappearance would be fresh enough to

---

* Properly the Sierra de la Giganta range, in eastern Baja California Sur (on the Baja California peninsula). The highest point is 3,858 feet, and the range is just over nine hundred miles long.

be spread abroad in the Associated Press despatches. From New Orleans they'd go on west by train."

"What I don't see is how they caught Roddy on such an old game. He's easy, but I didn't s'pose he was that easy."

"To do him justice, he isn't—quite. They put it up on him rather cleverly. In the period of waiting to hear from the geographical expert I've put in some fairly hard work, going over your son's effects. And, in the room over Silent Charley's bar, I found a newspaper with this in it."

He handed to Doctor Hoff a thin clipping, marked "*Daily Saw,* March 29":

LOST—Spanish letter and map. Of no value except to owner. Return to No. 16, this office, and receive heartfelt thanks.

"Well," said Doctor Hoff, after reading it over twice, "that don't tell me nothing."

"No? Yet it's pretty plain. The two crooks 'planted' the letter and map on your son. Probably slipped them into a pocket of his coat while he was drunk. Then they inserted their little ad, waited until he had time to find the letter, and casually called the advertisement to his attention. The rest would be easy. But I'll have something to say to my clerk, who failed to clip that ad."

"You're workin' for *me,* now," half blustered, half whined the old quack. "Whatche goin' to do next?"

"Pack for the night train."

"Where to?"

"Yuma or Calexico. Don't know which till I get a reply to two telegrams. I'll need five hundred dollars expense money."

"Say, you don't want much, do ye?" snarled the quack, his avaricious soul in revolt at the prospect of immediate outlay.

"When I hire a man I expect him to pay his own expenses and send me the bill."

"Quite so," agreed the other blandly. "But, you see, you aren't hiring me. I'm doing this on spec. And I don't propose to invest anything in a dubious proposition, myself. It isn't too late to call it off, you know."

"No, I do' wanta do that," said the other with contorted face. "I'll get the five hundred here for you in an hour."

"And about the five thousand dollars reward? I think I'd better have a word of writing on that."

"You mean you don't trust me?" snapped the other. "I'm good for five million dollars to-morrow in this town."

"I know you are—in writing," agreed the other equably. "That's why I want your valued signature. You see, to be quite frank, I haven't the fullest confidence in gentlemen in your line of business."

"I'll have my lawyer draw up a form of contract and mail it after you to-morrow," promised the quack with a crafty look.

"No, you wo—" began Average Jones; but he broke off with a smile. "Very well," he amended. "If things work out as I figure them, that will do. And," he added, dropping into his significant drawl and looking the quack flatly in the eye, "don't you—er—bank on my—er—not understanding your offer—and—er—you."

Uncomfortably pondering this reply, Doctor Hoff set about the matter of the expense money. Meantime a telegram came which settled the matter of immediate destination. It apprised Average Jones that, a fortnight previous, this paragraph had appeared in the paid columns of the Yuma *Yucca:*

WANTED—Small, flat-bottomed sailboat. Center-
board type preferred. Hasty, care this office.

Average Jones bought a ticket for Yuma.

Disembarking at the Yuma station three days later, Average Jones blinked in the harsh sunlight at a small, compactly built, keen-eyed man, roughly dressed for the trail.

"I'm Captain Funcke," said the stranger. His speech was gentle, slow, even hesitant; but there was something competent and reliable in his bearing which satisfied the shrewd young reader of men's characters from the outset. "Your wire got me two days since and I came right up."

"Any trace?"

"Left here two days ago."

"Three of them?"

"Yes. Flat-bottomed, narrow-beamed boat, sloop-rigged pretty light."

"Know anything of the men?"

"Only the big one. Calls himself Colonel Richford. Had a fake copper outfit in the mountains east of Alamo."

"Where do you think they're headed for?"

"Probably the wildest country they can find, if they want to get rid of young Hoff," said the other, who had been apprised of the main points of the situation. "That would likely be the Pinto range, to the southwest of the Laguna. Richford knows that country a little. He was in there two years ago."

"They would probably want to get rid of him without obvious murder," said Average Jones. "You see, his money is in certified checks which they'd have to get cashed. If some one should find his body with a bullet hole in it, they'd have some explaining to do."

"Nobody'd be likely to find it. Only about two parties a year get down there. Still, somebody might trail him. And I guess old Richford is too foxy to do any killing when he turns the trick just as well without it."

"Suppose it's the Pintos, then. How do we get there?"

"Hard-ash breeze,"* returned the other succinctly. "Our row-boat is outfitted and waiting."

"Good work!" said Jones heartily. "How far is it?"

"Sixty miles to the turn of the Laguna. There's a four-mile current to help. They've a scant two days' start, and we'll catch up some, for their boat is heavier and their sail is no good with the wind in this direction. If we don't catch up some," he added grimly, "I wouldn't want to insure our young friend's life. So it's all aboard, if you're ready."

For the first time since embarking upon the strange seas of advertising in his quest of the Adventure of Life, Average Jones now met the experience of grilling physical toil. All that day and all the night the two men swung at the oars; swung until every muscle in the young Easterner's back had turned to live nerve-fiber, and the flesh had begun to strip from the palms of his hands. Even so, the hardy captain had done most of the work. Aided by the current, they turned the shoulder of the Cocopah range as the dawn shone lurid in the east, and the captain swung the boat's head to the southern shore of the lake. Meantime, between spells at the oars, Average Jones had outlined the case in full to Funcke. He could have found no better coadjutor.

By nature and equipment every really expert hunter and tracker is a detective. The subtleties of the trial sharpen both physical and mental sensibility. Captain Funcke was, by instinct, a student of that continuous logic which constitutes the science of the chase, whether the prize of pursuit be a mountain sheep's horns or the scholar's meed† of praise for the interpreting of some

---

* Funcke means that they will have to row the boat; hard ash is a common material for the manufacture of oars.

---

† A recompense or reward.

half-obliterated inscription on a pre-Hittite tomb.* After long and silent consideration the captain gave his views.

"It isn't bunco. It's a hold-up. If Richford had wanted to stick young Hoff, he'd never have brought him here. There isn't 'color' enough within eighty miles to gild a cigar band. It looks to me like the scheme is this: They get him off in the mountains, out of sight of the lake, so he'll have no landmark to go by. Then they scare him into signing copartnership papers, and make him turn over those certified checks to them. With the papers to show for it, they go out by Calexico and cash the checks in Los Angeles. They could put up the bluff that their partner was guarding the mine while they bought machinery and outfitted. That'd be good enough to cash certified checks by."

"Yes; that's about the way I figure it out. You spoke of Richford's being able to get rid of young Hoff effectually, without actual murder."

"All he'd have to do would be to quit the boy while he was asleep. A tenderfoot would die of thirst over there in a short time."

"Is there no water?"

"There's a *tenaja* they're depending on. But I doubt if they find any water there now. It's been an extra dry season."

"A *tenaja*?" queried the Ad-Visor.

"Rock-basin holding rainwater," explained the hunter. "There's been no rainfall since August. If they find the *tenaja* empty they'll have barely enough in the canteens they pack to get them to the next water, the Tenaja Poquita, around behind the mountains and across the desert into the next range."

"What's the next water to that?"

"The Stream of Palms. That's a day and a half on foot."

For the space of a hundred oar-strokes Average Jones ruminated.

---

* The Hittite Empire occupied parts of the Anatolian peninsula and the Levant around 1600 BCE.

"Suppose—er—they didn't—er—find any water in the Tenaja Poquita, either?" he drawled.

"Then they *would* be up against it."

"And there's no other water in the Pintos?"

"Yes, there is," said the captain. "There's a *tenaja* that's so high up and so hidden that it's only known to one other man besides me, and he's an Indian. It's less than an hour from the *tenaja* that Richford will take his party to. And we're sure of finding water there. It never dries up this early."

"Get me to young Hoff, then, Captain. You're in command from the moment we land."

It was broad day when the keel pushed softly into the muddy bottom of a long, shallow arm of the lake. Captain Funcke rose, stretched the kinks out of his back, and jumped ashore.

"You say I'm in command?" he inquired.

"Absolute."

"Then you roll up under that *mesquite* and fall asleep. I'm going to cast about for their trail."

To the worn-out oarsman, it seemed only a few moments later that an insistent grip on his shoulder aroused him. But the overhead sun, whose direct rays were fairly boiling the sweat out of him, harshly corrected this impression.

"I've found their boat," said Captain Funcke. "The trail heads for the Pintos. They're traveling heavy. I don't believe they're twenty-four hours ahead of us."

Average Jones stumbled to his feet. "I'm ready," he said.

"It's a case of travel light." The hunter handed over a small bag of food and a large canteen full of water. He himself packed a much larger load, including two canteens and a powerful field glass. Taking a shotgun from the boat, he shouldered it, and set out at a long, easy stride.

To Average Jones the memory of that day has never been

wholly clear. Sodden with weariness, dazzled and muddled by the savage sun-glare, he followed, with eyes fixed, the rhythmically, monotonously moving feet of his leader, through an interminable desert of soft, clogging sand; a desert which dropped away into parched *arroyos,* and rose to scorched *mesas* whereon fierce cacti thrust at him with thorns and spikes; a desert dead and mummified in the dreadful heat; a lifeless Inferno wherein moved neither beast, bird nor insect. He remembers, dimly, lying as he fell, when the indefatigable captain called a halt, and being wakened in the chill breeze of evening, to see a wall of mountains blocking the advance. Food brought him to his normal self again, and in the crisp air of night he set his face to the task of climbing. Severe as this was upon his unaccustomed muscles, the firm rocks were still a welcome relief after the racking looseness of sand that interminably sank away from foothold. At midnight the wearied pursuers dropped down from a high plateau to a narrow *arroyo.* Here again was sand. Fortunately, this time, for in it footprints stood out clear, illuminated by the white moonlight. They led direct to a side *barranca.** There the pursuers found the camp. It was deserted.

Like a hound on the trail, Captain Funcke cast about him.

"Here's where they came in. No—yes—this is it. Confound the cross-tracks!....Here one of them cuts across the ridge to the *tenaja* for water....Wait!...What's this? Coyote trail? Yes, but...Trail brushed over, by thunder! They didn't do it carefully enough...Straight for the rocky *mesa....*That's it! They made their sneak while Hoff was asleep, probably covering trail behind them, and struck out for the inside desert route to the Tenaja Poquita." He took a quick look about the camp and picked up an empty canteen. "Of course, they wouldn't leave him any water."

---

* A deep ravine.

"Then he's gone to hunt it," suggested Average Jones. "Which way?"

"You can't tell which way a tenderfoot will go," said the hunter philosophically. "If he had any savvy at all he'd follow the old beaten track around by the *arroyo* to the water-hole. We'll try it."

On the way, Average Jones noticed his companion stop frequently to examine the sand for something which he evidently didn't find.

"These are fresh footsteps we're following, aren't they?" he asked.

"Yes. It isn't that. He went this way all right. But the *tenaja's* gone dry."

"How can you tell that?"

"No fresh sign of animals going this way. Must have been dry for weeks. Our mining friends have taken what little water there was and left young Hoff to die of thirst," said the other grimly.

"Well, that explains the empty canteen all right."

He turned and renewed his quick progress, leaping from boulder to boulder, between narrowing walls of gray-white rock. Just as Average Jones was spent and almost ready to collapse the leader checked.

"Hark!" he whispered.

Above the beating of the blood in his ears, Jones heard an irregular, insistent scuffing sound. He crouched in silence while the captain crept up to a ledge and cautiously peered over, then went forward in response to the other's urgent beckoning. They looked down into a rock-basin of wild and curious beauty. To this day Average Jones remembers the luminous grace and splendor of a Matilija poppy, which, rooted between two boulders, swayed gently in the white moonlight above a figure of dread. The figure, naked from the waist up, huddled upon the hard-baked mud, digging madly at the earth. A sharp exclamation broke from Average

Jones. The digger half rose, turned, collapsed to his knees, and pointed with bleeding fingers to his open mouth, in which the tongue showed black and swollen.

They went down to him.

An hour later, "Rickey" Hoff was sleeping the sleep of utter exhaustion in camp. Average Jones felt amply qualified to join him. But it was not in the Ad-Visor's character to quit an enterprise before it was wholly completed. So long as the two bandits were on their way to cash the young spendthrift's checks—Jones had heard from the victim a brief account of the extortion—success was not fully won.

"We've got to get that money back," he said to Captain Funcke with conviction.

The hunter made no reply in words. He merely leaned his shotgun against his thigh, reached around beneath his coat and produced a forty-five caliber revolver. This he held out toward Jones.

"Good thing to have," conceded the other. "But—well, no; not in this case. They got the booty with a show of legality, since Hoff signed the copartnership agreement and turned over the checks. It was under duress and threats, it's true, but who's to prove that, they being two to one, and this being Mexico? No; they're within the law, and I've a notion that we can get the swag back by straight sale and barter. Provided, always, we can catch them in time."

"They'll want to make pretty good time to the Tenaja Poquita," pointed out the captain. "They're shy on water."

"On wind, too. They've traveled hard, and they can't be in the pink of condition. According to Hoff, they deserted him while he was taking a nap, about four o'clock in the afternoon. It's a fair bet they'd camp for the night, as you say it's an eight-hour hike to the *tenaja*."

"Eight, the way they'd go."

"Then—er—there's a—er—shorter way?" drawled Average Jones, removing some sand from a wrinkle in his scarified and soiled trousers as carefully as if that were the one immediate and important consideration in life.

"Yes. Across the Padre Cliffs. It cuts off about four hours, and it takes us almost to the secret *tenaja* I spoke of. We can fill up there. But it's not what you'd call safe, even in daylight."

"But to a hunter, wouldn't it be well worth the risk for a record pair of horns—even if they were only tin horns?" queried Average Jones suggestively.

Captain Funcke relaxed into a grin. He nodded.

"What'll we do with *him?*" he asked, jerking his head toward the sleeper.

"Leave him water, food and a note. Now, about this Tenaja Poquita we're headed for. How much water do you think there is in it?"

"If there's a hundred gallons it's doing well, this dry season."

Average Jones got painfully to his feet. Looking carefully over the scattered camp outfit, he selected from it a collapsible pail. Captain Funcke glanced at it with curiosity, but characteristically forebore to ask any questions. He himself shouldered the largest canteen.

"This'll be enough for both until we reach the supply," he said. "Don't need so much water at night."

But the tenderfoot hung upon his own shoulder, not only the smallest of their three canteens, but also the empty one which they had found in the camp. Their own third tin, almost full, they left beside Hoff, with a note.

"I've a notion," said Jones, "that I'll need all these receptacles for water in my own peculiar business."

"All right," assented the other patiently. He took one of them and the pail from Jones and skillfully disposed them on his own back. "Ready? Hike, then."

Two hours of the roughest kind of climbing brought them to a landslide. These sudden shiftings of the slopes are a frequent feature of travel in the Lower California mountains, often obliterating trails and costing the wayfarer painful and perilous search for a new path. On the Padre Cliffs, however, had occurred that rare phenomenon, a benevolent avalanche, piling up a safe and feasible embankment around the angle of an impracticable precipice, and thus saving an hour of the most ticklish going of the journey. Thanks to this dispensation, the two men reached the Tenaja Poquita before dawn. Scouting ahead, the captain reported no fresh trail except coyotes and mule deer, and not more than seventy-five gallons of water in the basin. Of this they both drank deeply. Then after they had filled all the canteens, Average Jones unfolded his scheme to the captain.

"If any one caught us at it," commented that experienced hunter, "we'd be shot without warning. However, the water would be evaporated in a few days anyhow, and I'll post notices at the next water-camps. I'm with you."

Taking turn and turn about with the pail, they bailed out the rock-basin, scattering the water upon the greedy sand. What little moisture remained in the sticky mud at the bottom they blotted up with more sand. They then rolled in boulders. Average Jones looked down into the hollow with satisfaction, and moved his full canteens into a grotto.

"This company," he said, "is now open for business."

At eight o'clock there was a clatter of boots upon the rocks and two men came staggering up the defile. Colonel Richford and his partner did not look to be in good repair. The colonel's face was drawn and sun-blotched. His companion, the "Fred" of Silent Charley's bar, was bloated and shaken with liquor. Both panted with the hard, dry, open-lipped breath of the first stage of thirst-exhaustion. The colonel, who was in the lead, checked and started upon discovering astride of a rock a pleasant-visaged young man of a familiar American type, whose appearance was in nowise remarkable except as to locality. With a grunt that might have been greeting, but was more probably surprise, the new-comer passed the seated man. Captain Funcke he did not see at all. That astute hunter had dropped behind a boulder.

At the brink of the *tenaja* the colonel stopped dead. Then with an outburst of flaming language, he leaped in, burrowing among the rocks.

"Dry!" he yelled, lifting a furious and appalled face to his companion.

Fred stood staring from Average Jones to his three canteens. There was a murderous look on his sinister face.

"Got water?" he growled.

"Yes," replied the young man.

"Here, Colonel," said Fred. "Here's drink for us."

"For sale," added Average Jones calmly.

"People don't *buy* water in this country."

"You're not people," returned Average Jones cheerfully. "You're a corporation; a soulless corporation. The North Pinto Gold Mining Company."

"What's that!" cried the colonel thickly.

His hand flew back to his belt. Then it dropped, limp at his side, for he was gazing into the two barrels of a shotgun, which, materializing over a rock, were pointing accurately and disconcertingly at the pit of his stomach. From behind the gun Captain Funcke's quiet voice remarked:

"I wouldn't, Colonel. As for you," he added, turning to the other wayfarer, who carried a rifle, "you want to remember that a shotgun has two barrels, usually both loaded."

Stepping forward, Average Jones "lifted" the financier's

weapon. Then he deprived Fred of his rifle amid a surprisingly brilliant outburst of verbal pyrotechnics.

"Now we can talk business comfortably," he observed.

"I can't talk at all pretty quick if I don't git a moistener," said Fred piteously.

Pouring out a scant cupful of water into his hat, Average Jones handed it over. "Drink slowly," he advised. "You've got about a hundred dollars' worth there at present quotations."

Colonel Richford's head went up with a jerk.

"Hundred dollars' worth!" he croaked, his eyes fiery with suspicion. "Are you going to hold up two men dying of thirst?"

"There's been only one man in danger of that death around here. His name is Hoff."

The redoubtable colonel gasped, and leaned back against a rock.

"You'll be relieved to learn that he's safe. Now, to answer your question: No, I don't propose to hold up two men for anything. I propose to deal with the president and treasurer of the North Pinto Gold Mining Company. As a practical mining man you will appreciate the absolute necessity of water in your operations. The nearest available supply is some ten hours distant. Before you could reach it I fear that—er—your company would—er—have gone out of existence. Therefore I am fortunate in being able to offer you a small supply which I will put on the market at the low rate of ten thousand dollars. I may add that—er—certified checks will—er—be accepted."

For two hours the colonel, with the occasional objurgatory assistance of his partner, talked, begged, argued, threatened, and even wept. By the end of that time his tongue was making sounds like a muffled castanet, and his resolution was scorched out of him.

"You've got us," he croaked. "Here's your checks. Give me the water."

"In proper and legal form, please," said Average Jones.

He produced a contract and a fountain-pen. The contract was duly signed and witnessed. It provided for the transfer of the water, in consideration of one revolver and ten thousand dollars in checks. These checks were endorsed over to A. V. R. E. Jones, whereupon he turned over the pail of water and the largest canteen to the parched miners. Then, sorting out the checks, he pocketed two aggregating five thousand dollars, tore up three, and holding the other in his hand, turned to Captain Funcke.

"Will five hundred dollars pay you for keeping young Hoff down here a couple of months and making the beginning of a man of him?" he asked.

"Yes, and more," replied the captain.

"It's a go," said Average Jones. "I'd like to make the job complete."

Then, courteously bidding the North Pinto Gold Mining Company farewell, the two water-dealers clambered up the rocks and disappeared beyond the abrupt sky-line.

Once again Doctor Conrad Hoff sat in the private office of Average Jones, Ad-Visor. The young man was thinner, browner and harder of fiber than the Jones of two weeks previous. Doctor Hoff looked him over with shrewd eyes.

"Say, your trip ain't done you no harm, has it?" he exclaimed with a boisterous and false good nature. "You look like a fightin'-cock. Hope the boy comes out as good. You say he's all right?"

"You've got his letter, in which he says so himself. That's enough proof, isn't it?"

"Oh, I've got the letter all right. An' it's enough as far as it goes. But it ain't proof; not the kind of proof a man pays out reward money on," he added, cunningly. "You say you left Roddy down there with that Funcke feller, hey?"

"Yes. It'll make a man of him, if anything will. I threw that in as an extra."

"Yes; but what about them two crooks that gold-bricked him? What's become of them?"

"On their way to Alaska or Bolivia or Corea,* or anywhere else, for all I know—or care," said Average Jones indifferently.

"Is *that* so?" The quack's voice had taken on a sneering intonation. "You come back here with your job not half done, with the guilty fellers loose an' runnin', an' you expect me to pay over the five thousand dollars to you. Huh!"

"No, I—er—don't expect—er—anything of the sort," said Average Jones slowly.

Doctor Hoff's little, restless eyes puckered at the corners. He was puzzled. What did the young fellow mean?

"Don't, eh?" he said, groping in his mind for a solution.

"No. You forgot to send me that promised form of agreement, didn't you? Thought you'd fooled me, perhaps. Well, I wouldn't be so foolish as to expect anything in the way of fair and honorable dealing when I contract to do up a mining swindler for the benefit of the only meaner creature on God's earth—a patent medicine poisoner. So I took precautions."

"Say, be careful of what you say, young man," blustered the quack.

"I am—quite particular. And, before you leave, wouldn't you like to hear about the five thousand dollars I got for my little job?"

Doctor Hoff blinked rapidly.

"What didje say?" he finally inquired.

"Five—er—thousand—er—dollars."

---

* An alternate spelling for the country of Korea, then a single political unit (although it was also referred to as "the Koreas," likely in reference to its first-millennium division into three kingdoms).

"You got it?"

"In the bank."

"Where-dje get it?"

"From you, through your son's check, duly certified."

Doctor Hoff blinked more rapidly and moistened his lips with an effortful tongue.

"H-h-how-dje work it?" he asked in a die-away voice.

"By a forced sale of water rights to the North Pinto Gold Mining Company, dissolved, in which Mr. Roderick Hoff was vice-president and silent partner," replied Average Jones with an amiable smile, as he opened the door significantly.

CHAPTER IV
THE MERCY SIGN—ONE

"Want a job, Average?"

Bertram, his elegance undimmed by the first really trying weather of the early summer, drifted to the coolest spot in the Ad-Visor's sanctum and spread his languid length along a wicker settee.

"Give a man breathing space, can't you?" returned Average Jones. "This is hotter than Baja California."

"Why, I assumed that your quest of the quack's scion would have trained you down fit for anything."

"Haven't even caught up with the clippings that Simpson floods me with, since I came back," confessed the other. "What have you got up your faultlessly creased sleeve? It's got to be something different to rouse me from a well-earned lethargy."

"Because a man buncoes a loving father out of five thousand dollars"—Average Jones snorted gently—"is no reason why he should unanimously elect himself a life member of the Sons of Idleness," murmured Bertram.

He cast an eye around the uniquely decorated walls, upon which hung, here, the shrieking prospectus of a mythical gold mine; there a small but venomous political placard, and on all sides examples of the uncouth or unusual in paid print; exploitations of grotesque quackeries; appeals, business-like, absurd, or even passionate, in the form of "Wants;" threats thinly disguised as "Personals;" dim suggestions of crime, of fraud, of hope, of tragedy, of mania, all decorated with the stars of "paid matter" or designated by the *Adv.* sign, and each representing some case brought to A. Jones, Ad-Visor—to quote his hybrid and expressive door-plate—by some one of his numerous and incongruous clients.

"Something different?" repeated the visitor, reverting to Average Jones' last observation. "Well, yes; I think so. Where is Bellair Street?"*

"Ask a directory. How should I know?" retorted the other lazily. "Sounds like old Greenwich Village."

Bertram reached over with a cane of some pale, translucent green wood, selected to match his pale green tie and the marvelous green opal which held it in place, and prodded his friend severely in the ribs. "Double-up Lucy; the sun is in the sky!"† he proclaimed with unwonted energy. "Listen. I cut this out of yesterday's *Evening Register*. With my own fair hands I did it, to rouse you from your shameless sloth. With your kind attention, ladies and gentlemen—" He read:

"WANTED—A young man, unattached, competent to act as assistant in outdoor scientific work. Manual

---

* A fictional street.

---

† This is the punch line of an old anecdote: An instructor was teaching his pupil to spell and read. The pupil consistently spelled out two letters when the letter was doubled: For example, the word "feel" was spelled out by the pupil as "f-e-e-l" instead of, as the instructor insisted, "f-double e-l." The pupil finally learned his lesson, and when confronted with the sentence in the reading "Up, up, Lucy! The sun is in the sky!" read "Double-up, Lucy! The sun is in the sky!" (The anecdote can be found as early as 1886 in the magazine *Cottage Hearth* and is repeated in various newspapers and magazines in the 1890s.)

skill as desirable as experience. Emolument for one month's work generous. Man without family insisted upon. Apply after 8:30 p. m. in proper person. Smith, 74 Bellair Street."

Slowly whirling in his chair, Average Jones held out a hand, received the clipping, read it through with attention, laid it on the desk, and yawned.

"Is that all?" said the indignant Bertram. "Do you notice that 'unattached' in the opening sentence? And the specification that the applicant must be without family? Doesn't that inspire any notion above a yawn in your palsied processes of mind?"

"It does; several notions. I yawned," explained Average Jones with dignity, "because I perceive with pain that I shall have to go to work. What do you make of the thing, yourself?"

"Well, this man Smith—"

"What man Smith?"

"Smith, of 74 Bellair Street, who signs the ad."

Average Jones laughed. "There isn't any Smith," he said.

"What do you know about it?" demanded Bertram, sitting up.

"Only what the advertisement tells me. It was written by a foreigner; that's too obvious for argument. 'Emolument generous.' 'Apply in proper person.' Did a Smith ever write that? No. A Borgrevsky might have, or a Greiffenhauser, or even a Mavronovoupoulos.* But never Smith."

"Well, it's nothing to me what his name is. Only I thought you might be the aspiring young scientist he was yearning for."

"Wouldn't wonder if I were, thank you. Let's see. Bellair Street? Where's the directory? Thanks. Yes, it is Greenwich Village. Well, I think I'll just stroll down that way and have a look after dinner."

---

* That is, a Russian, German, or Greek, though these are intended to be comical permutations of common names.

Thus it was that Mr. Adrian Van Reypen Egerton Jones found himself on a hot May evening pursuing the Adventure of Life into the vestibule of a rather dingy old house which had once been the abode of solemn prosperity if not actual aristocracy in the olden days of New York City. Almost immediately the telegraphic click of the lock apprised him that he might enter, and as he stepped into the hallway the door of the right-hand ground-floor apartment opened to him.

"You will please come in," said a voice.

The tone was gentle and measured. Also it was, by its accent, alien to any rightful Smith. The visitor stepped into a passageway which was dim—until he entered it and the door swung behind him. Then it became pitch black.

"You will pardon this," said the voice. "A severe affection of the eyes compels me."

"You are Mr. Smith?" asked Average Jones.

"Yes. Your hand if you please."

The visitor, groping, brushed with his fingers the back of a hand which felt strangely hot and pulpy. Immediately the hand turned and closed, and he was led forward to an inner room and seated in a chair. The gentle, hot clasp relaxed and left his wrist free. A door facing him, if his ears could be trusted, opened and shut.

"You will find matches at your elbow," said the voice, coming dulled, from a further apartment. "Doubtless you would be more comfortable with a light."

"Thank you," returned Average Jones, enormously entertained by the dime-novel setting which his host had provided for him.

He lighted the gas and looked about a sparsely furnished room without a single distinguishing feature, unless a high and odd-shaped traveling-bag which stood on a chair near by could be so regarded. The voice interrupted his survey.

"You have come in answer to my advertisement?"

"Yes, sir."

"You are, then, of scientific pursuit?"

"Of scientific ambition, at least. I hope to meet your requirements."

"Your name, if you please."

"Jones; A. Jones, of New York City."

"You live with your family?"

"I have no family or near relatives."

"That is well. I will not conceal from you that there are risks. But the pay is high. Can you endure exposure? Laboring in all weathers? Subsisting on rough fare and sleeping as you may?"

"I have camped in the northern forests."

"Yes," mused the voice. "You look hardy."

Average Jones arose. "You—er—are spying upon me, then," he drawled quietly. "I might have—er—suspected a peep-hole."

He advanced slowly toward the door whence the voice came. A chair blocked his way. Without lowering his gaze he shoved at the obstacle with his foot.

"Have a care!" warned the voice.

The chair toppled and overturned. From it fell, with a light shock, the strange valise, which, striking the floor, flew open, disclosing a small cardboard cabinet.* Across the front of the cabinet was a strip of white paper labeled in handwriting, each letter being individual, with what looked to the young man like the word "MERCY." He stooped to replace the bag.

"Do not touch it," ordered the voice peremptorily.

Average Jones straightened up to face the door again.

"I will apologize for my clumsiness," he said slowly, "when you explain why you have tried to trick me."

---

* A small box.

There was a pause. Then—

"Presently," said the voice. "Meantime, after what you have accidentally seen, you will perhaps appreciate that the employment is not without its peril."

Average Jones stared from the door to the floored cabinet and back again in stupefaction.

"Perhaps I'm stupid," he said, "but a misshapen valise containing a cabinet with a girl's name on it doesn't seem calculated to scare an able-bodied man to death. It isn't full of dynamite, is it?"

"What is your branch of scientific work?" counter-questioned the other.

"Botany," replied the young man, at random.

"No other? Physics? Entomology? Astronomy? Chemistry? Biology?"

The applicant shook his head in repeated negation. "None that I've specialized on."

"Ah! I fear you will not suit my purpose."

"All right. But you haven't explained, yet, why you've been studying me through a peep-hole, when I am not allowed to see you."

After a pause of consideration the voice spoke again.

"You are right. Since I can not employ you, I owe you every courtesy for having put you to this trouble. You will observe that I am not very presentable."

The side door swung open. In the dimness of the half-disclosed apartment Average Jones saw a man huddled in a chair. He wore a black skull cap. So far as identification went he was safe. His whole face was grotesquely blotched and swollen. So, also, were the hands which rested on his knees.

"You will pardon me," said Average Jones, "but I am by nature cautious. You have touched me. Is it contagious?"

A contortion of the features, probably indicating a smile, made the changeling face more hideous than before.

"Be at peace," he said. "It is not. You can find your way out? I bid you good evening, sir."

"Now I wonder," mused Average Jones, as he jolted on the rear platform of an Eighth Avenue car, "by what lead I could have landed that job. I rather think I've missed something."

All that night, and recurrently on many nights thereafter, the poisoned and contorted face and the scrawled "MERCY" on the cabinet lurked troublously in his mind. Nor did Bertram cease to scoff him for his maladroitness until both of them temporarily forgot the strange "Smith" and his advertisement in the entrancement of a chase which led them for a time far back through the centuries to a climax that might well have cost Average Jones his life. They had returned from Baltimore and the society of the Man who spoke Latin* a few days when Bertram, at the club, called up Average Jones' office.

"I'm sending Professor Paul Gehren to you," was his message. "He'll call to-day or to-morrow."

Average Jones knew Professor Gehren by sight, knew of him further by repute as an impulsive, violent, warm-hearted and learned pundit who, for a typically meager recompense, furnished sundry classes of young gentlemen with amusement, alarm and instruction, in about equal parts, through the medium of lectures at the Metropolitan University. During vacations the professor pursued, with some degree of passion, experiments which added luster and selected portions of the alphabet to his name. Twice a week he walked down-town to the Cosmic Club, where he was

---

* "The Man Who Spoke Latin" was published in magazine form in January 1911, six months after "The Mercy Sign" was published in magazine form. Adams apparently forgot the order of the stories when he inserted this cross-reference to a story that had not yet appeared—not unlike the apparent confusion of Dr. Watson in the recounting of his Sherlock Holmes stories!

wont to dine and express destructive and anarchistic views upon the nature, conduct, motives and personality of the organization's governing committees.

On the day following Bertram's telephone, Professor Gehren entered Astor Court Temple, took the elevator to the ninth floor, and, following directions, found himself scanning a ground-glass window flaunting the capitalized and gilded legend,

A. JONES, AD-VISOR.

"Ad-Visor," commented the professor, rancorously. "A vicious verbal monstrosity!" He read on:

ADVICE UPON ADVERTISING IN ALL FORMS
Consultation Free. Step In

"Consultation free!" repeated the educator with virulence. "A trap! A manifest pitfall! I don't know why Mr. Bertram should have sent me hither. The enterprise is patently quack," he asseverated in a rising voice.

Upon the word a young man opened the door and, emerging, received the accusation full in the face. The young man smiled.

"Quack, I said," repeated the exasperated mentor, "and I repeat it. Quack!"

"If you're suffering from the delusion that you're a duck," observed the young man mildly, "you'll find a taxidermist on the top floor."

The caller turned purple. "If you are Mr. Jones, of the Cosmic Club—"

"I am."

"—there are certain things which Mr. Bertram must explain."

"Yes; Bertram said that you were coming, but I'd almost given you up. Come in."

"Into a—a—den where free advice is offered? Of all the patent and infernal rascalities, sir, the offer of free advice—"

"There, there," soothed the younger man. "I know all about the free swindles. This isn't one of them. It's just a fad of mine."

He led the perturbed scholar inside and got him settled in a chair. "Now, go ahead. Show me the advertisement and tell me how much you lost."

"I've lost my assistant. There is no advertisement about it. What I came for is advice. But upon seeing your tricky door-plate—"

"Oh, that's merely to encourage the timorous. Who is this assistant?"

"Harvey Craig, a youth, hardly more than a boy, for whom I feel a certain responsibility, as his deceased parents left him in my care."

"Yes," said Jones as the professor paused.

"He has disappeared."

"When?"

"Permanently, since ten days ago."

"Permanently?"

"Up to that time he had absented himself without reporting to me for only three or four days at a time."

"He lived with you?"

"No. He had been aiding me in certain investigations at my laboratory."

"In what line?"

"Metallurgy."

"When did he stop?"

"About four weeks ago."

"Did he give any reason?"

"He requested indefinite leave. Work had been offered him, he hinted, at a very high rate of remuneration."

"You don't know by whom?"

"No, I know nothing whatever about it."

"Have you any definite suspicions as to his absence?"

"I gravely fear that the boy has made away with himself."

"Why so?"

"After his first absence I called to see him at his room. He had obviously undergone a violent paroxysm of grief or shame."

"He told you this?"

"No. But his eyes, and, indeed, his whole face, were abnormally swollen, as with weeping."

"Ah, yes." Average Jones' voice had suddenly taken on a bored indifference. "Were—er—his hands, also?"

"His hands? Why should they?"

"Of course, why, indeed? You noted them?"

"I did not, sir."

"Did he seem depressed or morose?"

"I can not say that he did."

"Professor Gehren, what newspaper do you take?"

The scholar stared. "The *Citizen* in the morning, The *Register* in the evening."

"Are either of them delivered to your laboratory?"

"Yes; the *Register.*"

"Do you keep it on file?"

"No."

"Ah! That's a pity. Then you wouldn't know if one were missing?"

The professor reflected. "Yes, there was a copy containing a letter upon Von Studeborg's recent experiments—"

"Can you recall the date?"

"After the middle of June, I think."

Average Jones sent for a file and handed it to Professor Gehren.

"Is this it?" he asked, indicating the copy of June 18.

"That is the letter!" said that gentleman.

Average Jones turned the paper and found, upon an inside page, the strange advertisement from 74 Bellair Street.

"One more question, Professor," said he. "When did you last see Mr. Craig?"

"Nine or ten days ago. I think it was July 2."

"How did he impress you?"

"As being somewhat preoccupied. Otherwise normal."

"Was his face swollen then?"

"No."

"Where did you see him?"

"The first time at my laboratory, about eleven o'clock."

"You saw him again that day, then?"

"Yes. We met by accident at a little before two P. M. on Twenty-third Street. I was surprised, because he had told me he had to catch a noon train and return to his work."

"Then he hadn't done so?"

"Yes. He explained that he had, but that he had been sent back to buy some supplies."

"You believe he was telling the truth?"

"In an extensive experience with young men I have never known a more truthful one than he."

"Between the first day of his coming back to New York and the last, had you seen him?"

"I had talked with him over the telephone. He called up two or three times to say that he was well and working hard and that he hoped to be back in a few weeks."

"Where did he call up from?"

"As he did not volunteer the information, I am unable to say."

"Unfortunate again. Well, I think you may drop the notion

of suicide. If anything of importance occurs, please notify me at once. Otherwise, I'll send you word when I have made progress."

Having dismissed the anxious pundit, Average Jones, so immersed in thought as to be oblivious to outer things, made his way to the Cosmic Club in a series of caroms from indignant pedestrian to indignant pedestrian. There, as he had foreseen, he found Robert Bertram.

"Can I detach you from your usual bridge game this evening?" he demanded of that languid gentleman.

"Very possibly. What's the inducement?"

"Chapter Second of the Bellair Street advertisement. I've told you the first chapter. You've been the god-outside-the-machine so far.* Now, come on in."

Together they went to the Greenwich Village house. The name "Smith" had disappeared from the vestibule.

"As I expected," said Jones. "Our hope be in the landlord!"

The landlord turned out to be a German landlady, who knew little concerning her late ground-floor tenant and evinced no interest in the subject. The "perfessor," as she termed "Smith," had taken the flat by the month, was prompt in payment, quiet in habit, given to long and frequent absences; had been there hardly at all in the last few weeks. Where had he moved to? Himmel only knew! He had left no address. Where did his furniture go? Nowhere; he'd left it behind. Was any one in the house acquainted with him? Mrs. Marron in the other ground-floor flat had tried to be. Not much luck, she thought.

Mrs. Marron was voluble, ignorant, and a willing source of information.

"The perfessor? Sure! I knew'm. 'Twas me give'm the name. He was a Mejum. Naw! Not for money. Too swell for that. But

---

* The deus ex machina, once literally a god lowered onto a stage, now meaning an unexpected or contrived turn of situation.

a real-thing Mejum. A big one; one of the kind it comes to, nacheral. Spirit-rappin's! Somethin' fierce! My kitchen window is on the air-shaft. So's his. Many's the time in the still evenin's I've heard the rap-rap-rappin' on his window an' on the wall, but mostly on the window. Blip! out of the dark. It'd make you just hop! And him sittin' quiet and peaceful in the front room all the time. Yep; my little girl seen him there while I was hearin' the raps."

"Did you ask him about them?" inquired Jones.

"Sure! He wouldn't have it at first. Then he kinder smiled and half owned up. And once I seen him with his materializin' wand, sittin' in the room almost dark."

"His what?"

"Materializin' wand. Spirit-rod, you know. As tall as himself and all shiny and slick. It was slim and sort o' knobby like this wood—what's the name of it, now?—they make fish poles out of.* Only the real big-bugs in spiritualism use 'em. They're dangerous. You wouldn't catch me touchin' it or goin' in there even now. I says to Mrs. Kraus, I says—"

And so the stream of high-pitched, eager talk flowed until the two men escaped from it into the vacant apartment. This was much as Average Jones had seen on his former visit. Only the strange valise was missing. Going to the kitchen, which opened through intermediate doors on a straight line with the front room, Average Jones inspected the window. The glass was thickly marked with faint, bluish blurs, being, indeed, almost opaque from them in the middle of the upper pane. There was nothing indicative below the window, unless it were a considerable amount of crumbled putty, which he fingered with puzzled curiosity.

---

* Bamboo.

In the front room a mass of papers had been half burned. Some of them were local journals, mostly the *Evening Register*. A few were publications in the Arabic text.

"Oriental newspapers," remarked Bertram.

Average Jones picked them up and began to fold them. From between two sheets fluttered a very small bit of paper, narrow and half curled, as if from the drying of mucilage. He lifted and read it.

"Here we are again, Bert," he remarked in his most casual tone. "The quality of *this* Mercy is strained, all right."*

The two men bent over the slip, studying it. The word was, as Average Jones had said, in a strained, effortful handwriting, and each letter stood distinct. These were the characters:

$$Me \cdot 2 \, cy$$

"Is it mathematical, do you think, possibly?" asked Average Jones.

"All alone by itself like that? Rather not! More like a label, if you ask me."

"The little sister of the label on the cabinet, then."

"*Cherchez la femme,*" observed Bertram. "It sounds like perfect foolishness to me; a swollen-faced outlander who rules familiar spirits with a wand, and, between investigations in the realms of science, writes a girl's name all over the place like a lovesick school-boy! Is Mercy his spirit-control, do you suppose?"

"Oh, let's get out of here," said Average Jones. "I'm getting dizzy with it all. The next step," he observed, as they walked slowly up the street, "is by train. Want to take a short trip to-morrow, Bert? Or, perhaps, several short trips?"

---

* Referring to Portia's famous speech in Shakespeare's *The Merchant of Venice* (act 4, scene 1), in which, defending Antonio, she states, "The quality of mercy is not strained. It droppeth as the gentle rain from heaven."

"Whither away, fair youth?"

"To the place where the fake 'Smith' and the lost Craig have been doing their little stunts."

"I thought you said Professor Gehren couldn't tell you where Craig had gone."

"No more he could. So I've got to find out for myself. Here's the way I figure it out: The two men have been engaged in some out-of-door work that is extra hazardous. So much we know. Harvey Craig has, I'm afraid, succumbed to it. Otherwise he'd have sent some word to Professor Gehren. He may be dead or he may only be disabled by the dangerous character of the work, whatever it was. In any case our mysterious foreign friend has probably skipped out hastily. Now, I propose to find the railroad station they passed through, coming and going, and interview the ticket agent."

"You've got a fine large contract on your hands to find it."

"Not so large, either. All we have to do is to look for a place that is very isolated and yet quite near New York."

"How do you know it is quite near New York?"

"Because Harvey Craig went there and back between noon and two o'clock, Professor Gehren says. Now, we've got to find such a place which is near a stretch of deserted, swampy ground, very badly infested with mosquitoes. I'd thought of the Hackensack Meadows, just across the river in Jersey."

"That is all very well," said Bertram; "but why mosquitoes?"

"Why, the poisoned and swollen face and hands both of them suffered from," explained Average Jones. "What else could it be?"

"I'd thought of poison-ivy or some kind of plant they'd been grubbing at."

"So had I. But I happened to think that anything of that sort, if it had poisoned them once, would keep on poisoning them, while mosquitoes they could protect themselves against, if they didn't become immune, as they most likely would. As there must have been a lot of 'skeeters' to do the kind of job that 'Smith's' face showed, I naturally figured on a swamp."

"Average," said Bertram solemnly, "there are times when I conceive a sort of respect for your commonplace and plodding intellect. Now, let me have my little inning. I used to commute on the Jersey and Delaware Short Line. There's a station on that line, Pearlington by name, that's a combination of Mosquitoville, Lonesomehurst and Nutting Doon.* It's in the mathematical center of the ghastliest marsh anywhere between Here and Somewhere-else. I think that's our little summer resort, and I'm yours for the nine A. M. train to-morrow."

Dismounting from that rather casual accommodation on the following day, the two friends found Pearlington to consist of a windowed packing-box inhabited by a hermit in a brass-buttoned blue. This lonely official readily identified the subjects of Average Jones' inquiry.

"I guess I know your friends, all right. The dago was tall and thin and had white hair; almost snow-white. No, he wasn't old, neither. He talked very soft and slow. Used to stay off in the reeds three and four days at a time. No, ain't seen him for near a week; him nor his boat nor the young fellow that was with him. Sort of bugologists, or something, wasn't they?"

"Have you any idea where we could find their camp?"

The railroad man laughed.

"Fine chance you got of finding anything in that swamp. There's ten square miles of it, every square just like every other square, and a hundred little islands, and a thousand creeks and rivers winding through."

"You're right," agreed Average Jones. "It would take a month to search it. You spoke of a boat."

---

* Fictional nondescript small towns; "Podunk" is another such name.

"It's my notion they must have had a houseboat. They could a-rowed it up on the tide from the Kills*—a little one. I never saw no tent with 'em. And they had to have something over their heads. The boat I seen 'em have was a rowboat. I s'pose they used it to go back and forth in."

"Thanks," said Average Jones. "That's a good idea about the houseboat."

On the following day this advertisement appeared in the newspapers of several shore towns along the New Jersey and Staten Island coast.

ADRIFT—A small houseboat lost several days ago from the Hackensack Meadows. Fifty dollars reward paid for information leading to recovery. JONES, Advisor, Astor Court Temple, New York.

Two days later came a reply, locating the lost craft at Bayonne. Average Jones went thither and identified it. Within its single room was uttermost confusion, testifying to the simplest kind of housekeeping sharply terminated. Attempt had been made to burn the boat before it was given to wind and current, but certain evidences of charred wood, and the fact of a succession of furious thunder-showers in the week past, suggested the reason for failure. In a heap of rubbish, where the fire had apparently started, Average Jones found, first, a Washington newspaper, which he pocketed; next, with a swelling heart, the wreck of the pasteboard cabinet, but no sign of the strange valise which had held it. The "Mercy" sign was gone from the cabinet, its place being supplied by

---

* The "Kills" likely refers to Kill Van Kull, a tidal strait between Staten Island, New York, and Bayonne, New Jersey. "Kill" is derived from the Middle Dutch word *kille* for creek.

a placard, larger, in a different handwriting, and startlingly more specific:

"DANGER! IF FOUND DESTROY AT ONCE.
Do Not Touch With Bare Hands."

There was nothing else. Gingerly, Average Jones detached the sign. The cabinet proved to be empty. He pushed a rock into it, lifted it on the end of a stick and dropped it overboard. One after another eight little fishes glinted up through the water, turned their white bellies to the sunlight and bobbed, motionless. The investigator hastily threw away the label and cast his gloves after it. But on his return to the city he was able to give a reproduction of the writing to Professor Gehren which convinced that anxious scholar that Harvey Craig had been alive and able to write not long before the time when the houseboat was set adrift.

CHAPTER V
THE MERCY SIGN—TWO

Some days after the recovery of the houseboat, Average Jones sat at breakfast, according to his custom, in the café of the Hotel Palatia. Several matters were troubling his normally serene mind. First of these was the loss of the trail which should have led to Harvey Craig. Second, as a minor issue, the Oriental papers found in the deserted Bellair Street apartment had been proved, by translation, to consist mainly of revolutionary sound and fury, signifying, to the person most concerned, nothing. As for the issue of the Washington daily, culled from the houseboat, there was, amidst the usual mélange of social, diplomatic, political and city news, no marked passage to show any reason for its having been in the possession of "Smith." Average Jones had studied and restudied the columns, both reading matter and advertising, until he knew them almost by heart. During the period of waiting for his order to be brought he was brooding over the problem, when he felt a hand-pressure on his shoulder and turned to confront Mr. Thomas Colvin McIntyre, solemn of countenance and groomed with a supernal modesty of elegance, as befitted a rising young diplomat, already Fifth Assistant Secretary of State of the United States of America.

"Hello, Tommy," said the breakfaster. "What'll you have to drink? An *entente cordiale*?"*

"Don't joke," said the other. "I'm in a pale pink funk. I'm afraid to look into the morning papers."

"Hello! What have you been up to that's scandalous?"

"It isn't me," replied the diplomat ungrammatically. "It's Telfik Bey."

"Telfik Bey? Wait a minute. Let me think." The name had struck a response from some thought-wire within Average Jones' perturbed brain. Presently it came to him as vizualized print in small head-lines, reproduced to the mind's eye from the Washington newspaper which he had so exhaustively studied.

THIS TURK A QUICK JUMPER
Telfik Bey, Guest of Turkish Embassy, Barely
Escapes a Speeding Motor-Car

No arrest, it appeared, had been made. The "story," indeed, was brief, and of no intrinsic importance other than as a social note. But to Average Jones it began to glow luminously.

"Who is Telfik Bey?" he inquired.

"He isn't. Up to yesterday he was a guest of this hotel."

"Indeed! Skipped without paying his bill?"

"Yes—ah. Skipped—that is, left—suddenly—without paying his bill, if you choose to put it that way."

The tone was significant. Average Jones' good-natured face became grave.

"Oh, I beg your pardon, Tommy. Was he a friend of yours?"

"No. He was, in a sense, a ward of the Department, over here on invitation. This is what has almost driven me crazy."

---

* Literally, an informal treaty or alliance—the speaker here is punning on the word "cordial," meaning a liqueur.

Fumbling nervously in the pocket of his creaseless white waist-coat he brought forth a death notice.

"From the *Dial*," he said, handing it to Average Jones.

The clipping looked conventional enough.

DIED—July 21, suddenly at the Hotel Palatia: Telfik Bey of Stamboul, Turkey. Funeral services from the Turkish Embassy, Washington, on Tuesday. Ana Alhari.

"If the newspapers ever discover—" The young diplomat stopped short before the enormity of the hypothesis.

"It looks straight enough to me as a death notice, except for the tail. What does 'Ana Alhari' mean? Sort of a *requiescat*?"

"Yes; like a mice!"* said young Mr. McIntyre bitterly. "It means 'Hurrah!' That's the sort of *requiescat* it is!"

"Ah! Then they got him the second time."

"What do you mean by 'second time?'"

"The Washington incident, of course, was the first; the attempted murd—that is, the narrow escape of Telfik Bey."

Young Mr. McIntyre looked baffled. "I'm blessed if I know what you're up to, Jones," he said. "But if you *do* know anything of this case I need your help. In Washington, where they failed, we fooled the newspapers. Here, where they've succeeded—"

"Who are 'they?'" interrupted Jones.

"That's what I'm here to get at. The murderers of Telfik Bey, of course. My instructions are to find out secretly, if at all. For if it does get into the newspapers there'll be the very deuce to pay. It isn't desirable that even Telfik Bey's presence here should have been known for reasons which—ah—(here Average Jones

---

* A "requiescat" is a prayer for the repose of the dead. McIntyre responds with a punning answer to the "cat" portion of the word.

remarked the resumption of his friend's official bearing)—which, not being for the public, I need not detail to you."

"You need not, in point of fact, tell me anything about it at all," observed Average Jones equably.

Pomposity fell away from Mr. Thomas Colvin McIntyre, leaving him palpably shivering.

"But I need your help. Need it very much. You know something about handling the newspapers, don't you?"

"I know how to get things in; not how to keep them out."

The other groaned. "It may already be too late. What newspapers have you there?"

"All of 'em. Want me to look?"

Mr. McIntyre braced himself.

"Turk dies at Palatia," read Average Jones. "Mm—heart disease…wealthy Stamboul merchant…studying American methods…Turkish minister notified."

"Is that all?"

"Practically."

"And the other reports?"

Average Jones ran them swiftly over. "About the same. Hold on! Here's a little something extra in the *Universal.*"

"'Found on the floor…bell-boy who discovered the tragedy collapses…condition serious…Supposedly shock—'"

"What's that?" interrupted young Mr. McIntyre, half rising. "Shot?"

"You're nervous, Tommy. I didn't say 'shot.' I said 'shock.'"

"Oh, of course. Shock—the bell-boy, it means."

"See here; first thing you know you'll be getting me interested. Hadn't you better open up or shut up?"

Mr. McIntyre took a long breath and a resolution simultaneously.

"At any rate I can trust you," he said. "Telfik Bey is not a merchant. He is a secret, confidential agent of the Turkish government.

He came over to New York from Washington in spite of warnings that he would be killed."

"You're certain he was killed?"

"I only wish I could believe anything else."

"Shot?"

"The coroner and a physician whom I sent can find no trace of a wound."

"What do they say?"

"Apoplexy."*

"The refuge of the mystified medico. It doesn't satisfy you?"

"It won't satisfy the State Department."

"And possibly not the newspapers, eventually."

"Come up with me and look the place over, Average. Let me send for the manager."

That functionary came, a vision of perturbation in a pale-gray coat. Upon assurance that Average Jones was "safe" he led the way to the rooms so hastily vacated by the spirit of the Turkish guest.

"We've succeeded in keeping two recent suicides and a blackmail scheme in this hotel out of the newspapers," observed the manager morosely. "But this would be the worst of all. If I could have known, when the Turkish Embassy reserved the apartment—"

"The Turkish Embassy never reserved any apartment for Telfik Bey," put in the Fifth Assistant Secretary of State.

"Surely you are mistaken, sir," replied the hotel man. "I saw their emissary myself. He specified for rooms on the south side, either the third or fourth floor. Wouldn't have anything else."

"You gave him a definite reservation?" asked Jones.

"Yes; 335 and 336."

---

* A cerebral hemorrhage or stroke.

"Has the man been here since?"

"Not to my knowledge."

"A Turk, you think?"

"I suppose so. Foreign, anyway."

"Anything about him strike you particularly?"

"Well, he was tall and thin and looked sickly. He talked very soft, too, like a sick man."

The characterization of the Pearlington station agent recurred to the interrogator's mind. "Had he—er—white hair?" he half yawned.

"No," replied the manager, and, in the same breath, the budding diplomat demanded:

"What are you up to, Average? Why should he?"

Average Jones turned to him. "To what other hotels would the Turkish Embassy be likely to send its men?"

"Sometimes their *charge d'affaires* goes to the Nederstrom."

"Go up there and find out whether a room has been reserved for Telfik Bey, and if so—"

"They wouldn't reserve at two hotels, would they?"

"—by whom," concluded Average Jones, shaking his head at the interruption. "Find out who occupied or reserved the apartments on either side."

Mr. Thomas Colvin McIntyre lifted a wrinkling eyebrow. "Really, Jones," he observed, "you seem to be employing me rather in the capacity of a messenger boy."

"If you think a messenger boy could do it as well, ring for one," drawled Average Jones, in his mildest voice. "Meantime, I'll be in the Turk's room here."

Numbers 335 and 336, which the manager opened, after the prompt if somewhat sulky departure of Mr. McIntyre, proved to consist of a small sitting-room, a bedroom and a bath, each with a large window giving on the cross-street, well back from Fifth Avenue.

"Here's where he was found." The manager indicated a spot

near the wall of the sitting-room and opposite the window. "He had just pushed the button when he fell."

"How do you know that?"

"Bronson, the bell-boy on that call, answered. He knocked several times and got no answer. Then he opened the door and saw Mr. Telfik down, all in a heap."

"Where is Bronson?"

"At the hospital, unconscious."

"What from?"

"Shock, the doctors say."

"What—er—about the—er—shot?"

The manager looked startled. "Well, Bronson says that just as he opened the door he saw a bullet cross the room and strike the wall above the body."

"You can't see a bullet in flight."

"He saw this one," insisted the manager. "As soon as it struck it exploded. Three other people heard it."

"What did Bronson do?"

"Lost his head and ran out. He hadn't got halfway to the elevator when he fell, in a sort of fainting fit. He came to long enough to tell his story. Then he got terribly nauseated and went off again."

"He's sure the man had fallen before the explosion?"

"Absolutely."

"And he got no answer to his knocking?"

"No. That's why he went in. He thought something might be wrong."

"Had anybody else been in the room or past it within a few minutes?"

"Absolutely no one. The floor girl's desk is just outside. She must have seen any one going in."

"Has she anything to add?"

"She heard the shot. And a minute or two before, she had heard and felt a jar from the room."

"Corroborative of the man having fallen before the shot," commented Jones.

"When I got here, five minutes later, he was quite dead," continued the manager.

Evidence of the explosion was slight to the investigating eye of Average Jones. The wall showed an abrasion, but, as the investigator expected, no bullet hole. Against the leg of a desk he found a small metal shell, which he laid on the table.

"There's your bullet," he observed with a smile.

"It's a cartridge, anyway," cried the hotel man. "He must have been shot, after all."

"From inside the room? Hardly! And certainly not with that. It's a very small fulminate of mercury shell, and never held lead. No. The man was down, if not dead, before that went off."

Average Jones was now at the window. Taking a piece of paper from his pocket he brushed the contents of the window-sill upon it. A dozen dead flies rolled upon the paper. He examined them thoughtfully, cast them aside and turned back to the manager.

"Who occupy the adjoining rooms?"

"Two maiden ladies *did,* on the east. They've left," said the manager bitterly. "Been coming here for ten years, and now they've quit. If the facts ever get in the newspapers—"

"What's on the west, adjoining?"

"Nothing. The corridor runs down there."

"Then it isn't probable that any one got into the room from either side."

"Impossible," said the manager.

Here Mr. Thomas Colvin McIntyre arrived with a flushed face.

"You are right, Average," he said. "The same man had reserved rooms at the Nederstrom for Telfik Bey."

"What's the location?"

"Tenth floor; north side. He had insisted on both details. Nos. 1015, 1017."

"What neighbors?"

"Bond salesman on one side, Reverend and Mrs. Salisbury, of Wilmington, on the other."

"Um-m-m. What across the street?"

"How should I know? You didn't tell me to ask."

"It's the Glenargan office building, just opened, Mr. Jones," volunteered the manager.

Average Jones turned again to the window, closed it and fastened his handkerchief in the catch. "Leave that there," he directed the manager. "Don't let any one into this room. I'm off."

Stopping to telephone, Average Jones ascertained that there were no vacant offices on the tenth floor, south side of the Glenargan apartment building, facing the Nederstrom Hotel. The last one had been let two weeks before to—this he ascertained by judicious questioning—a dark, foreign gentleman who was an expert on rugs. Well satisfied, the investigator crossed over to the skyscraper across from the Palatia. There he demanded of the superintendent a single office on the third floor, facing north. He was taken to a clean and vacant room. One glance out of the window showed him his handkerchief, not opposite, but well to the west.

"Too near Fifth Avenue," he said. "I don't like the roar of the traffic."

"There's one other room on this floor, farther along," said the superintendent, "but it isn't in order. Mr. Perkins' time isn't up till day after to-morrow, and his things are there yet. He told the janitor, though, that he was leaving town and wouldn't bother to take away the things. They aren't worth much. Here's the place."

They entered the office. In it were only a desk, two chairs and a scrap basket. The basket was crammed with newspapers. One of them was the *Hotel Register.*[*] Average Jones found Telfik Bey's name, as he had expected, in its roster.

"I'll give fifty dollars for the furniture as it stands."

"Glad to get it," was the prompt response. "Will you want anything else, now?"

"Yes. Send the janitor here."

That worthy, upon receipt of a considerable benefaction, expressed himself ready to serve the new tenant to the best of his ability.

"Do you know when Mr. Perkins left the building?"

"Yes, sir. This morning, early."

"This morning! Sure it wasn't yesterday?"

"Am I sure? Didn't I help him to the street-car and hand him his little package? That sick he was he couldn't hardly walk alone."

Average Jones pondered a moment. "Do you think he could have passed the night here?"

"I know he did," was the prompt response. "The scrubwoman heard him when she came this morning."

"Heard him?"

"Yes, sir. Sobbing, like."

The nerves of Average Jones gave a sharp "kickback," like a mis-cranked motor-car. His trend of thought had suddenly been reversed. The devious and scientific slayer of Telfik Bey in tears? It seemed completely out of the picture.

"You may go," said he, and seating himself at the desk, proceeded to an examination of his newly acquired property. The newspapers in the scrap basket, mainly copies of the *Evening Register,* seemed to contain, upon cursory examination, nothing germane to the issue. But, scattered among them, the searcher found a number of fibrous chips. They were short and thick;

---

[*] An actual newspaper, founded sometime in the nineteenth century; after 1912, the *Hotel Register & Review.*

such chips as might be made by cutting a bamboo pole into cross lengths, convenient for carrying.

"The 'spirit-wand,'" observed Average Jones with gusto. "That was the 'little package,' of course."

Next, he turned his attention to the desk. It was bare, except for a few scraps of paper and some writing implements. But in a crevice there shone a glimmer of glass. With a careful finger-nail Average Jones pushed out a small phial. It had evidently been sealed with lead. Nothing was in it. Its discoverer leaned back and contemplated it with stiffened eyelids. For, upon its tiny, improvised label was scrawled the "Mercy sign;" mysterious before, now all but incredible.

For silent minutes Average Jones sat bemused. Then, turning in a messenger call, he drew to him a sheet of paper, upon which he slowly and consideringly wrote a few words.

"You get a dollar extra if this reaches the advertising desk of the *Register* office within half an hour," he advised the uniformed urchin who answered the call. The modern mercury seized the paper and fled forthwith.

Punctuality was a virtue which Average Jones had cultivated to the point of a fad. Hence it was with some discountenance that his clerk was obliged to apologize for his lateness, first, at 4 P. M. of July 23, to a very dapper and spruce young gentleman in pale mauve spats, who wouldn't give his name; then at 4:05 P. M. of the same day to Professor Gehren, of the Metropolitan University; and finally at 4:30 P. M. to Mr. Robert Bertram. When, only a moment before five, the Ad-Visor entered, the manner of his apology was more absent than fervent.

Bertram held out a newspaper to him.

"Cast your eye on that," said he. "The *Register* fairly reeks with freaks lately."

Average Jones read aloud.

SMITH-PERKINS, formerly 74 Bellair—Send map present location H. C. Turkish Triumph about smoked out. MERCY—Box 34, Office.

"Oh, I don't know about its being so freakish," said Average Jones.

"Nonsense! Look at it! Turkish Triumph—that's a cigarette, isn't it? H. C.—what's that? And signed Mercy. Why, it's the work of a lunatic!"

"It's my work," observed Average Jones blandly.

The three visitors stared at him in silence.

"Rather a forlorn hope, but sometimes a bluff will go," he continued.

"If H. C. indicates Harvey Craig, as I infer," said Professor Gehren impatiently, "are you so infantile as to suppose that his murderer will give information about him?"

Average Jones smiled, drew a letter from his pocket, glanced at it and called for a number in Hackensack.

"Take the 'phone, Professor Gehren," he said, when the reply came. "It's the Cairnside Hospital. Ask for information about Harvey Craig."

With absorbed intentness the other three listened to the one-sided conversation.

"Hello!...May I speak to Mr. Harvey Craig's doctor?...This is Professor Gehren of the Metropolitan University...Thank you, Doctor. How is he?...Very grave?...Ah, has been very grave.... Wholly out of danger?...What was the nature of his illness?... When may I see him?...Very well. I will visit the hospital to-morrow morning. Thank you....I should have expected that you would notify me of his presence." ...A long silence intervened, then "Good-by."

"It is most inexplicable," declared Professor Gehren, turning to the others. "The doctor states that Harvey was brought there at night, by a foreigner who left a large sum of money to pay for his care, and certain suggestions for his treatment. One detail, carefully set down in writing, was that if reddish or purple dots appeared under Harvey's nails, he was to be told that Mr. Smith released him and advised his sending for his friends at once."

"Reddish or purple dots, eh?" repeated Average Jones. "I should like—er—to have talked with—er—that doctor before you cut off."

"And I, sir," said the professor, with the grim repression of the thinker stirred to wrath, "should like to interview this stranger."

"Perfectly feasible, I think," returned Average Jones.

"You don't mean that you've located him already!" cried young Mr. McIntyre.

"He was so obliging as to save me the trouble."

Average Jones held up the letter from which he had taken the Cairnside Hospital's telephone number. "The advertisement worked to a charm. Mr. Smith gives his address in this, and intimates that I may call upon him."

Young Mr. McIntyre rose.

"You're going to see him, then?"

"At once."

"Did I understand you to imply that I am at liberty to accompany you?" inquired Professor Gehren.

"If you care to take the risk."

"Think there'll be excitement?" asked Bertram languidly. "I'd like to go along."

Average Jones nodded. "One or a dozen; I fancy it will be all the same to Smith."

"You think we'll find him dead." Young Mr. McIntyre leaped to this conclusion. "Count me in on it."

"N—no; not dead."

"Perhaps his friend 'Mercy' has gone back on him, then," suggested Mr. McIntyre, unabashed.

"Yes; I rather think that's it," said Average Jones, in a curious accent. "'Mercy' has gone back on him, I believe, though I can't quite accurately place her as yet. Here's the taxi," he broke off. "All aboard that's going aboard. But it's likely to be dangerous."

Across town and far up the East Side whizzed the car, over the bridge that leads away from Manhattan Island to the north, and through quiet streets as little known to the average New Yorker as are Hong Kong and Caracas. In front of a frame house it stopped. On a side porch, over which bright roses swarmed like children clambering into a hospitable lap, sat a man with a gray face. He was tall and slender, and his hair, a dingy black, was already showing worn streaks where the color had faded. At Average Jones he gazed with unconcealed surprise.

"Ah; it is *you!*" he exclaimed. "*You*," he smiled, "are the 'Mercy' of the advertisement?"

"Yes."

"And these gentlemen?"

"Are my friends."

"You will come in?"

Average Jones examined a nodding rose with an indulgent, almost a paternal, expression.

"If you—er—think it—er—safe," he murmured.

"Assuredly."

As if exacting a pledge the young man held out his hand. The older one unhesitatingly grasped it. Average Jones turned the long fingers, which enclosed his, back upward, and glanced at them.

"Ah," he said, and nodded soberly, "so, it is that."

"Yes; it is that," assented the other. "I perceive that you have communicated with Mr. Craig. How is he?"

"Out of danger."

"That is well. A fine and manly youth. I should have sorely regretted it if—"

Professor Gehren broke in upon him. "For the peril in which you have involved him, sir, you have to answer to me, his guardian."

The foreigner raised a hand. "He was without family or ties. I told him the danger. He accepted it. Once he was careless— and—one is not careless twice in that work. But he was fortunate, too. I, also, was fortunate in that the task was then so far advanced that I could complete it alone. I got him to the hospital at night; no matter how. For his danger and illness I have indemnified him in the sum of ten thousand dollars. Is it enough?"

Professor Gehren bowed.

"And you, Mr. Jones; are you a detective?"

"No; merely a follower of strange trails—by taste."

"Ah. You have set yourself to a dark one. You wish to know how Telfik Bey"—his eyes narrowed and glinted—"came to his reward. Will you enter, gentlemen?"

"I know this much," replied Average Jones as, followed by his friends, he passed through the door which their host held open. "With young Craig as assistant, you prepared, in the loneliest part of the Hackensack Meadows, some kind of poison which, I believe, can be made with safety only in the open air."

The foreigner smiled and shook his head.

"Not with safety, even then," he said. "But go on."

"You found that your man was coming to New York. Knowing that he would probably put up at the Palatia or the Nederstrom, you reserved rooms for him at both, and took an office across from each. As it was hot weather, you calculated upon his windows being open. You watched for him. When he came you struck him down in his own room with the poison."

"But how?" It was the diplomat who interrupted.

"I think with a long blow-gun."

"By George!" said Bertram softly. "So the spirit-wand of bamboo was a blow-gun! What led you to that, Average?"

"The spirit rappings which the talky woman in the Bellair Street apartment used to hear. That and the remnants of putty I found near the window. You see, the doors opening through the whole length of the apartment gave a long range, where Mr.—er—Smith could practise. He had a sort of target on the window, and every time he blew a putty ball Mrs. Doubletongue heard the spirit. Am I right, sir?"

The host bowed.

"The fumes, whatever they were, killed swiftly?"

"They did. Instantly; mercifully. Too mercifully."

"How could you know it was fumes?" demanded Mr. Thomas Colvin McIntyre.

"By the dead flies, the effect upon the bell-boy, and the fact that no wound was found on the body. Then, too, there was the fulminate of mercury shell."

"Of what possible use was that?" asked Professor Gehren.

"A question that I've asked myself, sir, a great many times over in the last twenty-four hours. Perhaps Mr. Smith could answer that best. Though—er—I think the shell was blown through the blowpipe to clear the deadly fumes from the room by its explosion, before any one else should suffer. Mr. Smith is, at least, not a wanton slaughterer."

"You are right, sir, and I thank you," said the foreigner. He drew himself up weakly but with pride. "Gentlemen, I am not a murderer. I am an avenger. It would have gone hard with my conscience had any innocent person met death through me. As for that Turkish dog, you shall judge for yourself whether he did not die too easily."

M·LEONE BRACKER·

From among the papers in a *tiroir** against the wall he took a French journal, and read, translating fluently. The article was a bald account of the torture, outrage and massacre of Armenian women and girls, at Adana, by the Turks. The most hideous portion of it was briefly descriptive of the atrocities perpetrated by order of a high Turkish official upon a mother and two young daughters. "An Armenian prisoner, being dragged by in chains, went mad at the sight," the correspondent stated.

"I was that prisoner," said the reader. "The official was Telfik Bey. I saw my naked daughter break from the soldiers and run to him, pleading for pity, as he sat his horse; and I saw him strike his spur into her bare breast. My wife, the mother of my children—"

"Don't!" The protest came from the Fifth Assistant Secretary of State.

He had risen. His smooth-skinned face was contracted, and the sweat stood beaded on his forehead. "I—I can't stand it. I've got my duty to do. This man has made a confession."

"Your pardon," said the foreigner. "I have lived and fed on and slept with that memory, ever since. On my release I left my country. The enterprise of which I had been the head, dye-stuff manufacturing, had interested me in chemistry. I went to England to study further. Thence I came to America to wait."

"You have heard his confession, all of you," said young Mr. McIntyre, rising. "I shall have him put under arrest pending advice from Washington."

"You may save yourself the trouble, I think, Tommy," drawled Average Jones. "Mr. Smith will never be called to account in this world for the murd—execution of Telfik Bey."

"You saw the marks on my finger-nails," said the foreigner.

---

* A chest of drawers.

"That is the sure sign. I may live twenty-four hours; I may live twice or three times that period. The poison does its work, once it gets into the blood, and there is no help. It matters nothing. My ambition is satisfied."

"And it is because of this that you let us find you?" asked Bertram.

"I had a curiosity to know who had so strangely traced my actions."

"But what was the poison?" asked Professor Gehren.

"I think Mr. Jones has more than a suspicion," replied the doomed man, with a smile. "You will find useful references on yonder shelf, Mr. Jones."

Moving across to the shelf, Average Jones took down a heavy volume and ran quickly over the leaves.

"Ah!" he said presently, and not noticing, in his absorption, that the host had crossed again to the *tiroir* and was quietly searching in a compartment, he read aloud:

"Little is known of cyanide of cacodyl,* in its action the swiftest and most deadly of existing poisons. In the '40's, Bunsen, the German chemist, combined oxide of cacodyl with cyanogen, a radical of prussic acid, producing cyanide of cacodyl, or dimethyl arsine cyanide. As both of its components are of the deadliest description, it is extremely dangerous to make. It can be made

---

* Discovered by Robert Bunsen in the 1840s, he wrote of it:

> This substance is extraordinarily poisonous, and for this reason its preparation and purification can only be carried on in the open air; indeed, under these circumstances, it is necessary for the operator to breathe through a long open tube so as to insure the inspiration of air free from impregnation with any trace of the vapor of this very volatile compound. If only a few grains of this substance be allowed to evaporate in a room at the ordinary temperature, the effect upon any one inspiring the air is that of sudden giddiness and insensibility, amounting to complete unconsciousness.

Quoted in *Nature* (April 28, 1881), 597.

only in the open air, and not without the most extreme precaution known to science. Mr. Lacelles Scott, of England, nearly lost his life experimenting with it in 1904. A small fraction of a grain gives off vapor sufficient to kill a human being instantly."

"Had you known about this stuff, Average?" asked Bertram.

"No, I'd never heard of it. But from its action and from the lettered cabinet I judged that—"

"This is all very well," broke in Mr. Assistant Secretary Thomas Colvin McIntyre, "but I want this man arrested. How can we know that he isn't shamming and may not escape us, after all?"

"By this," retorted their host. He held aloft a small glass vial, lead-sealed, and staggered weakly to the door.

"Stop him!" said Average Jones sharply.

The door closed on the words. There was a heavy fall without, followed by the light tinkle of glass.

Average Jones, who had half crossed the room in a leap, turned to his friends, warning them back.

"Too late. We can't go out yet. Wait for the fumes to dissipate."

They stood, the four men, rigid. Presently Average Jones, opening a rear window, leaped to the ground, followed by the others, and came around the corner of the porch. The dead man lay with a peaceful face. Professor Gehren uncovered.

"God forgive him," he said. "Who shall say that he was not right?"

"Not I," said the young assistant secretary in awed tones. "I'm glad he—escaped. But what am I to do? Here we are with a dead body on our hands, and a state secret to be kept from the prying police."

Average Jones stood thinking for a moment, then he entered the room and called up the coroner's office on the telephone.

"Listen, you men," he said to his companions. Then, to the official who answered: "There's a suicide at 428 Elliver Avenue, the Bronx. Four of us witnessed it. We had come to keep an appointment with the man in connection with a discovery he claimed in metallurgy, and found him dying. Yes; we will wait here. Good-by."

Returning to the porch again, he cleared away the fragments of glass, aided by Bertram. To one of these clung a shred of paper. For all his languid self-control the club dilettante shivered a little as he thrust at it with a stick.

"Look, Average; it's the 'Mercy' sign again. What a hideous travesty!"

Average Jones shook his head.

"It isn't 'Mercy,' Bert. It's the label that he attached, for precaution, to everything that had to do with his deadly stuff. The formula for cyanide of cacodyl is 'Me-2cy.'* It was the scrawly handwriting that misled; that's all."

"So I was right when I suggested that his 'Mercy' had gone back on him," said Mr. Thomas Colvin McIntyre, with a semi-hysterical giggle.

Average Jones looked from the peaceful face of the dead to the label, fluttering in the light breeze.

"No," he said gravely. "You were wrong. It was his friend to the last."

---

* Actually, the formula is C_3H_6AsN.

CHAPTER VI
BLUE FIRES*

"Cabs for comfort; cars for company," was an apothegm which Average Jones had evolved from experience. A professed student of life, he maintained, must keep in touch with life at every feasible angle. No experience should come amiss to a detective; he should be a pundit of all knowledge. A detective he now frankly considered himself; and the real drudgery of his unique profession of Ad-Visor was supportable only because of the compensating thrill of the occasional chase, the radiance of the Adventure of Life glinting from time to time across his path.

There were few places, Average Jones held, where human nature in the rough can be studied to better advantage than in the stifling tunnels of the subway or the close-packed sardine boxes of the metropolitan surface lines. It was in pursuance of this theory that he encountered the Westerner, on a Third Avenue car. By custom, Average Jones picked out the most interesting or unusual human being in any assembly where he found himself, for study and analysis. This man was peculiar in that he alone was not perspiring in the sodden August humidity. The clear-browned skin and the rangy strength of the figure gave him a certain distinction. He held in his sinewy hands a doubly folded newspaper. Presently it slipped from his hold to the seat beside him. He stared at the window opposite with harassed and unseeing eyes. Abruptly he rose and went out on the platform. Average Jones picked up the paper. In the middle of the column to which it was folded was a marked advertisement:

```
ARE you in an embarrassing position? Anything,
anywhere, any time, regardless of nature or loca-
tion. Everybody's friend. Consultation at all hours.
Suite 152, Owl Building, Brooklyn.
```

The car was nearing Brooklyn Bridge. Average Jones saw his man drop lightly off. He followed and at the bridge entrance caught him up.

"You've left your paper," said he.

The stranger whirled quickly. "Right," he said. "Thanks. Perhaps you can tell me where the Owl Building is."

"Are you going there?"

"Yes."

"I wouldn't."

A slight wrinkle of surprise appeared on the man's tanned forehead.

"Perhaps *you* wouldn't," he returned coolly.

"In other words, 'mind your business,'" said Average Jones, with a smile.

"Something of that sort," admitted the stranger.

"Nevertheless, I wouldn't consult with Everybody's Friend over in the Owl Building."

"Why?"

"Er—because—er—if I may speak plainly," drawled Average Jones, "I wouldn't risk a woman's name with a gang of blackmailers."

"You've got your nerve," retorted the stranger. The keen eyes, flattening almost to slits, fixed on the impassive face of the other.

"Well, I'll go you," he decided, after a moment. His glance swept the range of vision and settled upon a rathskeller* sign. "Come over there where we can talk."

They crossed the grilling roadway, and, being wise in the heat, ordered "soft" drinks.†

"Now," said the stranger, "you've declared in on my game. Make good. What's your interest?"

"None, personally. I like your looks, that's all," replied the other frankly. "And I don't like to see you run into that spider's web."

"You know them?"

"Twice in the last year I've made 'em change their place of business."

"But you don't know me. And you spoke of—of a woman."

"I've been studying you on the car," explained Average Jones. "You're hard as nails; yet you're nerves are on edge. It isn't illness, so it must be trouble. On your watch-chain you've got a solitaire diamond ring. Not for ornament; you aren't that sort of a dresser. It's there for convenience until you can find a place to put it. When a deeply troubled man wears an engagement ring on his watch-chain it's a fair inference that there's been an obstruction in the course of true love. Unless I'm mistaken, you, being a stranger newly come to town, were going to take your case to those man-eating sharks?"

"How do you know I've just come to town?"

"When you looked at your watch I noticed it was three hours slow. That must mean the Pacific coast, or near it. Therefore

---

* A beer hall, in a basement. The term comes from the German words for council (*rat*) and cellar (*keller*), as the original ones were in the basements of city halls.

† That is, a drink containing little or no alcohol. The *Oxford English Dictionary* traces the earliest written example of this meaning to 1843.

you've just got in from the Far West and haven't thought to rectify your time. At a venture I'd say you were a mining man from down around the Ray-Kelvin copper district in Arizona. That peculiar, translucent copper silicate in your scarfpin comes from those mines."

"The Blue Fire? I wish it had stayed there, all of it! Anything else?"

"Yes," returned Average Jones, warming to the game. "You're an Eastern college man, I think. Anyway, your father or some older member of your family graduated from one of the older colleges."

"What's the answer?"

"The gold of your Phi Beta Kappa key is a different color from your watch-chain. It's the old metal, antedating the California gold. Did your father graduate some time in the latter forties or early fifties?"

"Hamilton, '51. I'm '89. Name, Kirby."

A gleam of pleasure appeared in Average Jones' keen eyes. "That's rather a coincidence," he said. "Two of us from the Old Hill.* I'm Jones of '04. Had a cousin in your class, Carl Van Reypen."

They plunged into the intimate community of interest which is the peculiar heritage and asset of the small, close-knit old college. Presently, however, Kirby's forehead wrinkled again. He sat silent, communing with himself. At length he lifted his head like one who has taken a resolution.

"You made a good guess at a woman in the case," he said. "And you call this a coincidence? *She'd* say it was a case of intuition. She's very strong on intuition and superstition generally."

---

* Samuel Hopkins Adams and many of his ancestors were also Hamilton College alumni. Hamilton was founded in 1792 as Hamilton-Oneida Academy, and Alexander Hamilton was among its initial trustees. Located on College Hill Road in Clinton, New York, its location was fondly known as the "Old Hill."

There was a mixture of tenderness and bitterness in his tone. "Chance brought that advertisement to her eyes. A hat-pin she'd dropped stuck through it, or something of the sort. Enough for her. Nothing would do but that I should chase over to see the Owl Building bunch. At that, maybe her hunch was right. It's brought me up against you. Perhaps you can help me. What are you? A sort of detective?"

"Only on the side." Average Jones drew a card from his pocket, and tendered it:

A. JONES, AD-VISOR
Advice upon all matters connected with Advertising
Astor Court Temple 2 to 5 P.M.

"Ad-Visor, eh?" repeated the other. "Well, there's going to be an advertisement in the *Evening Truth* to-day, by me. Here's a proof of it."

Average Jones took the slip and read it.

LOST—Necklace of curious blue stones from Hotel Denton, night of August 6. Reward greater than value of stones for return to hotel. No questions asked.

"Reward greater than value of stones," commented Average Jones. "There's a sentimental interest, then?"

"Will you take the case?" returned Kirby abruptly.

"At least I'll look into it," replied Average Jones.

"Come to the hotel, then, and lunch with me, and I'll open up the whole thing."

Across a luncheon-table, at the quiet, old-fashioned Hotel Denton, Kirby unburdened himself.

"You know all that's necessary about me. The—the other party in the matter is Mrs. Hale. She's a young widow. We've been engaged for six months; were to be married in a fortnight. Now she insists on a postponement. That's where I want your help."

Average Jones moved uneasily in his chair. "Really, Mr. Kirby, lovers' quarrels aren't in my line."

"There's been no quarrel. We're as much engaged now as ever, in spite of the return of the ring. It's only her infern—her deep-rooted superstition that's caused this trouble. One can't blame her; her father and mother were both killed in an accident after some sort of 'ghostly warning.' The first thing I gave her, after our engagement, was a necklace of these stones"—he tapped his scarfpin—"that I'd selected, one by one, myself. They're beautiful, as you see, but they're not particularly valuable; only semiprecious. The devil of it is that they're the subject of an Indian legend. The Indians and Mexicans call them 'blue fires,'* and say they have the power to bind and loose in love. Edna has been out in that country; she's naturally high strung and responsive to that sort of thing, as I told you, and she fairly soaked in all that nonsense. To make it worse, when I sent them to her I wrote that—that—" a dull red surged up under the tan skin—"that as long as the fire in the stones burned blue for her my heart would be all hers. Now the necklace is gone. You can imagine the effect on a woman of that temperament. And you can see the result." He pointed with a face of misery to the solitaire on his watch-chain. "She insisted on giving this back. Says that a woman as careless as she proved herself can't be trusted with jewelry. And she's hysterically sure that misfortune will follow

* Few gemstones found in Mexico are blue in color. Turquoise hardly seems to be "blue fire"; perhaps the stones were chrysocolla, a silicate that might sparkle. Most likely, however, these were labradorites, feldspar derivatives that scintillate and are often termed "blue fire."

us for ever if we're married without recovering the fool necklace. So she's begged a postponement."

"Details," said Average Jones crisply.

"She's here at this hotel. Has a small suite on the third floor. Came down from her home in central New York to meet my mother, whom she had never seen. Mother's here, too, on the same floor. Night before last Mrs. Hale thought she heard a noise in her outer room. She made a look-see, but found nothing. In the morning when she got up, about ten (she's a late riser) the necklace was gone."

"Where had it been left?"

"On a stand in her sitting-room."

"Anything else taken?"

"That's the strange part of it. Her purse, with over a hundred dollars in it, which lay under the necklace, wasn't touched."

"Does she usually leave valuables around in that casual way?"

"Well, you see, she's always stayed at the Denton, and she felt perfectly secure here."

"Any other thefts in the hotel?"

"Not that I can discover. But one of the guests on the same floor with Mrs. Hale saw a fellow acting queerly that same night. There he sits, yonder, at that table. I'll ask him to come over."

The guest, an elderly man, already interested in the case, was willing enough to tell all he knew.

"I was awakened by some one fumbling at my door and making a clinking noise," he explained. "I called out. Nobody answered. Almost immediately I heard a noise across the hall. I opened my door. A man was fussing at the keyhole of the room opposite. He was very clumsy. I said, 'Is that your room?' He didn't even look at me. In a moment he started down the hallway. He walked very fast, and I could hear him muttering to himself. He seemed to be carrying something in front of him with both hands. It was his keys, I suppose. Anyway I could hear it clink. At the end of the hall he stopped, turned to the door at the left and fumbled at the keyhole for quite a while. I could hear his keys clink again. This time, I suppose, he had the right room, for he unlocked it and went in. I listened for fifteen or twenty minutes. There was nothing further."

Average Jones looked at Kirby with lifted brows of inquiry. Kirby nodded, indicating that the end room was Mrs. Hales'.

"How was the man dressed?" asked Average Jones.

"Grayish dressing-gown and bed-slippers. He was tall and had gray hair."

"Many thanks. Now, Mr. Kirby, will you take me to see Mrs. Hale?"

The young widow received them in her sitting-room. She was of the slender, big-eyed, sensitive type of womanhood; her piquant face marred by the evidences of sleeplessness and tears. To Average Jones she gave her confidence at once. People usually did.

"I felt sure the advertisement would bring us help," she said wistfully. "Now, I feel surer than ever."

"Faith helps the worst case," said the young man, smiling. "Mr. Kirby tells me that the intruder awakened you."

"Yes; and I'm a very heavy sleeper. Still I can't say positively that anything definite roused me; it was rather an impression of some one's being about. I came out of my bedroom and looked around the outer room, but there was nobody there."

"You didn't think to look for the necklace?"

"No," she said with a little gasp; "if I only had!"

"And—er—you didn't happen to hear any clinking noise, did you?"

"No."

"After he'd got into the room he'd put the key up, wouldn't he?" suggested Kirby.

"You're assuming that he had a key."

"Of course he had a key. The guest across the hall saw him trying it on the other doors and heard it clink against the lock."

"If he had a key to this room why did he try it on several other doors first?" propounded Average Jones. "As for the clinking noise, in which I'm a good deal interested—may I look at your key, Mrs. Hale?"

She handed it to him. He tried it on the lock, outside, jabbing at the metal setting. The resultant sound was dull and wooden. "Not much of the clink which our friend describes as having heard, is it?" he remarked.

"Then how could he get into my room?" cried Mrs. Hale.

"Are you sure your door was locked?"

"Certain. As soon as I missed the necklace I looked at the catch."

"That was in the morning. But the night before?"

"I always slip the spring. And I know I did this time because it had been left unsprung so that Mr. Kirby's mother could come in and out of my sitting-room, and I remember springing it when she left for bed."

"Sometimes these locks don't work." Slipping the catch back, Average Jones pressed the lever down. There was a click, but the ward failed to slip. At the second attempt the lock worked. But repeated trials proved that more than half the time the door did not lock.

"So," observed Average Jones, "I think we may dismiss the key theory."

"But the locked door this morning?" cried Mrs. Hale.

"The intruder may have done that as he left."

"I don't see why," protested Kirby, in a tone which indicated a waning faith in Jones.

"By way of confusing the trail. Possibly he hoped to suggest that he'd escaped by the fire-escape. Presumably he was on the balcony when Mrs. Hale came out into this room."

As he spoke Average Jones laid a hand on the heavy net curtains which hung before the balcony window. Instead of parting them, however, he stood with upturned eyes.

"Was that curtain torn before yesterday?" he asked Mrs. Hale.

"I hardly think so. The hotel people are very careful in the up-keep of the rooms."

Jones mounted a chair with scant respect for the upholstery, and examined the damaged drapery. Descending, he tugged tentatively at the other curtain, first with his right hand, then with his left; then with both. The fabric gave a little at the last test. Jones disappeared through the window.

When he returned, after five minutes, he held in his hand some scrapings of the rusted iron which formed the balcony railing.

"You're a mining man, Mr. Kirby," he said. "Would you say that assayed anything?"

Kirby examined the glinting particles. "Gold," he said decisively.

"Ah, then the necklace rubbed with some violence against the railing. Now, Mrs. Hale, how long were you awake?"

"Ten or fifteen minutes. I remember that a continuous rattling of wagons below kept up for a little while. And I heard one of the drivers call out something about taking the air."

"Er—really!" Average Jones became suddenly absorbed in his seal ring. He turned it around five accurate times and turned it back an equal number of revolutions. "Did he—er—get any answer?"

"Not that I heard."

The young man pondered, then drew a chair up to Mrs. Hale's escritoire, and, with an abrupt "excuse me," helped himself to pen, ink and paper.

"There!" he said, after five minutes' work. "That'll do for a starter. You see," he added, handing the product of his toil to Mrs. Hale, "this street happens to be the regular cross-town route for the milk that comes over by one of the minor ferries. If you heard a number of wagons passing in the early morning they were the milk-vans. Hence this."

Mrs. Hale read:

"MILK-DRIVERS, ATTENTION—Delaware Central mid-town route. Who talked to man outside hotel early morning of August 7? Twenty dollars to right man. Apply personally to Jones, Ad-Visor, Astor Court Temple, New York."

"For the coming issue of the *Milk-Dealers' Journal*," explained its author. "Now, Mr. Kirby, I want you to find out for me—Mrs. Hale can help you, since she has known the hotel people for years—the names of all those who gave up rooms on this floor, or the floors above or below, yesterday morning, and ask whether they are known to the hotel people."

"You think the thief is still in the hotel?" cried Mrs. Hale.

"Hardly. But I think I see smoke from your blue fires. To make out the figure through the smoke is not—" Average Jones broke off, shaking his head. He was still shaking his head when he left the hotel.

It took three days for the milk-journal advertisement to work. On the afternoon of August tenth, a lank, husky-voiced teamster called at the office of the Ad-Visor and was passed in ahead of the waiting line.

"I'm after that twenty," he declared.

"Earn it," said Average Jones with equal brevity.

"Hotel Denton. Guy on the third floor balcony."

"Right so far."

"Leanin' on the rail as if he was sick. I give him a hello. 'Takin' a nip of night air, Bill?' I says. He didn't say nothin'."

"Did he do anything?"

"Kinder fanned himself an' jerked his head back over his shoulder. Meanin' it was too hot to sleep inside, I reckon. It sure was hot!"

"Fanned himself? How?"

"Like this." The visitor raised his hands awkwardly, cupped them, and drew them toward his face.

"Er—with both hands?"

"Yep."

"Did you see him go in?"

"Nope."

"Here's your twenty," said Average Jones. "You're long on sense and short on words. I wish there were more like you."

"Thanks. Thanks again," said the teamster, and went out.

Meantime Kirby had sent his list of the guests who had given up their rooms on August seventh:

George M. Weaver, Jr., Utica, N. Y., well known to hotel people and vouched for by them.

Walker Parker, New Orleans, ditto.

Mr. and Mrs. Charles Hull; quiet elderly people; first visit to hotel.

Henry M. Gillespie, Locke, N. Y. Middle-aged man; new guest.

C. F. Willard, Chicago; been going to hotel for ten years; vouched for by hotel people.

Armed with the list, Average Jones went to the Hotel Denton and spent a busy morning.

"I've had a little talk with the hotel servants," said he to Kirby, when the latter called to make inquiries. "Mr. Henry M. Gillespie, of Locke, New York, had room 168. It's on the same floor with Mrs. Hale's suite, at the farther end of the hall. He had only one piece of luggage, a suitcase marked H. M. G. That information I got from the porter. He left his room in perfect order except for one thing: one of the knobs on the headboard of the old-fashioned bed was broken off short. He didn't mention the matter to the hotel people."

"What do you make of that?"

"It was a stout knob. Only a considerable effort of strength exerted in a peculiar way would have broken it as it was broken. There was something unusual going on in room 168, all right."

"Then you think Henry M. Gillespie, of Locke, New York, is our man."

"No," said Average Jones.

The Westerner's square jaw fell. "Why not?"

"Because there's no such person as Henry M. Gillespie, of Locke, New York. I've just sent there and found out."

Three stones of the fire-blue necklace returned on the current of advertised appeal. One was brought in by the night bartender of a "sporting" club. He had bought it from a man who had picked it up in a gutter; just where, the finder couldn't remember. For the second a South Brooklyn pawnbroker demanded (and received) an exorbitant reward. A florist in Greenwich, Connecticut, contributed the last. With that patient attention to detail which is the A. B. C. of detective work, Average Jones traced down these apparently incongruous wanderings of the stones and then followed them all back to Mrs. Hale's fire-escape.

The bartender's stone offered no difficulties. The setting which the pawnbroker brought in had been found on the city refuse heap by a scavenger. It had fallen through a grating into the hotel cellar, and had been swept out with the rubbish to go to the municipal "dump." The apparent mystery of the florist was lucid when Jones found that the hotel exchanged its shop-worn plants with the Greenwich Floral Company. His roaming eye, keen for every detail, had noticed a row of tubbed azaleas within the ground enclosure of the Denton. Recalling this to mind, it was easy for the Ad-Visor to surmise that the gem had dropped from the fire-escape into a tub, which was, shortly after, shipped to the florist. Thus it was apparent that the three jewels had been stripped from the necklace by forcible contact with the iron rail of the fire-escape at the point where Average Jones had found the "color" of precious metal. The stones were identified by Kirby, from a peculiarity in the setting, as the end three, nearest the clasp at the back; a point which Jones carefully noted. But there the trail ended. No more fire-blue stones came in.

For three weeks Average Jones issued advertisements like commands. The advertisements would, perhaps, have struck the formal-minded Kirby as evidences of a wavering intellect. Indeed, they present a curious and incongruous appearance upon the page of Average Jones' scrapbook, where they now mark a successful conclusion.

The first reads as follows:

OH, YOU HOTEL MEN! Come through with the dope on H. M. G. What's he done to your place? Put a stamp on it and we'll swap dates on his past performances. A. Jones, Astor Court Temple, New York City.

This was spread abroad through the medium of *Mine Host's Weekly* and other organs of the hotel trade.

It was followed by this, of a somewhat later date:

WANTED—Slippery Sams, Human Eels, Fetter Kings, etc. Liberal reward to artist who sold second-hand props to amateur, with instructions for use. Send full details, time and place to A. Jones, Astor Court Temple, New York City.

Variety, the *Clipper* and the *Billboard* scattered the appeal broadcast throughout "the profession." Thousands read it, and one answered it. And within a few days after receiving that answer Jones wired to Kirby:

"Probably found. Bring Mrs. Hale to-morrow at 11.
Answer.

A. JONES."

Kirby answered. He also telegraphed voluminously to his ex-fiancée, who had returned to her home, and who replied that she would leave by the night train. Some minutes before the hour the pair were at Average Jones' office. Kirby fairly pranced with impatience while they were kept waiting in a side room. The only other occupant was a man with a large black dress-suit case, who sat at the window in a slump of dejection. He raised his head for a moment when they were summoned and let it sag down again as they left.

Average Jones greeted his guests cordially. Their first questions to him were significant of the masculine and feminine differences in point of view.

"Have you got the necklace?" cried Mrs. Hale.

"Have you got the thief?" queried Kirby.

"I haven't got the necklace and I haven't got the thief," announced Average Jones; "but I think I've got the man who's got the necklace."

"Did the thief hand it over to him?" demanded Kirby.

"Are you conversant with the Baconian* system of thought, which Old Chips used to preach to us at Hamilton?" countered Average Jones.

"Forgotten it if I ever knew it," returned Kirby.

"So I infer from your repeated use of the word 'thief.' Bacon's principle—an admirable principle in detective work—is that we should learn from things and not from the names of things. You are deluding yourself with a name. Because the law, which is always rigid and sometimes stupid, says that a man who takes that which does not belong to him is a thief, you've got your mind fixed on the name 'thief,' and the idea of theft. If I had gone off on that tack I shouldn't have the interesting privilege of introducing to you Mr. Harvey M. Greene, who now sits in the outer room."

"H. M. G.," said Kirby quickly. "Is it possible that that decent-looking old boy out there is the man who stole—"

"It is *not*," interrupted Average Jones with emphasis, "and I shall ask you, whatever may occur, to guard your speech from offensive expressions of that sort while he is here."

"All right, if you say so," acquiesced the other. "But do you mind telling me how you figure out a man traveling under an alias and helping himself to other people's property on any other basis than that he's a thief?"

"A, B, C," replied Average Jones; "as thus: A—Thieves don't wander about in dressing-gowns. B—Nor take necklaces and leave purses. C—Nor strip gems violently apart and scatter them like largess from fire-escapes. The rest of the alphabet I postpone. Now for Mr. Greene."

---

* Sir Francis Bacon (1561–1626), that is, whose philosophy emphasized inductive reasoning (commonly and incorrectly referred to as "deductive reasoning." Sherlock Holmes used Baconian methods).

The man from the outer room entered and nervously acknowledged his introduction to the others.

"Mr. Greene," explained Jones, "has kindly consented to help clear up the events of the night of August sixth at the Hotel Denton and"—he paused for a moment and shifted his gaze to the new-comer's narrow shoes—"and—er—the loss of—er—Mrs. Hale's jeweled necklace."

The boots retracted sharply, as under the impulse of some sudden emotion; startled surprise, for example. "What?" cried Greene, in obvious amazement. "I don't know anything about a necklace."

A twinkle of satisfaction appeared at the corners of Average Jones' eyes.

"That also is possible," he admitted. "If you'll permit the form of an examination; when you came to the Hotel Denton on August sixth, did you carry the same suitcase you now have with you, and similarly packed?"

"Ye-es. As nearly as possible."

"Thank you. You were registered under the name of Henry M. Gillespie?"

The other's voice was low and strained as he replied in the affirmative.

"For good reasons of your own?"

"Yes."

"For which same reasons you left the hotel quite early on the following morning?"

"Yes."

"Your business compels you to travel a great deal?"

"Yes."

"Do you often register under an alias?"

"Yes," returned the other, his face twitching.

"But not always?"

"No."

"In a large city and a strange hotel, for example, you'd take any name which would correspond to the initials, H. M. G., on your dress-suit case. But in a small town where you were known, you'd be obliged to register under your real name of Harvey M. Greene. It was that necessity which enabled me to find you."

"I'd like to know how you did it," said the other gloomily.

From the left-hand drawer of his desk Jones produced a piece of netting, with hooks along one end.

"Do you recognize the material, Mrs. Hale?" he asked.

"Why, it's the same stuff as the Hotel Denton curtains, isn't it?" she asked.

"Yes," said Average Jones, attaching it to the curtain rod at the side door. "Now, will you jerk that violently with one hand?"

"It will tear loose, won't it?" she asked.

"That's just what it will do. Try it."

The fabric ripped from the hooks as she jerked.

"You remember," said Jones, "that your curtain was torn partly across, and not ripped from the hook at all. Now see."

He caught the netting in both hands and tautened it sharply. It began to part.

"Awkward," he said, "yet it's the only way it could have been done. Now, here's a bedpost, exactly like the one in room 168, occupied by Mr. Greene at the Denton. Kirby, you're a powerful man. Can you break that knob off with one hand?"

He wedged the post firmly in a chair for the trial. The bedpost resisted.

"Could you do it with both hands?" he asked.

"Probably, if I could get a hold. But there isn't surface enough for a good hold."

"No, there isn't. But now." Jones coiled a rope around the

post and handed the end to Kirby. He pulled sharply. The knob snapped and rolled on the floor.

"Q. E. D.," said Kirby. "But it doesn't mean anything to me."

"Doesn't it? Let me recall some other evidence. The guest who saw Mr. Greene in the hallway thought he was carrying something in both hands. The milk-driver who hailed him on the balcony noticed that he gestured awkwardly with both hands. In what circumstances would a man use both hands for action normally performed with one?"

"Too much drink," hazarded Kirby, looking dubiously at Greene, who had been following Jones' discourse with absorbed attention.

"Possibly. But it wouldn't fit this case."

"Physical weakness," suggested Mrs. Hale.

"Rather a shrewd suggestion. But no weakling broke off that bedpost in Henry M. Gillespie's room. I assumed the theory that the phenomena of that night were symptomatic rather than accidental. Therefore, I set out to find in what other places the mysterious H. M. G. had performed."

"How did you know my initials really were H. M. G.?" asked Mr. Greene.

"The porter at the Denton had seen them on 'Henry M. Gillespie's' suitcase. So I sent out a loudly printed call to all hotel clerks for information about a troublesome H. M. G."

He handed the "OH, YOU HOTEL MEN" advertisement to the little group.

"Plenty of replies came. You have, if I may say it without offense, Mr. Greene, an unfortunate reputation among hotel proprietors. Small wonder that you use an alias! From the Hotel Carpathia in Boston I got a response more valuable than I had dared to hope. An H. M. G. guest—H. Morton Garson, of Pillston, Pennsylvania (Mr. Greene nodded)—had wrecked his room and left behind him this souvenir."

Leaning over, Jones pulled, clinking from the scrap basket, a fine steel chain. It was endless and some twelve feet in total length, and had two small loops, about a foot apart. Mrs. Hale and Kirby stared at it in speechless surprise.

"Yes, that is mine," said Mr. Greene with composure. "I left it because it had ceased to be serviceable to me."

"Ah! That's very interesting," said Average Jones with a keen glance. "Of course when I examined it and found no locks, I guessed that it was a trick chain, and that there were invisible springs in the wrist loops."

"But why should any one chain Mr. Greene to his bed with a trick chain?" questioned Mrs. Hale, whose mind had been working swiftly.

"He chained himself," explained Jones, "for excellent reasons. As there is no regular trade in these things, I figured that he probably bought it from some juggler whose performance had given him the idea. So," continued Jones, producing a specimen of his advertisements in the theatrical publications, "I set out to find what professional had sold a 'prop' to an amateur. I found the sale had been made at Barsfield, Ohio, late in November of last year, by a 'Slippery Sam,' termed 'The Elusive Edwardes.' On November twenty-eighth of last year Mr. Harvey M. Greene, of Richmond, Virginia, was registered at the principal, in fact the only decent hotel, at Barsfield. I wrote to him and here he is."

"Yes; but where is my necklace?" cried Mrs. Hale.

"On my word of honor, madam, I know nothing of your necklace," asserted Greene, with a painful contraction of his features. "If this gentleman can throw any more light—"

"I think I can," said Average Jones. "Do you remember anything of that night's events after you broke off the bedpost and left your room—the meeting with a guest who questioned you in the hall, for example?"

"Nothing. Not a thing until I awoke and found myself on the fire-escape."

"Awoke?" cried Kirby. "Were you asleep all the time?"

"Certainly. I'm a confirmed sleep-walker of the worst type. That's why I go under an alias. That's why I got the trick handcuff chain and chained myself up with it, until I found it drove me fighting crazy in my sleep when I couldn't break away. That's why I slept in my dressing-gown that night at the Denton. There was a red light in the hall outside, and any light, particularly a colored one, is likely to set me going. I probably dreamed I was escaping from a locomotive—that's a common delusion of mine—and sought refuge in the first door that was open."

"Wait a minute," said Average Jones. "You—er—say that you are—er—peculiarly susceptible to—er—colored light."

"Yes."

"Mrs. Hale, was the table on which the necklace lay in line with any light outside?"

"I think probably with the direct ray of an electric globe shining through the farther window."

"Then, Mr. Greene," said Average Jones, "the glint of the fire-blue stones undoubtedly caught your eye. You seized on the necklace and carried it out on the fire-escape balcony, where the cool air or the milk-driver's hail awakened you. Have you no recollection of seeing such a thing?"

"Not the faintest, unhappily."

"Then he must have dropped it to the ground below," said Kirby.

"I don't think so," controverted Jones slowly. "Mr. Greene must have been clinging to it tenaciously when it swung and caught against the railing, stripping off the three end stones. If the whole necklace had dropped it would have broken up fine, and more than three stones would have returned to us in reply to the advertisements. And in that case, too, the chances against the end stones alone returning, out of all the thirty-six, are too unlikely to be considered. No, the fire-blue necklace never fell to the ground."

"It certainly didn't remain on the balcony," said Kirby. "It would have been discovered there."

"Quite so," assented Average Jones. "We're getting at it by the process of exclusion. The necklace didn't fall. It didn't stay. Therefore?"—he looked inquiringly at Mrs. Hale.

"It returned," she said quickly.

"With Mr. Greene," added Average Jones.

"I tell you," cried that gentleman vehemently, "I haven't set eyes on the wretched thing."

"Agreed," returned Average Jones; "which doesn't at all affect the point I wish to make. You may recall, Mr. Greene, that in my message I asked you to pack your suitcase exactly as it was when you left the hotel with it on the morning of August seventh."

"I've done so with the exception of the conjurer's chain, of course."

"Including the dressing-gown you had on, that night, I assume. Have you worn it since?"

"No. It hung in my closet until yesterday, when I folded it to pack. You see, I—I've had to give up the road on account of my unhappy failing."

"Then permit me." Average Jones stooped to the dress-suit case, drew out the garment and thrust his hand into its one pocket. He turned to Mrs. Hale.

"Would you—er—mind—er—leaning over a bit?" he said.

She bent her dainty head, then gave a startled cry of delight as the young man, with a swift motion, looped over her shoulders a chain of living blue fires which gleamed and glinted in the sunlight.

"They were there all the time," she exclaimed; "and you knew it."

"Guessed it," he corrected, "by figuring out that they couldn't well be elsewhere—unless on the untenable hypothesis that our friend, Mr. Greene here, was a thief."

"Which only goes to prove," said Kirby soberly, "that evidence may be a mighty deceptive accuser."

"Which only goes to prove," amended Average Jones, "that there's no fire, even the bluest, without traceable smoke."

CHAPTER VII
PIN-PRICKS

"The thing is a fake," declared Bertram. He slumped heavily into a chair, and scowled at Average Jones' well-littered desk, whereon he had just tossed a sheet of paper. His usually impeccable hair was tousled. His trousers evinced a distinct tendency to bag at the knees, and his coat was undeniably wrinkled. That the elegant and flawless dilettante of the Cosmic Club should have come forth, at eleven o'clock of a morning, in such a state of comparative disreputability, argued an upheaval of mind little short of phenomenal.

"A fake," he reiterated. "I've spent a night of pseudo-intellectual riot and ruin over it. You've almost destroyed a young and innocent mind with your infernal palimpsest,* Average."

"You would have it," returned Average Jones with a smile. "And I seem to recall a lofty intimation on your part that there never *was* a cipher so tough but what you could rope, throw, bind, and tie a pink ribbon on its tail in record time."

"Cipher, yes," returned the other bitterly. "That thing isn't a cipher. It's an alphabetical riot. Maybe," he added hopefully, "there was some mistake in my copy."

---

* A palimpsest is a manuscript that has been overwritten with another text. Bertram is speaking figuratively here.

"Look for yourself," said Average Jones, handing him the original.

It was a singular document, this problem in letters which had come to light up the gloom of a November day for Average Jones; a stiffish sheet of paper, ornamented on one side with color prints of alluring "spinners," and on the other inscribed with an appeal, in print. Its original vehicle was an envelope, bearing a one-cent stamp, and addressed in typewriting:

Mr. William H. Robinson,
The Caronia,
Broadway and Evenside Ave.,
New York City.

The advertisement on the reverse of the sheet ran as follows:

ANGLERS—When you are looking for "Baits That Catch Fish," do you see these spinners in the store where you buy tackle? You will find here twelve baits, every one of which has a record and has literally caught tons of fish. We call them "The 12 Surety Baits." We want you to try them for casting and trolling these next two months, because all varieties of bass are particularly savage in striking these baits late in the season.

DEALERS—You want your customers to have these 12 Shoemaker "Surety Baits" that catch fish. This case will sell itself empty over and over again, for every bait is a record-breaker and they catch fish. We want you to put in one of these cases so that the anglers will not be disappointed and have to

wait for baits to be ordered. It will be furnished
FREE, charges prepaid, with your order for the
dozen baits it contains.

The peculiar feature of the communication was that it was
profusely be-pimpled with tiny projections, evidently made by
thrusting a pin through, from the side which bore the illustrations.
These perforations were liberally scattered. Most, though not all
of them, transfixed certain letters. Accepting this as indicative,
Bertram had copied out all the letters thus distinguished, with
the following cryptic result:

b-n-o-k-n-o-a-h-t (doubtful) *i* (doubtful) *d-o-o-u-t-s-e-
h-w-h e-u-a-l-e-w-f-i-h-t-e-l-y-a-n-u-t-t-m-a-n* (doubtful *g-e-x-c-s* (doubtful) *s-e M-e-p-c* (two punctures)
l-y-w-u-s-o-m-e-r-s-h-a-s 1 *S-k-t-s-a-s-e-l-e-v-a-h*
(twice) *W-y-o-u* (doubtful) *h-c-s-e-v-t-l-t-f-r* (perforated twice) *c-a-o-u-c-e-o-u-c* (doubtful) *m-t* (perforated twice) *n-o-h-a-e-f-o-u-w-o-r-t-h-t-r-e-d-w-l-l-b*
(perforated three times) *f-u-h-g-e-p-dh-o-d* (doubtful)
e-f-h-g-b-t-n-t.

"Yes, the copy's all right," growled Bertram. "Tell me again
how you came by it."

"Robinson came here twice and missed me. Yesterday I
got the note from him which you've seen, with the enclosure
which has so threatened your reason. You know the rest. Perhaps
you'd have done well to study the note for clues to the other
document."

Something in his friend's tone made Bertram glance up sus-
piciously. "Let me see the note," he demanded.

Average Jones handed it to him. There was no stamp on it;

it had been left by the writer. It was addressed, in rather scrawly chirography, to "A. Jones, Ad-Visor," and read:

The Caronia, Nov. 18.

Mr. A. Jones, *Astor Court Temple:*

I have tried unsuccessfully to see you twice. Enclosed you will find the reason. Please read through it carefully. Then I am sure you will see and help me. Money is no object. I will call to-morrow at noon.

Respectfully,

William H. Robinson.

"Well, I see nothing out of the ordinary in that," observed Bertram.

"Nothing?" inquired Average Jones.

Bertram read the message again. "Of course the man is rattled. That's obvious in his handwriting. Also, he has inverted one sentence in his haste and said 'read through it,' instead of 'read it through.' Otherwise, it's ordinary enough."

"It must be vanity that keeps you from eyeglasses, Bert," Average Jones observed with a sigh. "Well, I'm afraid I set you on the wrong track, myself!"

Bertram lifted an eyebrow with an effort. "Meaning, I suppose, that you're on the right one and have solved the cipher."

"Cipher be jiggered. You were right in your opening remark. There isn't any cipher. If you'd read Mr. Robinson's note correctly, and if you'd had the advantage of working on the original of the bait advertisement as I have, you'd undoubtedly have noticed at once—"

"Thank you," murmured Bertram.

"—that fully one-third of the pin-pricks don't touch any letters at all."

"Then we should have taken the letters which lie between the holes?"

"No. The letters don't count. It's the punctures. Force your eyes to consider those alone, and you will see that the holes themselves form letters and words. Read *through* it carefully, as Robinson directed."

He held the paper up to the light. Bertram made out in straggling characters, formed in skeleton by the perforations, this legend:

ALL POINTS TO
YOU TAKE THE
SHORT CUT DEATH
IS EASIER THAN
SOME THINGS.

"Whew! That's a cheery little greeting," remarked Bertram. "But why didn't friend Robinson point it out definitely in his letter?"

"Wanted to test my capacity perhaps. Or, it may have been simply that he was too frightened and rattled to know just what he was writing."

"Know anything of him?"

"Only what the directory tells, and directories don't deal in really intimate details of biography, you know. There's quite an assortment of William H. Robinsons, but the one who lives at the Caronia appears to be a commission merchant on Pearl Street. As the Caronia is one of the most elegant and quite the most enormous of those small cities within themselves which we call apartment houses, I take it that Mr. Robinson is well-to-do, and probably married. You can ask him, yourself, if you like. He's due any moment, now."

Promptly, as befitted a business man, Mr. William H. Robinson arrived on the stroke of twelve. He was a well-made, well-dressed citizen of forty-five, who would have been wholly ordinary save for one peculiarity. In a room more than temperately cool he was sweating profusely, and that, despite the fact that his light overcoat was on his arm. Not polite perspiration, be it noted, such as would have been excusable in a gentleman of his pale and sleek plumpness, but soul-wrung sweat, the globules whereof gathered in the grayish hollows under his eyes, and assailed, not without effect, the glistening expanse of his tall white collar. He darted a glance at Bertram, then turned to Average Jones.

"I had hoped for a private interview," he said in a high piping voice.

"Mr. Bertram is my friend and business confidant."

"Very good. You—you have read it?"

"Yes."

"Then—then—then—" The visitor fumbled, with nerveless fingers, at his tightly buttoned cutaway coat. It resisted his efforts. Suddenly, with a snarl of exasperation, he dragged violently at the lapel, tearing the button outright from the cloth. "Look what I have done," he said, staring stupidly for a moment at the button which had shot across the room. Then, to the amazed consternation of the others, he burst into tears.

Average Jones pushed a chair behind him, while Bertram brought him a glass of water. He gulped out his thanks, and, mastering himself after a moment's effort, drew a paper from his inner pocket which he placed on the desk. It was a certified check for one hundred dollars, made payable to A. Jones.

"There's the rest of a thousand ready, if you can help me," he said.

"We'll talk of that later," said the prospective beneficiary. "Sit tight until you're able to answer questions."

"Able now," piped the other in his shrill voice. "I'm ashamed of myself, gentlemen, but the strain I've been under—When you've heard my story—"

"Just a moment, please," interrupted Average Jones, "let me get at this my own way."

"Any way you like," returned the visitor.

"Good! Now what is it that points to you?"

"I don't know any more than you."

"What are the 'some things' that are worse than death?"

Mr. Robinson shook his head. "I haven't the slightest notion in the world."

"Nor of the 'short cut' which you are advised to take?"

"I suppose it means suicide." He paused for a moment. "They can't drive me to that—unless they drive me crazy first." He wiped the sweat from under his eyes, breathing hard.

"Who are 'they?'"

Mr. Robinson shook his head. In the next question the interrogator's tone altered and became more insistent.

"Have you ever called in a doctor, Mr. Robinson?"

"Only once in five years. That was when my nerves broke down—under this."

"When you do call in a doctor, is it your habit to conceal your symptoms from him?"

"Of course not. I see what you mean. Mr. Jones, I give you my word of honor, as I hope to be saved from this persecution, I don't know any more than yourself what it means."

"Then—er—I am—er—to believe," replied Jones, drawling, as he always did when interest, in his mind, was verging on excitement, "that a simple blind threat like this—er—without any backing from your own conscience—er—could shake you—er—as this has done? Why, Mr. Robinson, the thing—er—may be—er—only a raw practical joke."

"But the others!" cried the visitor. His face changed and fell. "I believe I *am* going crazy," he groaned. "I didn't tell you about the others."

Diving into his overcoat pocket he drew out a packet of letters which he placed on the desk with a sort of dismal flourish.

"Read those!" he cried.

"Presently." Average Jones ran rapidly over the eight envelopes. With one exception, each bore the imprint of some firm name made familiar by extensive advertising. All the envelopes were of softish Manila paper varying in grade and hue, under one-cent stamps.

"Which is the first of the series?" he asked.

"It isn't among those. Unfortunately it was lost, by a stupid servant's mistake, pin and all."

"Pin?"

"Yes. Where I cut open the envelope—"

"Wait a moment. You say you cut it open. All these, being one-cent postage, must have come unsealed.* Was the first different?"

"Yes. It had a two-cent stamp. It was a circular announcement of the Swift-Reading Encyclopedia, in a sealed envelope. There was a pin bent over the fold of the letter so you couldn't help but notice it. Its head was stuck through the blank part of the circular. Leading from it were three very small pins arranged as a pointer to the message."

"Do you remember the message?"

"Could I forget it! It was pricked out quite small on the blank fold of the paper. It said: 'Make the most of your freedom. Your

---

* As early as 1879, the US postal system permitted third-class mail (printed material with no handwritten message) to be sent at a lower rate than first-class mail. However, third-class mail had to remain unsealed to allow inspection. For example, many sent printed holiday greeting cards in this manner. This rule was eliminated in 1968 with the advent of mail-sorting machines, because the unsealed envelopes got stuck in the machines.

time is short. Call at General Delivery, Main P. O., for your warning.'"

"You went there?"

"The next day."

"And found—?"

"An ordinary sealed envelope, addressed in pinpricks connected by pencil lines. The address was scrawly, but quite plain."

"Well, what did it contain?"

"A commitment blank to an insane asylum."

Average Jones absently drew out his handkerchief, elaborately whisked from his coat sleeve an imaginary speck of dust, and smiled benignantly where the dust was supposed to have been.

"Insane asylum," he murmured. "Was—er—the blank—er—filled in?"

"Only partly. My name was pricked in, and there was a specification of dementia from drug habit, with suicidal tendencies."

With a quick signal, unseen by the visitor, Average Jones opened the way to Bertram, who, in a wide range of experience and study had once specialized upon abnormal mental phenomena.

"Pardon me," that gentleman put in gently, "has there ever been any dementia in your family?"

"Not as far as I know."

"Or suicidal mania?"

"All my people have died respectably in their beds," declared the visitor with some vehemence.

"Once more, if I may venture. Have you ever been addicted to any drug?"

"Never, sir."

"Now," Average Jones took up the examination, "will you tell me of any enemy who would have reason to persecute you?"

"I haven't an enemy in the world."

"You're fortunate," returned the other smiling, "but surely,

some time in your career—business rivalry—family alienation—
any one of a thousand causes?"

"No," answered the harassed man. "Not for me. My business
runs smoothly. My relations are mostly dead. I have no friends
and no enemies. My wife and I live alone, and all we ask," he
added in a sudden outburst of almost childish resentment, "is
to be left alone."

The inquisitor's gaze returned to the packet of letters. "You
haven't complained to the post-office authorities?"

"And risk the publicity?" returned Robinson with a shudder.

"Well, give me over night with these. Oh! and I may want to
'phone you presently. You'll be at home? Thank you. Good day."

"Now," said Average Jones to Bertram, as their caller's plump
back disappeared, "this looks pretty queer to me. What did you
think of our friend?"

"Scared but straight," was Bertram's verdict.

"Glad to hear it. That's my idea, too. Let's have a look at the
material. We've already got the opening threat, and the General
Delivery follow-up."

"Which shows, at least, that it isn't a case of somebody in the
apartment house tampering with the mail."

"Not only that. It's a dodge to find out whether he got the first
message. People don't always read advertisements, even when
sealed, as the first message-bearing one was. Therefore, our mysterious persecutor says: 'I'll just have Robinson prove it to me if
he *did* get the first message, by calling for the second.' Then, after
a lapse of time, he himself goes to the General Delivery, asks for a
letter for Mr. William H. Robinson, finds it's gone, and is satisfied."

"Yes, and he'd be sure then that Robinson would go through
all the mailed ads with a fine-tooth comb after that. But why the
pin-pricks? Just to disguise his hand?"

"Possibly. It's a fairly effectual disguise."

"Why didn't he address the envelope that way then?"

"The address wouldn't be legible against the white background of the paper inside. On the other hand, if he'd addressed all his envelopes by pinpricks filled in with pencil lines, the post-office people might get curious and look into one. Sending threats through the mail is a serious matter."

Average Jones ran over the letter again. "Good man, Robinson!" he observed. "He's penciled the date of receipt on each one, like a fine young methodical business gent. Here we are: 'Rec'd July 14. Card from Goshorn & Co., Oriental Goods.' Message pricked in through the cardboard: 'You are suspected by your neighbors. Watch them.' Not bad for a follow-up, is it?"

"It would look like insanity, if it weren't that—that 'through the letters one increasing purpose runs,'" parodied Bertram.[*]

"Here's one of July thirty-first; an advertisement of the Croiset Line tours to the Orient. Listen here, Bert: 'Whither can guilt flee that vengeance may not follow?'"

"I can't quite see Robinson in the part of guilt," mused Bertram. "What's next?"

"More veiled accusation. The medium is a church society announcement of a lecture on Japanese Feudalism. Date, August seventeenth. Inscription: 'If there is no blood on your soul, why do you not face your judges?'"

"Little anti-climactic, don't you think?"

"What about this one of September seventh, then? Direct reference back to the drug habit implied in the commitment blank. It's a testimonial booklet of one of the poisonous headache dopes, Lemona Powders. The message is pricked through the cover. 'Better these than the hell of suspense.'"

"Trying the power of suggestion, eh?"

---

[*] Bertram is parodying Alfred, Lord Tennyson's "Locksley Hall" (1835): "thro' the ages one increasing purpose runs."

"Quite so. The second attempt at it is even more open. An advertisement of Shackleton's Safeguard Revolvers. Date, September twenty-second. Advice, by pin: 'As well this as any other way.'"

"Drug or suicide," remarked Bertram. "The man at the other end doesn't seem particular which."

"There's the insane asylum always to fall back on. Under date of October first, comes the Latherton Soap Company's impassioned appeal to self-shaving manhood. Great Cæsar! No wonder poor Robinson was upset. Listen to this: 'God himself hates you.' After that there's a three-weeks respite, for there's October twenty-second on this one, Kirkby and Dunn's offering of five per cent. water bonds. 'The commission has its spies watching you constantly.' Calculated to inspire confidence in the most timid soul! Now we come to the soup course: Smith and Perkins' Potted Chowder. Date of November third. Er—Bert—here's something—er—really worth while, now. Hark to the song of the pin."

He read sonorously:

> "*Animula, vagula, blandula,*
> *Hospes, comesque corporis;*
> *Quae nunc abibis in loca?*" *

---

* The Roman emperor Hadrian (76–138 CE) also wrote poetry. He was devoted to his lover Antinoüs and wrote numerous verses, though only four survive. The message of the pinpricks is the first three lines of Hadrian's most famous poem, "Little Soul"—said to have been written on his deathbed—translated here by Alexander Pope:

Ah! Fleeting Spirit! wand'ring Fire,
That long hast warm'd my tender Breast,
Must thou no more this Frame inspire?
No more a pleasing, chearful Guest?

Whither, ah whither art thou flying!
To what dark, undiscover'd Shore?
Thou seem'st all trembling, shiv'ring, dying,
And Wit and Humour are no more!

"Hadrian, isn't it?" cried Bertram, in utter amazement. "Of course it is! Hadrian's terrified invocation to his own parting spirit. 'Guest and companion of my body; into what places will you now go?' Average, it's uncanny! Into what place of darkness and dread is the Demon of the Pin trying to drive poor Robinson's spirit?"

Average Jones shook his head. "'*Pallidula, nudula, rigida,*'" he completed the quatrain. "'Ghost-pale, stark, and rigid.' He's got a grisly imagination, that pin-operator. I shouldn't care to have him on my trail."

"But Robinson!" protested Bertram feebly. "What has a plump, commonplace, twentieth-century, cutaway-wearing, flat-inhabiting Robinson to do with a Roman emperor's soul-questionings?"

"Perhaps the last entry of the lot will tell us. *Palmerton's Magazine's* feature announcement, received November ninth. No; it doesn't give any clue to the Latinity. It isn't bad, though. 'The darkness falls.' That's all there is to it. And enough."

"I should say the darkness did fall," confirmed Bertram. "It falls—and remains."

Average Jones pushed the collection of advertisements aside and returned to the opening phase of the problem, the fish-bait circular which Robinson had mailed him. So long after, that Bertram hardly recognized it as a response to his last remark, the investigator drawled out:

"Not such—er—impenetrable darkness. In fact,—er— Eureka, or words to that effect. Bert, when does the bass season end?"

"November first, hereabouts, I believe."

"The postmark on the envelope that carried this advertisement to our friend advises the use of the baits for 'these next two months.' Queer time to be using bass-lures, after the season is closed. Bert, it's a pity I can't waggle my ears."

"Waggle your ears! For heaven's sake, why?"

"Because then I'd be such a perfect jackass that I could win medals at a show. I ought to have guessed it at first glance, from the fact that the advertisement couldn't well have been mailed to Robinson originally, anyhow."

"Why not?"

"Because he's not in the sporting-goods business, and the advertisement is obviously addressed to the retail trade. Don't you remember: it offers a show-case, free. What does a man living in an apartment want of a show-case to keep artificial bait in? What we—er—need here is—er—steam."

A moment's manipulation of the radiator produced a small jet. In this Average Jones held the envelope. The stamp curled up and dropped off. Beneath it were the remains of a small portion of a former postmark.

"I thought so," murmured Average Jones.

"Remailed!" exclaimed Bertram.

"Remailed," corroborated his friend. "I expect we'll find the others the same."

One by one he submitted the envelopes to the steam bath. Each of them, as the stamp was peeled off, exhibited more or less fragmentary signs of a previous cancellation.

"Careless work," criticized Average Jones. "Every bit of the mark should have been removed, instead of trusting to the second stamp to cover what little was left, by shifting it a bit toward the center of the envelope. Look; you can see on this one where the original stamp was peeled off. On this the traces of erasure are plain enough. That's why Manila paper was selected: it's easier to erase from."

"Is Robinson faking?" asked Bertram. "Or has some one been rifling his waste-basket?"

"That would mean an accomplice in the house, which would

be dangerous. I think it was done at longer range. As for the question of our friend's faking in his claim of complete ignorance of all this, I propose to find that out right now."

Drawing the telephone to him, he called the Caronia apartments. Thus it was that Mr. William H. Robinson, for two unhappy minutes, profoundly feared that at last he had really lost his mind. This is the conversation in which he found himself implicated.

"Hello! Mr. Robinson? This is Mr. A. Jones. You hear me?"

"Yes, Mr. Jones. What is it?"

"Integer vitae, scelerisque purus."

"I—I—beg your pardon!"

"Non egit Mauris jaculis nec arcu."

"This is Mr. Robinson: Mr. William H. Rob—"

*"Nec venenatis gravida sag—*Hello! Central, don't cut off! Mr. Robinson, do you understand me?"

"God knows, I don't!"

("If he doesn't recognize the *Integer Vitae*," said Average Jones in a swift aside to Bertram, "he certainly wouldn't know the more obscure Latin of the late Mr. Hadrian.") "One more question, Mr. Robinson. Is there, in all your acquaintance, any person who never goes out without an attendant? Take time to think, now."

"Why—why—why," stuttered the appalled subject of this examination, and fell into silence. From the depths of the silence he presently exhumed the following: "I *did* have a paralytic cousin who always went out in a wheeled chair. But she's dead."

---

* The twenty-second poem in the Roman poet Horace's first book of *Odes*, written in the first century BCE. The Latin phrases are the first three lines (the third incomplete), and roughly translate as:

The man who is pure of life, and free of sin,
has no need for Moorish javelins,
nor a bow and a quiver, fully loaded.

"And there's no one else?"

"No. I'm quite sure."

"That's all. Good-by."

"Thank Heaven! Good-by."

"What was that about an attendant?" inquired Bertram, as his friend replaced the receiver.

"Oh, I've just a hunch that the sender of those messages doesn't go out unaccompanied."

"Insane? Or semi-insane? It does rather look like delusional paranoia."

As nearly as imperfect humanity may, Average Jones appeared to be smiling indulgently at the end of his own nose.

"Dare say you're right—er—in part, Bert. But I've also a hunch that our man Robinson is himself the delusion as well as the object."

"I wish you wouldn't be cryptic, Average," said his friend pathetically. "There's been enough of that without your gratuitously adding to the sum of human bewilderment."

Average Jones scribbled a few words on a pad, considered, amended, and handed the result over to Bertram, who read:

"WANTED—Professional envelope eraser to remove marks from used envelopes. Experience essential. Apply at once.—A. Jones, Ad-Visor, Astor Court Temple."

"Would it enlighten your gloom to see that in every New York and Brooklyn paper to-morrow?" inquired its inventor.

"Not a glimmer."

"We'll give this ad a week's repetition if necessary, before trying more roundabout measures. As soon as I have heard from it I'll drop in at the club and we'll write—that is to say, compose a letter."

"To whom?"

"Oh, that I don't know yet. When I do, you'll see me."

Three days later Average Jones entered the Cosmic Club, with that twinkling up-turn of the mouth corners which, with him, indicated satisfactory accomplishment.

"Really, Bert," he remarked, seeking out his languid friend, in the laziest corner of the large divan. "You'd be surprised to know how few experienced envelope erasers there are in four millions of population. Only seven people answered that advertisement, and they were mostly tyros."

"Then you didn't get your man?"

"It was a woman. The fifth applicant. Got a pin about you?"

Bertram took a pearl from his scarf.

"That's good. It will make nice, bold, inevitable sort of letters. Come over here to this desk."

For a few moments he worked at a sheet of paper with the pin, then threw it down in disgust.

"This sort of thing requires practise," he muttered. "Here, Bert, you're cleverer with your fingers than I. You take it, and I'll dictate."

Between them, after several failures, they produced a fair copy of the following:

> "Mr. Alden Honeywell will choose between making explanation to the post-office authorities or calling at 3:30 P. M. to-morrow on A. Jones, Ad-Visor, Astor Court Temple."

This Average Jones enclosed in an envelope which he addressed in writing to Alden Honeywell, Esq., 550 West Seventy-fourth Street, City, afterward pin-pricking the letters in outline. "Just for moral effect," he explained. "In part this ought to give him a taste of the trouble he made for poor Robinson. You'll be there to-morrow, Bert?"

"Watch me!" replied that gentleman with unwonted emphasis. "But will Alden Honeywell, Esquire?"

"Surely. Also Mr. William H. Robinson, of the Caronia. Note that 'of the Caronia.' It's significant."

At three-thirty the following afternoon three men were waiting in Average Jones' inner office. Average Jones sat at his desk sedulously polishing his left-hand fore-knuckle with the tennis callous of his right palm. Bertram lounged gracefully in the big chair. Mr. Robinson fidgeted. There was an atmosphere of tension in the room. At three-forty there came a tap-tapping across the floor of the outer room, and a knock at the door brought them all to their feet. Average Jones threw the door open, took the man who stood outside by the arm, and pushing a chair toward him, seated him in it.

The new-comer was an elderly man dressed with sober elegance. In his scarf was a scarab of great value; on his left hand a superb signet ring. He carried a heavy, gold-mounted stick. His face was curiously divided against itself. The fine calm forehead and the deep setting of the widely separated eyes gave an impression of intellectual power and balance. But the lower part of the face was mere wreckage; the chin quivering and fallen, from self-indulgence, the fine lines of the nose coarsened by the spreading nostrils; the mouth showing both the soft contours of sensuality and the hard, fine lines of craft and cruelty. The man's eyes were unholy. They stared straight before him, and were dead. With his entrance there was infused in the atmosphere a sense of something venomous.

"Mr. Alden Honeywell?" said Average Jones.

"Yes." The voice had refinement and calm.

"I want to introduce you to Mr. William H. Robinson."

The new-comer's head turned slowly to his right shoulder then back. His eyes remained rigid.

"Why, the man's blind!" burst out Mr. Robinson in his piping voice.

"Blind!" echoed Bertram. "Did you know this, Average?"

"Of course. The pin-pricks showed it. And the letter mailed to Mr. Robinson at the General Delivery, which, if you remember, had the address penciled in from pin-holes."

"When you have quite done discussing my personal misfortune," said Honeywell patiently, "perhaps you will be good enough to tell me which is William Robinson."

"I am," returned the owner of that name. "And do *you* be good enough to tell me why you hound me with your hellish threats."

"That is not William Robinson's voice!" said the blind man. "Who are you?"

"William H. Robinson."

"Not William Honeywell Robinson!"

"No; William Hunter Robinson."

"Then why am I brought here?"

"To make a statement for publication in to-morrow morning's newspaper," returned Average Jones crisply.

"Statement? Is this a yellow journal trap?"

"As a courtesy to Mr. Robinson, I'll explain. How long have you lived in the Caronia, Mr. Robinson?"

"About eight months."

"Then, some three or four months before you moved in, another William H. Robinson lived there for a short time. His middle name was Honeywell. He is a cousin, and an object of great solicitude to this gentleman here. In fact, he is, or will be, the chief witness against Mr. Honeywell in his effort to break the famous Holden Honeywell will, disposing of some ten million dollars. Am I right, Mr. Honeywell?"

"Thus far," replied the blind man composedly.

"Five years ago William Honeywell Robinson became addicted to a patent headache 'dope.' It ended, as such habits do, in insanity. He was confined two years, suffering from psychasthenia,* with suicidal melancholia and delusion of persecution. Then he was released, cured, but with a supersensitive mental balance."

"Then the messages were intended to drive him out of his mind again," said Bertram in sudden enlightenment. "What a devil!"

"Either that, or to impel him, by suggestion, to suicide or to revert to the headache powders, which would have meant the asylum again. Anything to put him out of the way, or to make his testimony incompetent for the will contest. So, when the ex-lunatic returned from Europe a year ago, our friend Honeywell here, in some way located him at the Caronia. He matured his little scheme. Through a letter broker who deals with the rag and refuse collectors, he got all the second-hand mail from the Caronia. Meantime, William Honeywell Robinson had moved away, and as chance would have it, William Hunter Robinson moved in, receiving the pinprick letters which, had they reached their goal, would probably have produced the desired effect."

"If they drove a sane man nearly crazy, what wouldn't they have done to one whose mind wasn't quite right!" cried the wronged Robinson.

"But since Mr. Honeywell is blind," said Bertram, "how could he see to erase the cancellations?"

"Ah! That's what I asked myself. Obviously, he couldn't. He'd have to get that done for him. Presumably he'd get some stranger to do it. That's why I advertised for a professional eraser who was *experienced*, judging that it would fetch the person who had done Honeywell's work."

---

* An old term, meaning a mental condition in which the patient is subject to obsessions, phobias, compulsions, or excessive anxiety.

"Is there any such thing as a professional envelope eraser?" asked Bertram.

"No. So a person of experience in this line would be almost unique. I was sure to find the right one, if he or she saw my advertisement. As a matter of fact, it turned out to be an unimaginative young woman who has told me all about her former employment with Mr. Honeywell, apparently with no thought that there was anything strange in erasing cancellations from hundreds of envelopes—for Honeywell was cautious enough not to confine her to the Robinson mail alone—and then pasting on stamps to remail them."

"You appear to have followed out my moves with some degree of acumen, Mr.—er—Jones," said the blind schemer suavely.

"Yet I might not have solved your processes so easily if you had not made one rather—if you will pardon me—stupid mistake."

For the first time, the man's bloated lips shook. His evil pride of intellectuality was stung.

"You lie!" he said hastily. "I do not make mistakes."

"No? Well, have it as you will. The point is that you are to sign here a statement, which I shall read to you before these witnesses, announcing for publication the withdrawal of your contest for the Honeywell millions."

"And if I decline?"

"The painful necessity will be mine of turning over these instructive documents to the United States postal authorities. But not before giving them to the newspapers. How would you look in court, in view of this attempt to murder a fellow-man's reason?"

Mr. Honeywell had now gained his composure. "You are right," he assented. "You seem to have a singular faculty for being right. Be careful it does not fail you—some time."

"Thank you," returned Average Jones. "Now you will listen, please, all of you."

He read the brief document, placed it before the blind man, and set a pin between his finger and thumb. "Sign there," he said.

Honeywell smiled as he pricked in his name.

"For identification, I suppose," he said. "Am I to assign no cause to the newspapers for my sudden action?"

A twinkle of malice appeared in Average Jones' eye.

"I would suggest waning mental acumen," he said.

The blind man winced palpably as he rose to his feet. "That is the second time you have taunted me on that. Kindly tell me my mistake."

Average Jones led him to the door and opened it.

"Your mistake," he drawled as he sped his parting guest into the grasp of a waiting attendant, "was—er—in not remembering that—er—you mustn't fish for bass in November."

CHAPTER VIII
BIG PRINT

In the Cosmic Club Mr. Algernon Spofford was a figure of distinction. Amidst the varied, curious, eccentric, brilliant, and even slightly unbalanced minds which made the organization unique, his was the only wholly stolid and stupid one. Club tradition declared that he had been admitted solely for the beneficent purpose of keeping the more egotistic members in a permanent and pleasing glow of superiority. He was very rich, but otherwise quite harmless. In an access of unappreciated cynicism, Average Jones had once suggested to him, as a device for his newly acquired coat-of-arms, "Rocks et Praeterea Nihil."*

But the "praeterea nihil" was something less than fair to Mr. Spofford, with whom it was not strictly a case of "nothing further" besides his "rocks." Ambition, the vice of great souls, burned in Mr. Spofford's pigeon-breast. He longed to distinguish himself in the line of endeavor of his friend Jones and was prone to proffer suggestions, hints, and even advice, to the great tribulation of the recipient.

Hence it was with misgiving that the Ad-Visor opened the door

---

* A pun on the old motto "vox et praeterea nihil," "voice and nothing more," that is, sound without substance.

of his sanctum to Mr. Spofford, on a harsh December noon. But the misgivings were supplanted by pleased surprise when the caller laid in his hand a clipping from a small country town paper, to this effect:

RANSOM—Lost lad from Harwick not drowned nor harmed. Retained for ransom. Safe and sound to parents for $50,000. Write, Mortimer Morley, General Delivery, N. Y. Post-Office.

"Thought that'd catch you," chuckled Mr. Spofford, in great self-congratulation. "'Jones'll see into this,' I says to myself. 'If he don't, I'll explain.' Somethin' to that, ay?"

Average Jones looked from the advertisement to the vacuous smile of Mr. Algernon Spofford. "Oh, you'll explain, will you?" he said softly. "Well, the thing I'd like to have explained is—come over here to the window a minute, will you, Algy?"

Mr. Spofford came, and gazed down upon a dispiriting area of rain-swept street and bedraggled wayfarers.

"See that ten-story office building across the way?" pursued Average Jones. "What would you do if, coming in here at midnight, you were to see twenty-odd rats ooze out of that building and disperse about their business?"

"I—I'd quit," said the startled Spofford promptly.

"That's the obvious solution," retorted the other, "but my question wasn't intended to elicit your brand of music-hall humor."

Spofford contemplated the building uneasily. "I don't know what you're up to, Average," he complained. "Is it a catch?"

"No; it's a test case. What would you do?"

"I'd think it was Billy-be-dashed* queer," answered Spofford with profound conviction.

---

* A polite version of "Billy-be-damned," an emphatic, intensive comparison found in written use as early as 1837.

"You're getting on," said Jones tartly. "What next?"

"Ay? How do I know? What're you devilin' me this way for?"

"You wouldn't call a policeman?"

"No," said Spofford, staring.

"You wouldn't hustle around and 'phone Central?"

"Bosh!"

"Yet if any one told you you hadn't the sense of a policeman, you'd resent it."

"Of course, I would!"

"Well, Jimmy McCue, the night special, who patrols past the corner, saw that very thing happen a few nights ago at the Sterriter Building.* Knowing that rats don't go out at midnight for a saunter, two dozen strong, he began to suspect."

"Suspect what?" growled Spofford.

"That there must be some abnormal cause for so abnormal a proceeding. Think, now, Algy."

"I've heard of rats leavin' a sinkin' ship. The building might have been sinkin'," suggested the visitor hopefully.

"Is that the best you can do? I'll give you one more try."

"I know," said Spofford. "A cat."

"On my soul," declared Average Jones, gazing at his club-mate with increased interest, "you're the most remarkable specimen of inverted mentality I've ever encountered. D'you think a cat habitually rounds up two dozen rats and then chivies 'em out into the street for sport? McCue didn't have any cat theory. He figured that when rats come out of a place that way the place is afire. So he turned in an alarm and saved a two hundred and fifty thousand dollar building."

"Umph!" grunted Spofford. "Well, what's that got to do with the advertisement I brought you?"

---

* A fictional building.

"Nothing in the world, directly. I'm merely trying to figure out, in my own way, how a mind like yours could see under the surface print into the really interesting peculiarity of this clipping. Now I know that your mind didn't do anything of the sort. Come on, now, Algy, who sent this to you?"

"Cousin of mine up in Harwick.* I wish you weren't so Billy-be-dashed sharp, Average. I used to visit in Harwick, so they asked me to get you interested in Bailey Prentice's case. He's the lost boy."

"You've done it. Now tell me all you know."

Spofford produced a letter which gave the outlines of the case. Bailey Prentice's disappearance, it was set forth, was the lesser of two simultaneous phenomena which violently jarred the somnolent New England village of Harwick from its wonted calm. The greater was the "Harwick meteor." At ten-fifteen on the night of December twelfth, the streets being full of people coming from the moving picture show, there was a startling concussion from the overhanging clouds and the astounded populace saw a ball of flame plunging earthward, to the northwest of the town, and waxing in intensity as it fell. Darkness succeeded. But, within a minute, a lurid radiance rose and spread in the night. The aerial bolt had gone crashing through an old barn on the Tuxall place, setting it afire.

Bailey Prentice was among the very few who did not go to the fire. Taken in connection with the fact that he was fourteen years old and very thoroughly a boy, this, in itself, was phenomenal. In the excitement of the occasion, however, his absence was not noted. But when, on the following morning, the Reverend Peter Prentice, going up to call his son, found the boy's room empty and the bed untouched, the second sensation of the day was launched. Bailey Prentice had, quite simply, vanished.

---

* There was a Hartwick in New York, near Cooperstown, but this village is fictional.

Some one offered the theory that, playing truant from the house while his father was engaged in work below stairs, he had been overwhelmed and perhaps wholly consumed by a detached fragment from the fiery visitant. This picturesque suggestion found many supporters until, on the afternoon of December fourteenth, a coat and waistcoat were found on the seashore a mile north of the village. The Reverend Mr. Prentice identified the clothes as his son's. Searching parties covered the beach for miles, looking for the body. Preparations were made for the funeral services, when a new and astonishing factor was injected into the situation. An advertisement, received by mail from New York, with stamps affixed to the "copy" to pay for its insertion, appeared in the local paper.

"And here's the advertisement," concluded Mr. Algernon Spofford, indicating the slip of paper which he had turned over to Average Jones. "And if you are going up to Harwick and need help there, why I've got time to spare."

"Thank you, Algy," replied Average Jones gravely. "But I think you'd better stay here in case anything turns up at this end. Suppose," he added, with an inspiration, "you trace this Mortimer Morley through the General Delivery."

"All right," agreed Spofford innocently satisfied with this wild-goose errand. "Lemme know if anything good turns up."

Average Jones took the train for Harwick, and within a few hours was rubbing his hands over an open-fire in the parsonage, whose stiff and cheerless aspect bespoke the lack of a woman's humanizing touch, for the Reverend Mr. Prentice was a widower. Overwrought with anxiety and strain, the haggard clergyman, as soon as he had taken his visitor's coat, began a hurried, inconsequential narrative, broke off, tried again, fell into an inextricable confusion of words, and, dropping his head in his hands, cried:

"I can't tell you. It is all a hopeless jumble."

"Come!" said the younger man encouragingly. "Comfort your-self with the idea that your son is alive, at any rate."

"But how can I be sure, even of that?"

Average Jones glanced at a copy of the advertisement which he held. "I think we can take Mr. Morley's word so far."

"Even so; fifty thousand dollars ransom!" said the minister, and stopped with a groan.

"Nonsense!" said Average Jones heartily. "That advertisement counts for nothing. Professional kidnappers do not select the sons of impecunious ministers for their prey. Nor do they give addresses through which they may be found. You can dismiss the advertisement as a blind; the second blind, in fact."

"The second?"

"Certainly. The first was the clothing on the shore. It was put there to create the impression that your son was drowned."

"Yes; we all supposed that he must be."

"By what possible hypothesis a boy should be supposed to take off coat and waistcoat and wade off-shore into a winter sea is beyond my poor powers of conjecture," said the other. "No. Somebody 'planted' the clothes there."

"It seems far-fetched to me," said the Reverend Mr. Prentice doubtfully. "Who would have any motive for doing such a thing?"

"That is what we have to find out. What time did your son go to his room the night of his disappearance?"

"Earlier than usual, as I remember. A little before nine o'clock."

"Any special reason for his going up earlier?"

"He wanted to experiment with a new fishing outfit just given him for his birthday."

"I see. Will you take me to his room?"

They mounted to the boy's quarters, which overlooked the roof of the side porch from a window facing north. The charred ruins of a barn about half a mile away were plainly visible through this window.

"The barn which the meteor destroyed," said the Reverend Mr. Prentice, pointing it out.

One glance was all that Average Jones bestowed upon a spot which, for a few days, had been of national interest. His concern was inside the room. A stand against the wall was littered with bits of shining mechanism. An unjointed fishing-rod lay on the bed. Near at hand were a small screw-driver and a knife with a broken blade.

"Were things in this condition when you came to call Bailey in the morning and found him gone?" asked Average Jones.

"Nothing has been touched," said the clergyman in a low voice.

Average Jones straightened up and stretched himself languidly. His voice when he spoke again took on the slow drawl of boredom. One might have thought that he had lost all interest in the case—but for the thoughtful pucker of the broad forehead which belied his halting accents.

"Then—er—when Bailey left here he hadn't any idea—of—er—running away."

"I don't follow you, Mr. Jones."

"Psychology," said Average Jones. "Elementary psychology. Here's your son's new reel. A normal boy doesn't abandon a brand-new fad when he runs away. It isn't in boy nature. No, he was taking this reel apart to study it when some unexpected occurrence checked him and drew him outside."

"The meteor."

"I made some inquiries in the village on my way up. None of the hundreds of people who turned out for the fire, remembers seeing Bailey about."

"That is true."

"The meteor fell at ten-fifteen. Bailey went up-stairs before nine. Allow half an hour for taking apart the reel. I don't believe he'd have been longer at it. So, it's probable that he was out of the house before the meteor fell."

"I should have heard him go out of the front door."

"That is, perhaps, why he went out of the window," observed Average Jones, indicating certain marks on the sill. Swinging his feet over, he stepped upon the roof of the porch, and peered at the ground below.

"And down the lightning rod," he added.

For a moment he stood meditating. "The ground is now frozen hard," he said presently. "Bailey's footprints where he landed are deeply marked. Therefore the soil must have been pretty soft at the time."

"Very," agreed the clergyman. "There had been a three-day downpour, up to the evening of Bailey's disappearance. About nine o'clock the wind shifted to the northeast, and everything froze hard. There has been no thaw since."

"You seem very clear on these points, Mr. Prentice."

"I noted them specially, having in mind to write a paper on the meteorite for the *Congregationalist*."

"Ah! Perhaps you could tell me, then, how soon after the meteor's fall, the barn yonder was discovered to be afire."

"Almost instantly. It was in full blaze within a very short time after."

"How short? Five minutes or so?"

"Not so much. Certainly not more than two."

"H'm! Peculiar! Ra—a—a—ather peculiar," drawled Average Jones. "Particularly in view of the weather."

"In what respect?"

"In respect to a barn, water-soaked by a three-day rain bursting into flame like tinder."

"It had not occurred to me. But the friction and heat of the meteorite must have been extremely great."

"And extremely momentary except as to the lower floor, and the fire should have taken some time to spread, from that. However, to turn to other matters—" He swung himself over the edge of the roof and went briskly down the lightning rod. Across the frozen ground he moved, with his eyes on the soil, and presently called up to his host:

"At any rate, he started across lots in the direction of the barn. Will you come down and let me in?"

Back in the study, Average Jones sat meditating a few moments. Presently he asked:

"Did you go to the spot where your son's clothes were found?"

"Yes. Some time after."

"Where was it?"

"On the seashore, some half a mile to the east of the Tuxall place, and a little beyond."

"Is there a roadway from the Tuxall place to the spot?"

"No; I believe not. But one could go across the fields and through the barn to the old deserted roadway."

"Ah. There's an old roadway, is there?"

"Yes. It skirts the shore to join Boston Pike about three miles up."

"And how far from this roadway were your son's clothes found?"

"Just a few feet."

"H'm. Any tracks in the roadway?"

"Yes. I recall seeing some buggy tracks and being surprised, because no one ever drives that way."

"Then it is conceivable that your son's clothes might have been tossed from a passing vehicle, to the spot where they were discovered."

"Conceivable, certainly. But I can see no ground for such a conjecture."

"How far down the road, in this direction, did the tracks run?"

"Not beyond the fence-bar opening from the Tuxall field, if that is what you mean."

"It is, exactly. Do you know this Tuxall?"

"Hardly at all. He is a recent comer among us."

"Well, I shall probably want to make his acquaintance, later."

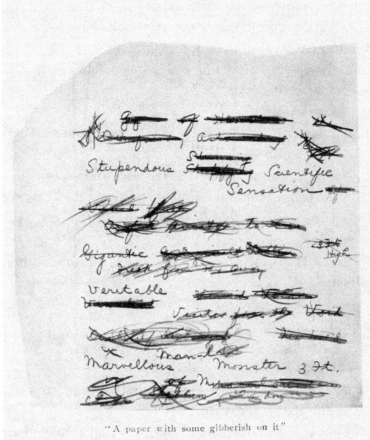

"A paper with some gibberish on it"

"Have a care, then. He is very jealous of his precious meteor, and guards the ruins of the barn, where it lies, with a shot gun."

"Indeed? He promises to be an interesting study. Meantime, I'd like to look at your son's clothes."

From a closet Mr. Prentice brought out a coat and waistcoat of the "pepper-and-salt" pattern which is sold by the hundreds of thousands the whole country over. These the visitor examined carefully. The coat was caked with mud, particularly thick on one shoulder. He called the minister's attention to it.

"That would be from lying wet on the shore," said the Reverend Mr. Prentice.

"Not at all. This is mud, not sand. And it's ground or pressed in. Has any one tampered with these since they were found?"

"I went through the pockets."

Average Jones frowned. "Find anything?"

"Nothing of importance. A handkerchief, some odds and ends of string—oh, and a paper with some gibberish on it."

"What was the nature of this gibberish?"

"Why it might have been some sort of boyish secret code, though it was hardly decipherable enough to judge from. I remember some flamboyant adjectives referring to something three feet high. I threw the paper into the waste-basket."

Turning that receptacle out on the table, Average Jones discovered in the debris a sheet of cheap, ruled paper, covered with penciled words in print characters. Most of these had been crossed out in favor of other words or sentences, which in turn had been "scratched." Evidently the writer had been toilfully experimenting toward some elegance or emphasis of expression, which persistently eluded him. Amidst the wreck and ruin of rhetoric, however, one phrase stood out clear:

"Stupendous scientific sensation."

Below this was a huddle and smudge of words, from which adjectives darted out like dim flames amidst smoke. "Gigantic" showed in its entirety, followed by an unintelligible erasure. At the end of this line was the legend "3 Feet High." "Veritable Visitor," appeared below, and beyond it, what seemed to be the word

"Void." And near the foot of the sheet the student of all this chaos could make out, faintly but unmistakably, "Marvelous Man-l— (the rest of the word being cut off by a broad smear of black) Monster 3 Feet." The remainder was wholly undecipherable.

Average Jones looked up from this curio, and there was a strange expression in the eyes which met the minister's.

"You—er—threw this in the—er—waste-basket," he drawled. "In which pocket was it?"

"The waistcoat. An upper one, I believe. There was a pencil there, too."

"Have you an old pair of shoes of Bailey's?" asked the visitor abruptly.

"Why, I suppose so. In the attic somewhere."

"Please bring them to me."

The Reverend Mr. Prentice left the room. No sooner had the door closed after him than Average Jones jumped out of his chair stripped to his shirt, caught up the pepper-and-salt waistcoat, tried it on, buttoned it across his chest without difficulty; then thrust his arm into the coat which went with it, and wormed his way, effortfully, partly into that. He laid it aside only when he had determined that he could get it no farther on. He was clothed and in his right garments when the Reverend Mr. Prentice returned with a much-worn pair of shoes.

"Will these do?" he asked.

Average Jones hardly gave them the courtesy of a glance. "Yes," he said indifferently, and set them aside. "Have you a time-table here?"

"You're going to leave?" cried the clergyman, in sharp disappointment.

"In just half an hour," replied the visitor, holding his finger on the time-table.

"But," cried Mr. Prentice, "that is the train back to New York."

"Exactly."

"And you're not going to see Tuxall?"

"No."

"Nor to examine the place where the clothes were found?"

"Haven't time."

"Mr. Jones, are you giving up the attempt to discover what became of my boy?"

"I know what became of him."

The minister put out a hand and grasped the back of a chair for support. His lips parted. No sound came from them. Average Jones carefully folded the paper of "gibberish" and tucked it away in his card case.

"Bailey has been carried away by two people in a buggy. They were strangers to the town. He was injured and unconscious. They still have him. Incidentally, he has seriously interfered with a daring and highly ingenious enterprise. That is all I can tell you at present."

The clergyman found his voice. "In the name of heaven, Mr. Jones," he cried, "tell me who and what these people are."

"I don't know who they are. I do know what they are. But it can do no good to tell you the one until I can find out the other. Be sure of one thing. Bailey is in no further danger. You'll hear from me as soon as I have anything definite to report."

With that, the Reverend Mr. Prentice had to be content; that and a few days later, a sheet of letter paper bearing the business imprint of the Ad-Visor, and enclosing this advertisement:

WANTED—3 Ft. type for sensational Bill Work. Show samples. Delivery in two weeks. A. JONES, Ad-Visor, Astor Court Temple, N. Y. City.

Had the Reverend Mr. Prentice been a reader of journals devoted to the art and practice of printing, he might have observed that message widely scattered to the trade. It was answered by a number of printing shops. But, as the answers came in to Average Jones, he put them aside, because none of the seekers for business was able to "show samples." Finally there came a letter from Hoke and Hollins of Rose Street. They would like Mr. Jones to call and inspect some special type upon which they were then at work. Mr. Jones called. The junior member received him.

"Quite providential, Mr. Jones," he said. "We're turning out some single-letter, hand-made type of just the size you want. Only part of the alphabet, however. Isn't that a fine piece of lettering!"

He held up an enormous M to the admiration of his visitor.

"Excellent!" approved Average Jones. "I'd like to see other letters; A, for example."

Mr. Hollins produced a symmetrical A.

"And now, an R, if you please; and perhaps a V."

Mr. Hollis looked at his visitor with suspicion. "You appear to be selecting the very letters which I have," he remarked.

"Those which—er—would make up the—er—legend, 'Marvelous Man-Like Monster," drawled Average Jones.

"Then you know the Farleys," said the print man.

"The Flying Farleys?" said Average Jones. "They used to do ascensions with firework trimmings, didn't they? No; I don't exactly know them. But I'd like to."

"That's another matter," retorted Mr. Hollins, annoyed at having betrayed himself. "This type is decidedly a private—even a secret—order. I had no right to say anything about it or the customers who ordered it."

"Still, you could see that a letter left here for them reached them, I suppose."

After some hesitation, the other agreed. Average Jones sat down to the composition of an epistle which should be sufficiently imperative without being too alarming. Having completed this delicate task to his satisfaction he handed the result to Mr. Hollins.

"If you haven't already struck off a proof of that line, you might do so," he suggested. "I've asked the Farleys for a print of it; and I fancy they'll be sending for one."

Leaving the shop he went direct to a telegraph office, whence he despatched two messages to Harwick. One was to the Reverend Peter Prentice. The other was to the local chief of police.

On the following afternoon Mr. Prentice stood trembling in the anteroom of the Ad-Visor's suite. With the briefest word of greeting Average Jones led him into his private office, where a white-faced, clear-eyed boy, with his head swathed in bandages, sat waiting. As the Ad-Visor closed the door after him, he heard the breathless, boyish "Hello, father," merged in the broken cry of the Reverend Peter Prentice.

Five minutes he gave father and son. When he returned to the room, carrying a loose roll of reddish paper, he was followed by a strange couple. The woman was plumply muscular. Her attractive face was both defiant and uneasy. Behind her strode a wiry man of forty. His chief claim to notice lay in an outrageously fancy waistcoat, which was ill-matched with his sober, commonplace, "pepper-and-salt" suit.

"Mr. and Mrs. Farley, the Reverend Mr. Prentice," said Average Jones in introduction.

"The strangers in the wagon?" asked the clergyman quickly.

"The same," admitted the woman briefly.

The Reverend Mr. Prentice turned upon Farley. "Why did you want to steal my boy away?" he demanded.

"Didn't want to. Had to," replied that gentleman succinctly.

"Let's do this in order," suggested Average Jones. "The principal actor's story first. Speak up, Bailey."

"Don't know my own story," said the boy with a grin. "Only

part of it. Mrs. Farley's been awful good to me, takin' care of me an' all that. But she wouldn't tell me how I got hurt or where I was when I woke up."

"Naturally. Well, we must piece it out among us. Now, Bailey, you were working over your reel the night the meteor fell, when—"

"What meteor? I don't know anything about a meteor."

"Of course you don't," said Average Jones laughing. "Stupid of me. For the moment I had forgotten that you were out of the world then. Well, about nine o'clock of the night you got the reel, you looked out of your window and saw a queer light over at the Tuxall place."

"That's right. But say, Mr. Jones, how do you know about the light?"

"What else but a light could you have seen, on a pitch-black night?" counter-questioned Average Jones with a smile. "And it must have been something unusual, or you wouldn't have dropped everything to go to it."

"That's what!" corroborated the boy. "A kind of flame shot up from the ground. Then it spread a little. Then it went out. And there were people running around it."

"Ah! Some one must have got careless with the oil," observed Average Jones.

"That fool Tuxall!" broke in Farley with an oath. "It was him gummed the whole game."

"Mr. Tuxall, I regret to say," remarked Average Jones, "has left for parts unknown, so the Harwick authorities inform me, probably foreseeing a charge of arson."

"Arson?" repeated the Reverend Mr. Prentice in astonishment.

"Of course. Only oil and matches could have made a barn flare up, after a three-days' rain, as his did. Now, Bailey, to continue. You ran across the fields to the Tuxall place and went around— let me see; the wind had shifted to the northeast—yes; to the northeast of the barn and quite a distance away. There you saw a man at work in his shirt."

"Well—I'll—be—jiggered!" said the boy in measured tones. "Where were you hiding, Mr. Jones?"

"Not behind the tree there, anyway," returned the Ad-Visor with a chuckle. "There is a tree there, I suppose?"

"Yes; and there was something alive tied up in it with a rope."

"Well, not exactly alive," returned Average Jones, "though the mistake is a natural one."

"I tell you, I *know*," persisted Bailey. "While Mr. and Mrs. Farley were workin' over some kind of a box, I shinned up the tree."

"Bold young adventurer! And what did you find?"

"One of the limbs was shakin' and thrashin'. I crawled out on it. I guess it was kind o' crazy in me, but I was goin' to find out what was what if I broke my neck. There was a rope tied to it, and some big thing up above pullin' and jerkin' at it, tryin' to get away. Pretty soon, Mr. and Mrs. Farley came almost under me. He says: 'Is Tuxall all ready?' and she says: 'He thinks we ought to wait half an hour. The street'll be full of folks then.' Then he says: 'Well, I hate to risk it, but maybe it's better.' Just then, the rope gave a twist and came swingin' over on me, and knocked me right off the limb. I gave a yell and then I landed. Next I knew I was in bed. And that's all."

"Now I'll take up the wondrous tale," said Average Jones. "The Farleys, naturally discomfited by Bailey's abrupt and informal arrival, were in a quandary. Here was an inert boy on their hands. He might be dead, which would be bad. Or, he might be alive, which would be worse, if they left him."

"How so?" asked the Reverend Mr. Prentice.

"Why, you see," explained Average Jones, "they couldn't tell how much he might have seen and heard before he made his hasty descent. He might have enough information to spoil their whole careful and elaborate plan."

"But what in the world was their plan?" demanded the minister.

"That comes later. They took off Bailey's coat and waistcoat, perhaps to see if his back was broken (Farley nodded), and finding him alive, tossed his clothes into the buggy, where Farley had left his own, and completed their necessary work. Of course, there was danger that Bailey might come to at any moment and ruin everything. So they worked at top speed, and left the final performance to Tuxall. In their excitement they forgot to find out from their accomplice who Bailey was. Consequently, they found themselves presently driving across country with an unknown and undesired white elephant of a boy on their hands. One of them conceived the idea of tossing his clothes upon the sea-beach to establish a false clue of drowning, until they could decide what was to be done with him. In carrying this out they made the mistake which lighted up the whole trail."

"Well, I don't see it at all," said Farley glumly. "How did you ever get to us?"

Average Jones mildly contemplated the mathematical center of his questioner.

"New waistcoat?" he asked.

Farley glanced down at the outrageous pattern with pride.

"Yep. Got it last week."

"Lost the one that came with the pepper-and-salt suit you're wearing?"

"Damn!" exploded Farley in sudden enlightenment.

"Just so. Your waistcoat got mixed with the boy's clothes, which are of the same common pattern, and was tossed out on the beach with his coat."

"Well, I didn't leave a card in it, did I?" retorted the other.

"Something just as good."

"The ad, Tim!" cried the woman. "Don't you remember, you couldn't find the rough draft you made while we were waiting?"

"That's right, too," he said. "It was in that vest-pocket. But it didn't have no name on it."

"Then, that," put in the Reverend Peter Prentice, "was the scrawled nonsense—"

"Which you—er—threw into the waste-basket," drawled Average Jones with a smile.

"Those were not Bailey's clothes at all?"

"The coat was his; not the waistcoat. His waistcoat may have fallen out of the buggy, or it may be there yet."

"But what does all this talk of people at work in the dark, and arson, and a mysterious creature tied in a tree lead to?"

"It leads," said Average Jones, "to a very large rock, much scorched, and with a peculiar carving on it, which now lies imbedded in the earth beneath Tuxall's barn."

"If you've seen that," said Farley, "it's all up."

"I haven't seen it. I've inferred it. But it's all up, nevertheless."

"Serves us right," said the woman disgustedly. "I wish we'd never heard of Tuxall and his line of bunk."

"Mystification upon mystification!" cried the clergyman. "Will some one please give a clue to the maze?"

"In a word," said Average Jones. "The Harwick meteor."

"What connection—"

"Pardon me, one moment. The 'live thing' in the tree was a captive balloon. The box on the ground was a battery. The wire from the battery was connected with a firework bomb, which, when Tuxall pressed the switch, exploded, releasing a flaming 'dropper.' About the time the 'dropper' reached the earth Tuxall lighted up his well-oiled barn. All Harwick, having had its attention attracted by the explosion, and seen the portent with its own eyes, believed that a huge meteor had fired the building. So Tuxall and Company had a well-attested wonder from the heavens. That's the little plan which Bailey's presence threatened to wreck. Is it your opinion that the stars are inhabited, Mr. Prentice?"

"What!" cried the minister, gaping.

"Stars—inhabited—living, sentient creatures."

"How should I know!"

"You'd be interested to know, though, wouldn't you?"

"Why, certainly. Any one would."

"Exactly the point. Any one would, and almost any one would pay money to see, with his own eyes, the attested evidence of human, or approximately human, life in other spheres. It was a big stake that Tuxall, Farley and Company were playing for. Do you begin to see the meaning of the big print now?"

"I've heard nothing about big prints," said the puzzled clergyman.

"Pardon me, you've heard but you haven't understood. However, to go on, Tuxall and our friends here fixed up a plan on the prospects of a rich harvest from public curiosity and credulity. Tuxall planted a big rock under the barn, fixed it up appropriately with torch and chisel and sent for the Farleys, who are expert firework and balloon people, to counterfeit a meteor."

"Amazing!" cried the clergyman.

"Such a meteor, furthermore, as had never been dreamed of before. If you were to visit Tuxall's barn, you would undoubtedly find on the boulder underneath it a carving resembling a human form, a hoax more ambitious than the Cardiff Giant.* He carted the rock in from some quarry and did the scorching and carving himself, I suppose."

"And you discovered all that in a half-day's visit to Harwick?" asked the Reverend Mr. Prentice incredulously.

---

* In 1869, a "petrified man" was reportedly discovered on the farm of William C. "Stub" Newell in Cardiff, New York. Newell and his cousin George Hull attempted to pass it off as genuine, and P. T. Barnum attempted to purchase the figure. Failing that, Barnum created a wax replica and exhibited it widely until both were debunked in a courtroom battle between Hull and Barnum.

"No, but in half-minute's reading of the 'gibberish' which you threw away."

Taking from the desk the reddish roll which he had brought into the room with him, he sent the loose end of it wheeling across the floor, until it lay, fully outspread. In black letters against red, the legend glared and blared its announcement:

MARVELOUS MAN-LIKE MONSTER!

"Those letters, Mr. Prentice," pursued the Ad-Visor, "measure just three feet from top to bottom. The phrase 'three feet high' which so puzzled you, as combined with the adjectives of great size, was obviously a printer's direction. All through the smudged 'copy,' which you threw away, there run alliterative lines, 'Stupendous Scientific Sensation,' 'Veritable Visitor Void' and finally 'Marvelous Man-l—Monster.' Only one trade is irretrievably committed to and indubitably hall-marked by alliteration, the circus trade. You'll recall that Farley insensibly fell into the habit even in his advertisement; 'lost lad,' 'retained for ransom' and 'Mortimer Morley.' Therefore I had the combination of a circus poster, an alleged meteor which burned down a barn in a highly suspicious manner, and an apparently purposeless kidnapping. The inference was as simple as it was certain. The two strangers, with Tuxall's aid, had prepared the fake meteor with a view to exploiting the star-man. Bailey had literally tumbled into the plot. They didn't know how much he had seen. The whole affair hinged on his being kept quiet. So they took him along. All that I had to do, then, was to find the deviser of the three-foot poster. He was sure to be Bailey's abductor."

"Say," said Farley with conviction, "I believe you're the devil's first cousin."

"When you left me in Harwick," said the Reverend Peter Prentice, before Average Jones could acknowledge this flattering surmise, "you said that strangers had done the kidnapping. How could you tell they were strangers then?"

"From the fact that they didn't know who Bailey was, and had to advertise him, indefinitely, as 'lost lad from Harwick.'"

"And that there were two of them?" pursued the minister.

"I surmised two minds: one that schemed out the 'planting' of the clothes on the shore; the other, more compassionate, that promulgated the advertisement."

"Finally, then, how could you know that Bailey was injured and unconscious?"

"If he hadn't been unconscious then and for long after, he'd have revealed his identity to his captors, wouldn't he?" explained the Ad-Visor.

There was a long pause. Then the woman said timidly:

"Well, and now what?"

"Nothing," answered Average Jones. "Tuxall has got away. Mr. Prentice has recovered his son. You and Farley have had your lesson. And I—"

"Yes, and you, Mr. Detective-man," said the woman, as he paused. "What do you get out of it?"

Average Jones cast an affectionate glance at the sprawling legend which disfigured his floor.

"A unique curio in my own special line," he replied. "An ad which never has been published and never will be. That's enough for me."

There was a double knock at the door, and Mr. Algernon Spofford burst in, wearing a face of gloom.

"Say, Average," he began, but broke off with a snort of amazement. "You've found him!" he cried. "Hello, Mr. Prentice. Well, Bailey, alive and kicking, eh?"

"Yes; I've found him and them," replied Average Jones.

"You've done better than me, then. I've gone through the

post-office department from the information window here to the postmaster-general in Washington, and nobody'll help me find Mortimer Morley."

"Then let me introduce him; Algy, this is Mr. Mortimer Morley; in less private life Mr. Tim Farley, and his wife, Mrs. Farley, Mr. Spofford."

"Well, I'll be Billy-be-dashed," exploded Mr. Spofford. "How did you work it out, Average?"

"On the previously enunciated principle," returned Average Jones with a smile, "that when rats leave a sinking ship or a burning building there's usually something behind, worth investigating."

CHAPTER IX
THE MAN WHO SPOKE LATIN

Mementos of Average Jones' exploits in his chosen field hang on the walls of his quiet sanctum. Here the favored visitor may see the two red-ink dots on a dated sheet of paper, framed in with the card of a chemist and an advertised sale of lepidopteræ, which drove a famous millionaire out of the country. Near by are displayed the exploitation of a lure for black-bass, strangely perforated (a man's reason hung on those pin-pricks), and a scrawled legend which seems to spell "Mercy" (two men's lives were sacrificed to that); while below them, set in somber black, is the funeral notice of a dog worth a million dollars; facing the call for a trombone player which made a mayor, and the mathematical formula which saved a governor. But nowhere does the observer find any record of one of the Ad-Visor's most curious cases, running back two thousand years; for its owner keeps it in his desk drawer, whence the present chronicler exhumed it, by accident, one day. Average Jones has always insisted that he scored a failure on this, because, through no possible fault of his own, he was unable to restore a document of the highest historical and literary importance. Of that, let the impartial reader judge.

It was while Average Jones was awaiting the break of that deadlock of events which, starting from the flat-dweller with the poisoned face, finally worked out the strange fate of Telfik Bey, that he sat, one morning, breakfasting late. The cool and breezy inner portico of the Cosmic Club, where the small tables overlook a gracious fountain shimmering with the dart and poise of goldfish, was deserted save for himself, a summer-engagement star actor, a specialist in carbo-hydrates, and a famous adjuster of labor troubles; the four men being fairly typical of the club's catholicity of membership. Contrary to his impeccant* habit, Average Jones bore the somewhat frazzled aspect of a man who has been up all night. Further indication of this inhered in the wide yawn, of which he was in mid-enjoyment, when a hand on his shoulder cut short his ecstasy.

"Sorry to interrupt so valuable an exercise," said a languid voice. "But—" and the voice stopped.

"Hello, Bert," returned the Ad-Visor, looking up at the faultlessly clad slenderness of his occasional coadjutor, Robert Bertram. "Sit down and keep me awake till the human snail who's hypothetically ministering to my wants can get me some coffee."

"What particular phase of intellectual debauchery have you been up to now?" inquired Bertram, lounging into the chair opposite.

"Trying to forget my troubles by chasing up a promising lead which failed to pan out. 'Wanted: a Tin Nose,' sounds pretty good, eh?"

"It is music to my untutored ear," answered Bertram.

"But it turned out to be merely the error of the imbecile, or perhaps facetious printer, who sets up the *Trumpeter's* personal column. It should have read, Wanted—a Tea Rose.'"

---

* Without sin or error.

"Even that seems far from commonplace."

"Only a code summons for a meeting of the Rosicrucians.*
I suppose you know that the order has been revived here in
America."

"Not the true Rosicrucians, surely!" said Bertram.

"They pretend to be. A stupid lot, who make child's play of
it," said Average Jones impatiently. "Never mind them. I'd rather
know what's on your mind. You made an observation, when you
came in, rather more interesting than your usual output of table-
talk. You said 'but' and nothing further. The conjunction 'but,' in
polite grammar, ordinarily has a comet-like tail to it."

"Apropos of polite grammar, do you speak Latin?" asked
Bertram carelessly.

"Not enough to be gossipy in it."

"Then you wouldn't care to give a job to a man who can't
speak anything else?"

"On that qualification alone?"

"No-o, not entirely. He is a good military engineer, I believe."

"So that's the other end of the 'but,' is it?" said Average Jones.
"Go on. Elaborate."

Bertram laid before his friend a printed clipping in clear, large
type, saying: "When I read this, I couldn't resist the notion that
somehow or other it was in your line; pursuit of the Adventure
of Life, and all that. Let's see what you make of it."

Average Jones straightened in his chair.

"Latin!" he said. "And an ad, by the look of it. Can our blind
friend, J. Alden Honeywell, have taken to the public prints?"

"Hardly, I think. This is from the *Classical Weekly,* a Baltimore
publication of small and select patronage."

"Hm. Looks ra-a-a-ather alluring," commented Average Jones

---

* Christian mystics; the modern Rosicrucian Fellowship was founded in 1909, though
other orders also came into existence in the twentieth century.

with a prolonged drawl. "Better than the Rosicrucian fakery, anyhow."

He bent over the clipping, studying these words:

L. Livius M. F. Praenestinus, quodlibet in negotium non inhonestum qui victum meream locare velim. Litteratus sum; scriptum facere bene scio. Stipendia multa emeritus, scientiarum belli, præsertim muniendi, sum peritus. Hac de re pro me spondebit M. Agrippa. Latine tantum scio. Siquis me velit convenire, quovis die mane adesto in publicis hortis urbis Batltimorianæ ad signum apri.

"Can you make it out?" asked Bertram.

"Hm-m-m. Well—the general sense. Livius seems to yearn in modern print for any honest employment, but especially scrapping of the ancient variety or secretarying. Apply to Agrippa for references. Since he describes his conversation as being confined to Latin, I take it he won't find many jobs reaching out eagerly for him. Anybody who wants him can find him in the Park of the Wild Boar in Baltimore. That's about what I make of it. Now, what's his little lay, I wonder."

"Some lay of Ancient Rome, anyhow," suggested Bertram. "Association with Agrippa would put him back in the first century, B. C., wouldn't it? Besides, my informant tells me that Mr. Livius, who seems to have been an all-around sort of person, helped organize fire brigades for Crassus,[*] and was one of the circle of minor poets who wrote rhapsodies to the fair but frail Clodia's eyebrows, ear-lobes and insteps."[†]

---

[*] Marcus Licinius Crassus (115–53 BCE), a Roman general and statesman who amassed a great fortune through real estate speculation. He was part of the "First Triumvirate," the informal alliance with Julius Caesar and Pompey that essentially launched the Roman Empire.

[†] Clodia, born ca. 95 BCE, was a daughter of Appius Claudius Pulcher, a poet herself, and probably "Lesbia," the lover of Catullus immortalized in his poetry and the writings of Cicero. Clodia reputedly had numerous lovers and was often involved in controversies, including a trial of her former lover Marcus Caelius Rufus, whom she accused of attempted poisoning.

"Your informant? The man's actually been seen, then?"

"Oh, yes. He's on view as per advertisement, I understand."

Average Jones rose and stretched his well-knit frame. "Baltimore will be hotter than the Place-as-Isn't," he said plaintively. "Martyrdom by fire! However, I'm off by the five-o'clock train. I'll let you know if anything special comes of it, Bert."

Barye's splendid bronze boar* couches, semi-shaded, in the center of Monument Park, Baltimore's social hill-top. There Average Jones lounged and strolled through the longest hour of a glaring July morning.† People came and went; people of all degrees and descriptions, none of whom suggested in any particular the first century, B. C. One individual only maintained any permanency of situation. He was a gaunt, powerful, freckled man of thirty who sprawled on a settee and regarded Average Jones with obvious and amused interest. In time this annoyed the Advisor, who stopped short, facing the settee.

"He's gone," said the freckled man.

"Meaning Livius the Roman?" asked Average Jones.

"Exactly. Lucius Livius, son of Marcus Praenestinus."

"Are you the representative of this rather peculiar person, may I ask?"

"It would be a dull world, except for peculiar persons," observed the man on the settee philosophically. "I've seen very many peculiar persons lately by the simple process of coming here day after day. No, I'm not Mr. Livius' representative. I'm only a town-bound and interested observer of his."

* Antoine-Louis Barye (1795–1875) was a French sculptor. In the Mount Vernon neighborhood (surrounding the Washington Monument) in Baltimore, his "Lion" is on display. Though Barye sculpted wild boars, there is no record of such a sculpture in Baltimore.

† Although it is winter in the previous story, "The Man Who Spoke Latin" takes place in the middle of "The Mercy Sign" story, thus this reference to July, even if Adams included this story out of order. See note on page 94.

"There you've got the better of me," said Average Jones. "I was rather anxious to see him myself."

The other looked speculatively at the trim, keen-faced young man. "Yet you do not look like a Latin scholar," he observed; "if you'll pardon the comment."

"Nor do you," retorted Jones; "if the apology is returnable."

"I suppose not," owned the other with a sigh. "I've often thought that my classical capacity would gain more recognition if I didn't have a skin like Bob Fitzsimmons* and hands like Ty Cobb.† Nevertheless, I'm in and of the department of Latin of Johns Hopkins University. Name, Warren. Sit down."

"Thanks," said the other. "Name, Jones. Profession, advertising advisor. Object, curiosity."

"A. V. R. E. Jones; better known as Average Jones, I believe?"

"*Experto crede!* Being dog-Latin for 'You seem to know all about it.'" The new-comer eyed his vis-à-vis. "Perhaps you—er—know Mr. Robert Bertram," he drawled.

"*Oculus*—the eye—*tauri*—of the bull. Bull's-eye!" said the freckled one, with a grin. "I'd heard of your exploits through Bertram, and thought probably you'd follow the bait contained in my letter to him."

"Nothing wrong with your nerve-system, is there?" inquired Average Jones with mock anxiety. "Now that I'm here, where is L. Livius And-so-forth?"

"Elegantly but uncomfortably housed with Colonel Ridgway Graeme in his ancestral barrack on Carteret Street."

"Is this Colonel Graeme a friend of yours?"

"Friend and foe, tried and true. We meet twice a week, usually

---

* The British professional boxer (1863–1917) and the sport's first three-division champion.

† Professional baseball player (1866–1961), an outfielder, ranked third on the 1999 *Sporting News* list of the greatest one hundred players of all time.

at his house, to squabble over his method of Latin pronunciation and his construction of the ablative case.* He's got a theory of the ablative absolute," said Warren with a scowl, "fit to fetch Tacitus howling from the shades."

"A scholar, then?"

"A very fine and finished scholar, though a faddist of the rankest type. Speaks Latin as readily as he does English."

"Old?"

"Over seventy."

"Rich?"

"Not in money. Taxes on his big place keep him pinched; that and his passion for buying all kinds of old and rare books. He's got, perhaps, an income of five thousand, clear, of which about three thousand goes in book auctions."

"Any family?"

"No. Lives with two ancient colored servants who look after him."

"How did our friend from B. C. connect up with him?"

"Oh, he ran to the old colonel like a chick to its hen. You see, there aren't so very many Latinists in town during the hot weather. Perhaps eighteen or twenty in all came from about here and from Washington to see the prodigy in 'the Park of the Boar,' after the advertisement appeared. He wouldn't have anything to do with any of us. Pretended he didn't understand our kind of Latin. I offered him a place, myself, at a wage of more *denarii* than I could well afford. I wanted a chance to study him. Then came the colonel and fairly grabbed him. So I sent for you—in my artless professional way."

"Why such enthusiasm on the part of Colonel Graeme?"

---

* A "case" in Latin refers to the ending of a noun or adjective indicating the construction of that word relative to other words in the sentence. Latin has six distinct cases, "ablative" being one of them.

"Simple enough. Livius spoke Latin with an accent which bore out the old boy's contention. I believe they also agreed on the ablative absolute."

"Yes—er—naturally," drawled Average Jones. "Does our early Roman speak pretty ready Latin?"

"He's fairly fluent. Sometimes he stumbles a little on his constructions, and he's apt to be—well—monkish—rather than classical when in full course."

"Doesn't wear the *toga virilis*,* I suppose."

"Oh, no. Plain American clothes. It's only his inner man that's Roman, of course. He met with a bump on the head—this is his story, and he's got the scar to show for it—and when he came to, he'd lost ground a couple of thousand years and returned to his former existence. No English. No memory of who or what he'd been. No money. No connection whatsoever with the living world."

"Humph! Wonder if he's been a student of Kipling. You remember 'The Greatest Story in the World'; the reincarnated galley slave?[+] Now as to Colonel Graeme; has he ever published?"

"Yes. Two small pamphlets, issued by the Classicist Press, which publishes the *Classical Weekly*."

"Supporting his fads, I suppose."

"Right. He devoted one pamphlet to each." Average Jones contemplated with absorbed attention an ant which was making a laborious spiral ascent of his cane. Not until it had gained a vantage point on the bone handle did be speak again.

"See here, Professor Warren: I'm a passionate devotee of the Latin tongue. I have my deep and dark suspicions of our present

---

* The stereotypical white toga assumed by boys upon attaining manhood in ancient Rome.

+ Published as "The Greatest Story Ever Written" and "The Finest Story in the World," written by Rudyard Kipling and first published in September 1891.

modes of pronunciation, all three of 'em. As for the ablative absolute, its reconstruction and regeneration have been the inspiring
principle of my studious manhood. Humbly I have sat at the
feet of Learning, enshrined in the Ridgway Graeme pamphlets.
I must meet Colonel Graeme—after reading the pamphlets. I
hope they're not long."

Warren frowned. "Colonel Graeme is a gentleman and my
friend, Mr. Jones," he said with emphasis. "I won't have him made
a butt."

"He shan't be, by me," said Average Jones quietly. "Has it perhaps struck you, as his friend, that—er—a close daily association
with the psychic remnant of a Roman citizen might conceivably
be non-conducive to his best interest?"

"Yes, it has. I see your point. You want to approach him on his
weak side. But, have you Latin enough to sustain the part? He's
shrewd as a weasel in all matters of scholarship, though a child
whom any one could fool in practical affairs."

"No; I haven't," admitted Average Jones. "Therefore, I'm a
mute. A shock in early childhood paralyzed my centers of speech.
I talk to you by sign language, and you interpret."

"But I hardly know the deaf-mute alphabet."

"Nor I. But I'll waggle my fingers like lightning if he says anything
to me requiring an answer, and you'll give the proper reply. Does
Colonel Graeme implicitly credit the Romanism of his guest?"

"He does, because he wants to. To have an educated man of the
classic period of the Latin tongue, a friend of Cæsar, an auditor
of Cicero and a contemporary of Virgil, Horace and Ovid come
back and speak in the accent he's contended for, makes a powerful support for his theories. He's at work on a supplementary
thesis already."

"What do the other Latin men who've seen Livius think of
the metempsychosis claim?"

"They don't know. Livius explained his remote antecedents only after he had got Colonel Graeme's private ear. The colonel has kept it quiet. 'Don't want a rabble of psychologists and soul-pokers worrying him to death,' he says."

"Making it pretty plain sailing for the Roman. Well, arrange to take me there as soon as possible."

At the Graeme house, Average Jones was received with simple courtesy by a thin rosy-cheeked old gentleman with a dagger-like imperial and a dreamy eye, who, on Warren's introduction, made him free of the unkempt old place's hospitality. They conversed for a time, Average Jones maintaining his end with nods and gestures, and (ostensibly) through the digital mediumship of his sponsor. Presently Warren said to the host:

"And where is your visitor from the past?"

"Prowling among my books," answered the old gentleman.

"Are we not going to see him?"

The colonel looked a little embarrassed. "The fact is, Professor Warren, Livius has taken rather an aversion to you."

"I'm sorry. How so?"

A twinkle of malice shone in the old scholar's eye. "He says your Latin accent frets his nerves," he explained.

"In that case," said Warren, obeying a quick signal from his accomplice, "I'll stroll in the garden, while you present Mr. Jones to Livius."

Colonel Graeme led the way to a lofty wing, once used as a drawing-room, but now the repository for thousands of books, which not only filled the shelves but were heaped up in every corner.

"I must apologize for this confusion, sir," said the host. "No one is permitted to arrange my books but myself. And my efforts, I fear, serve only to make confusion more confounded. There are four other rooms even more chaotic than this."

At the sound of his voice a man who had been seated behind a tumulus of volumes rose and stood. Average Jones looked at him keenly. He was perhaps forty-five years of age, thin and sinewy, with a close-shaven face, pale blue eyes, and a narrow forehead running high into a mop of grizzled locks. Diagonally across the front part of the scalp a scar could be dimly perceived through the hair. Average Jones glanced at the stranger's hands, to gain, if possible, some hint of his former employment. With his faculty of swift observation, he noticed that the long, slender fingers were not only mottled with dust, but also scuffed, and, in places, scarified, as if their owner had been hurriedly handling a great number of books.

Colonel Graeme presented the new-comer in formal Latin. He bowed. The scarred man made a curious gesture of the hand, addressing Average Jones in an accent which, even to the young man's long-unaccustomed ears, sounded strange and strained.

"*Di illi linguam astrinxere; mutus est,*" said Colonel Graeme, indicating the younger man, and added a sentence in sonorous metrical Greek.

Average Jones recalled the Æschylean line, "Well, though 'a great ox hath stepped on my tongue,' it hasn't trodden out my eyes, praises be!" said he to himself as he caught the uneasy glance of the Roman.

By way of allaying suspicion, he scribbled upon a sheet of paper a few complimentary Latin sentences, in which Warren had sedulously coached him for the occasion, and withdrew to the front room, where he was presently joined by the Johns Hopkins man. Fortunately, the colonel gave them a few moments together.

"Arrange for me to come here daily to study in the library," whispered Jones to the Latin professor.

The other nodded.

"Now, sit tight," added Jones.

He stepped, soft-footed, on the thick old rug, across to the library door and threw it open. Just inside stood Livius, an expression of startled anger on his thin face. Quickly recovering himself, he explained, in his ready Latin, that he was about to enter and speak to his patron.

"Shows a remarkable interest in possible conversation," whispered Jones, on his withdrawal, "for a man who understands no English. Also does me the honor to suspect me. He must have been a wily chap—in the Consulship of Plancus."*

Before leaving, Average Jones had received from Colonel Graeme a general invitation to spend as much time as he chose, studying among the books. The old man-servant, Saul, had orders to admit him at any hour. He returned to his hotel to write a courteous note of acknowledgment.

Many hours has Average Jones spent more tediously than those passed in the cool seclusion of Colonel Ridgway Graeme's treasure-house of print. He burrowed among quaint accumulations of forgotten classics. He dipped with astonishment into the savage and ultra-Rabelaisian satire of Von Hutten's *"Epistolæ Obscurorum Virorum,"*† which set early sixteenth century Europe a-roar with laughter at the discomfited monks; and he cleansed himself from that tainted atmosphere in the fresh air and free English of a splendid Audubon "first"—and all the time he was conscious that the Roman watched, watched, watched. More than once Livius offered aid, seeking to apprise himself of the supposed mute's line of investigation; but the other smilingly fended him off. At the end of four days, Average Jones had satisfied himself that if Livius were seeking anything in particular, he had an indefinite task before him, for the colonel's bound treasures

---

* Lucius Munatius Plancus was a Roman senator and consul who lived from approximately 87 BCE to 15 BCE.

† A celebrated text of satirical letters that appeared in 1515.

were in indescribable confusion. Apparently he had bought from far and near, without definite theme or purpose. As he bought he read, and having read, cast aside; and where a volume fell, there it had license to lie. No cataloguer had ever sought to restore order to that bibliographic riot. To seek any given book meant a blind voyage, without compass or chart, throughout the mingled centuries.

Often Colonel Graeme spent hours in one or the other of the huge book-rooms talking with his strange protégé and making copious notes. Usually the old gentleman questioned and the other answered. But one morning the attitude seemed, to the listening Ad-Visor, to be reversed. Livius, in the far corner of the room, was speaking in a low tone. To judge from the older man's impatient manner, the Roman was interrupting his host's current of queries with interrogations of his own. Average Jones made a mental note, and, in conference with Warren that evening, asked him to ascertain from Colonel Graeme whether Livius's inquiries had indicated a specific interest in any particular line of reading.

On the following day, however, an event of more immediate import occupied his mind. He had spent the morning in the upstairs library, at the unevadable suggestion of Colonel Graeme, while the colonel and his Roman collogued below. Coming down about noon, Average Jones entered the colonel's small study just in time to see Livius, who was alone in the room, turn away sharply from the desk. His elbow was held close to his ribs in a peculiar manner. He was concealing something under his coat. With a pretense of clumsiness, Average Jones stumbled against him in passing. Livius drew away, his high forehead working with suspicion. The Ad-Visor's expression of blank apology, eked out with a bow and a grimace, belied the busy-working mind within. For, in the moment's contact, he had heard the crisp rustle of paper from beneath the ill-fitting coat.

What paper had the man from B. C. taken furtively from his benefactor's table? It must be large; otherwise he could have readily thrust it into his pocket. No sooner was Livius out of the room than Average Jones scanned the desk. His face lighted with a sudden smile. Colonel Graeme never read a newspaper; boasted, in fact, that he wouldn't have one about the place. But, as Average Jones distinctly recalled, he had, himself, that very morning brought in a copy of the *Globe* and dropped it into the scrap basket near the writing-table. It was gone. Livius had taken it.

"If he's got the newspaper-reading habit," said Average Jones to himself, "I'll set a trap for him. But Warren must furnish the bait."

He went to look up his aide. The conference between them was long and exhaustive, covering the main points of the case from the beginning.

"Did you find out from Colonel Graeme," inquired Average Jones, "whether Livius affected any particular brand of literature?"

"Yes. He seems to be specializing on late seventeenth century British classicism. Apparently he considers that the flower of British scholarship of that time wrote a very inferior kind of dog-Latin."

"Late seventeenth century Latinity," commented Average Jones. "That—er—gives us a fair start. Now as to the body-servant."

"Old Saul? I questioned him about strange callers. He said he remembered only two, besides an occasional peddler or agent. They were looking for work."

"What kind of work?"

"Inside the house. One wanted to catalogue the library."

"What did he look like?"

"Saul says he wore glasses and a worse tall hat than the colonel's and had a full beard."

"And the other?"

"Bookbinder and repairer. Wanted to fix up Colonel Graeme's

collection. Youngish, smartly dressed, with a small waxed moustache."

"And our Livius is clean-shaven," murmured Average Jones. "How long apart did they call?"

"About two weeks. The second applicant came on the day of the last snowfall. I looked that up. It was March 27."

"Do you know, Warren," observed Average Jones, "I sometimes think that part of your talents, at least, are wasted in a chair of Latin."

"Certainly, there is more excitement in this hide-and-seek game, as you play it, than in the pursuits of a musty pedant," admitted the other, crackling his large knuckles. "But when are we going to spring upon friend Livius and strip him of his fake toga?"

"That's the easiest part of it. I've already caught him filling a fountain-pen as if he'd been brought up on them, and humming the spinning chorus from *The Flying Dutchman;*[*] not to mention the lifting of my newspaper."

"*Nemo mortalium omnibus horis sapit,*"[†] murmured Warren.

"No. As you say, no fellow can be on the job all the time. But our problem is not to catch Livius, but to find out what it is he's been after for the last three months."

"Three months? You're assuming that it was he who applied for work in the library."

"Certainly. And when he failed at that he set about a very carefully developed scheme to get at Colonel Graeme's books anyway. By inquiries he found out the old gentleman's fad and proceeded to get in training for it. You don't know, perhaps, that I have a corps of assistants who clip, catalogue and file all unusual

---

[*] The "spinning chorus" ("Summ und brumm, du gutes Rädchen"—"Whir and whirl, good wheel") appears at the beginning of act 2 of Richard Wagner's 1843 opera, *The Flying Dutchman.*

[†] "No man is wise all the time."

advertisements. Here is one which they turned up for me on my order to send me any queer educational advertisements: 'Wanted—Daily lessons in Latin speech from competent Spanish scholar. Write, Box 347, *Banner* office.' That is from the New York *Banner* of April third, shortly after the strange caller's second abortive attempt to get into the Graeme library."

"I suppose our Livius figured out that Colonel Graeme's theory of accent was about what a Spaniard would have. But he couldn't have learned all his Latin in four months."

"He didn't. He was a scholar already; an accomplished one, who went wrong through drink and became a crook, specializing in rare books and prints. His name is Enderby; you'll find it in the Harvard catalogue. He's supposed to be dead. My assistant traced him through his Spanish-Latin teacher, a priest."

"But even allowing for his scholarship, he must have put in a deal of work perfecting himself in readiness of speech and accent."

"So he did. Therefore the prize must be big. A man of Enderby's caliber doesn't concoct a scheme of such ingenuity, and go into bondage with it, for nothing. Do you belong to the Cosmic Club?"

The assistant professor stared. "No," he said.

"I'd like to put you up there. One advantage of membership is that its roster includes experts in every known line of erudition, from scarabs to skeeing.* For example, I am now going to telegraph for aid from old Millington, who seldom misses a book auction and is a human bibliography of the wanderings of all rare volumes. I'm going to find out from him what British publication of the late seventeenth century in Latin is very valuable; also what volumes of that time have changed hands in the last six months."

---

* Apparently an archaic spelling of "skiing." It developed as a sport in the late nineteenth century, primarily in the form of what is now known as "cross-country skiing." Arthur Conan Doyle was an early exponent.

"Colonel Graeme went to a big book auction in New York early in March," volunteered Warren, "but he told me he didn't pick up anything of particular value."

"Then it's something he doesn't know about and Livius does. I'm going to take advantage of our Roman's rather un-B.-C.-like habit of reading the daily papers by trying him out with this advertisement."

Average Jones wrote rapidly and tossed the result to his coadjutor who read:

> "LOST—Old book printed in Latin. Buff leather binding, a little faded ('It's safe to be that,' explained Average Jones). No great value except to owner. Return to Colonel Ridgway Graeme, 11 Carteret Street, and receive reward."

The advertisement made its appearance in big type on the front pages of the Baltimore paper of the following day. That evening Average Jones met Warren, for dinner, with a puckered brow.

"Did Livius rise to the bait?" asked the scholar.

"Did he!" chuckled Average Jones. "He's been nervous as a cat all day and hardly has looked at the library. But what puzzles me is this." He exhibited a telegram from New York.

> *"Millington says positively no book of that time and description any great value. Enderby at Barclay auction in March and made row over some book which he missed because it was put up out of turn in catalogue. Barclay auctioneer thinks it was one of Percival privately bound books 1680–1703. An anonymous book of Percival library, De Meritis Librorum Britannorum, was sold to*

Colonel Graeme for $47, a good price. When do I get in on this?

"(Signed) Robert Bertram.*"*

"I know that treatise," said Warren. "It isn't particularly rare."

Average Jones stared at the telegram in silence. Finally he drawled: "There are—er—books and—er—books—and—er—things in books. Wait here for me."

Three hours later he reappeared with collar wilted, but spirits elate, and abruptly announced:

"Warren, I'm a cobbler."

"A what?"

"A cobbler. Mend your boots, you know."

"Are you in earnest?"

"Certainly. Haven't you ever remarked that a serious-minded earnestness always goes with cobbling? Though I'm not really a practical cobbler, but a proprietary one. Our friend, Bertram, will dress and act the practical part. I've wired him and he's replied, collect, accepting the job. You and I will be in the background."

"Where?"

"No. 27 Jasmine Street. Not a very savory locality. Why is it, Warren, that the beauty of a city street is generally in inverse ratio to the poetic quality of its name? There I've hired the shop and stock of Mr. Hans Fichtel for two days, at the handsome rental of ten dollars per day. Mr. Fichtel purposes to take a keg of beer a-fishing. I think two days will be enough."

"For the keg?"

"For that noble Roman, Livius. He'll be reading the papers pretty keenly now. And in to-morrow's, he'll find this advertisement."

Average Jones read from a sheet of paper which he took from his pocket:

"FOUND—Old book in foreign language, probably Latin, marked 'Percival.' Owner may recover by giving satisfactory description of peculiar and obscure feature and refunding for advertisement— Fichtel, 27 Jasmine Street."

"What is the peculiar and obscure feature, Jones?" asked Warren.

"I don't know."

"How do you know there is any?"

"Must be something peculiar about the book or Enderby wouldn't put in four months of work on the chance of stealing it. And it must be obscure, otherwise the auctioneer would have spotted it."

"Sound enough!" approved the other. "What could it be? Some interpolated page?"

"Hardly. I've a treatise in my pocket on seventeenth century book-making, which I'm going to study to-night. Be ready for an early start, to meet Bertram."

That languid and elegant gentleman arrived by the first morning train. He protested mightily when he was led to the humble shoe-shop. He protested more mightily when invited to don a leather apron and smudge his face appropriately to his trade. His protests, waxing vehement and eventually profane, as he barked his daintily-kept fingers, in rehearsal for giving a correct representation of an honest artisan cobbling a boot, died away when Average Jones explained to him that on pretense of having found a rare book, he was to worm out of a cautious and probably suspicious criminal the nature of some unique and hidden feature of the volume.

"Trust me for diplomacy," said Bertram airily.

"I will because I've got to," retorted Average Jones. "Well, get to work. To you the outer shop: to Warren and me this rear room.

And, remember, if you hear me whetting a knife, that means come at once."

Uncomfortably twisted into a supposedly professional posture, Bertram wrought with hammer and last, while putting off, with lame, blind and halting excuses, such as came to call for their promised footgear. By a triumph of tact he had just disposed of a rancid-tongued female who demanded her husband's boots, a satisfactory explanation, or the arbitrament of the lists, when the bell tinkled and the two watchers in the back room heard a nervous, cultivated voice say:

"Is Mr. Fichtel here?"

"That's me," said Bertram, landing an agonizing blow on his thumb-nail.

"You advertised that you had found an old book."

"Yes, sir. Somebody left it in the post-office."

"Ah; that must have been when I went to mail some letters to New York," said the other glibly, "From the advertised description, the book is without doubt mine. Now as to the reward—"

"Excuse me, but you wouldn't expect me to give it up without any identification, sir?"

"Certainly not. It was the *De Meritis Libror*—"

"I can't read Latin, sir."

"But you could make that much out," said the visitor with rising exasperation. "Come; if it's a matter of the reward—how much?"

"I wouldn't mind having a good reward; say ten dollars. But I want to be sure it's your book. There's something about it that you could easily tell me, sir, for any one could see it."

"A very observing shoemaker," commented the other with a slight sneer. "You mean the—the half split cover?"

"Whish—swish; whish-swish," sounded from the rear room.

"Excuse me," said Bertram, who had not ceased from his pretended work. "I have to get a piece of leather."

He stepped into the back room where Average Jones, his face alight, held up a piece of paper upon which he had hurriedly scrawled:

"Mss. bound into cover. Get it out of him. Tell him you've a brother who is a Latin scholar."

Bertram nodded, caught up a strip of calf-skin and returned.

"Yes, sir," he said, "the split cover and what's inside?"

The other started. "You didn't get it out?" he cried. "You didn't tear it!"

"No, sir. It's there safe enough. But some of it can be made out."

"You said you didn't read Latin."

"No, sir; but I have a brother that went through the Academy. He reads a little." This was thin ice, but Bertram went forward with assumed assurance. "He thinks the manuscript is quite rare. Oh, Fritz! Come in."

"Any letter of Bacon's is rare, of course," returned the other impatiently. "Therefore, I propose offering you fifty dollars reward."

He looked up as Average Jones entered. The young man's sleeves were rolled up, his face was generously smudged, and a strip of cobbler's wax beneath the upper lip, puffed and distorted the firm line of his mouth. Further, his head was louting low on his neck, so that the visitor got no view sufficient for recognition.

"Lord Bacon's letter—er—must be pretty rare, Mister," he drawled thickly. "But a letter—er—from Lord Bacon—er— about Shakespeare—*that* ought to be worth a lot of money."

Average Jones had taken his opening with his customary incisive shrewdness. The mention of Bacon had settled it, to his mind. Only one imaginable character of manuscript from the philosopher-scholar-politician could have value enough to tempt a thief of Enderby's caliber. Enderby's expression told that the shot was a true one. As for Bertram, he had dropped his shoe-maker's knife and his shoemaker's rôle.

"Bacon on Shakespeare! Shades of the departed glory of Ignatius Donnelly!"*

The visitor drew back. Warren's gaunt frame appeared in the doorway. Jones' head lifted.

"It ought to be as—er—unique," he drawled, "as an—er—Ancient Roman speaking perfect English."

Like a flash, the false Livius caught up the knife from the bench where the false cobbler had dropped it and swung toward Average Jones. At the same moment the ample hand of Professor Warren, bunched into a highly competent fist, flicked across and caught the assailant under the ear. Enderby, alias Livius, fell as if smitten by a cestus.† As his arm touched the floor, Average Jones kicked unerringly at the wrist and the knife flew and tinkled in a far corner. Bertram, with a bound, landed on the fallen man's chest and pinned him.

"Did he get you, Average?" he cried.

"Not—er—this time. Pretty good—er—team work," drawled the Ad-Visor. "We've got our man for felonious assault, at least."

Enderby, panting under Bertram's solid knee, blinked and struggled.

"No use, Livius," said Average Jones. "Might as well quiet down and confess. Ease up a little on him, Bert. Take a look at that scar of his first though."

"Superficial cut treated with make-up paint; a clever job," pronounced Bertram after a quick examination.

---

* Donnelly (1831–1901) was a US congressman but is principally remembered for being a proponent of various pseudoscience and pseudohistory, including his 1888 book *The Great Cryptogram*, in which he asserted that Francis Bacon was the true author of the works of Shakespeare.

---

† An ancient battle glove, often filled with plates of iron or spikes.

"As I supposed," said Average Jones.

"Let me in on the deal," pleaded Livius. "That letter is worth ten thousand, twelve thousand, fifteen thousand dollars—anything you want to ask, if you find the right purchaser. And you can't manage it without me. Let me in."

"Thinks we're crooks, too?" remarked Average Jones. "Exactly what's in this wonderful letter?"

"It's from Bacon to the author of the book, who wrote about 1610. Bacon prophesies that Shakespeare, 'this vagabond and humble mummer' would outshine and outlive in fame all the genius of his time. That's all I could make out by loosening the stitches."

"Well, that *is* worth anything one could demand," said Warren in a somewhat awed tone.

"Why didn't you get the letter when you were examining it at the auction room?" inquired Average Jones.

"Some fool of a binder had overlooked the double cover, and sewed it in. I noticed it at the auction, gummed the opening together while no one was watching, and had gone to get cash to buy the book; but the auctioneer put it up out of turn and old Graeme got it. Bring it to me and I'll show you the 'pursed' cover. Many of the Percival books were bound that way."

"We've never had it, nor seen it," replied Average Jones. "The advertisement was only a trap into which you stepped."

Enderby's jaw dropped. "Then it's still at the Graeme house," he cried, beating on the floor with his free hand. "Take me back there!"

"Oh, we'll take you," said Warren grimly.

Close-packed among them in a cab, they drove him back to Carteret Street. Colonel Ridgway Graeme was at home and greeted them courteously.

"You've found Livius," he said, with relief. "I had begun to fear for him."

"Colonel Graeme," began Average Jones, "you have—"

"What! Speech!" cried the old gentleman. "And you a mute! What does this mean?"

"Never mind him," broke in Enderby Livius. "There's something more important."

But the colonel had shrunk back. "English from you, Livius!" he cried, setting his hand to his brow.

"All will be explained in time, Colonel," Warren assured him. "Meanwhile, you have a document of the utmost importance and value. Do you remember buying one of the Percival volumes at the Barclay auction?"

The collector drew his brows down in an effort to remember.

"An octavo, in fairly good condition?" he asked.

"Yes, yes!" cried Enderby eagerly. "Where is it? What did you do with it?"

"It was in Latin—very false Latin." The four men leaned forward, breathless. "Oh, I remember. It slipped from my pocket and fell into the river as I was crossing the ferry to Jersey."

There was a dead, flat, stricken silence. Then Average Jones turned hollow eyes upon Warren.

"Professor," he said, with a rueful attempt at a smile, "what's the past participle, passive, plural, of the Latin verb, 'to sting'?"

CHAPTER X
THE ONE BEST BET*

"Morrison has jammed the Personal Liberty bill through," said Waldemar, scrawling a head on his completed editorial, with one eye on the clock, which pointed to midnight.

"That was to be expected, wasn't it?" asked Average Jones.

"Oh, yes," replied the editor-owner of the *Universal* in his heavy bass. "And now the governor announces he will veto it."

"Thereby bringing the whole power of the gambling ring down on him like an avalanche."

"Naturally. Morrison has declared open war against 'Pharisee Phil,' as he calls Governor Arthur.† Says he'll pass the bill over his veto. In his heart he knows he can't do it. Still, he's a hard fighter."

Average Jones tipped his chair back against the wall of the editorial sanctum. "What do you suppose," he inquired with an air of philosophic speculation, "that the devil will do with Carroll Morrison's soul when he gets it? Deodorize it?"

"Harsh words, young sir! Harsh words and treasonable against

---

* Originally published as "Flash-Light."

† Charles Evans Hughes was the actual governor of New York from 1907 to 1910; Hughes later served as the US secretary of state and as chief justice of the US Supreme Court for eleven years.

one of our leading citizens; multimillionaire philanthropist, social leader, director of banks, insurance companies and railroads, and emperor of the race-track, the sport of kings."

"The sport of kings—maintained on the spoils of clerks," retorted Average Jones. "'To improve the breed of horses,' if you please! To make thieves of men and harlots of women, because Carroll Morrison must have his gambling-game dividends! And now he has our 'representative' legislature working for him to that honorable end!"

"Man to see you, Mr. Waldemar," said an office boy, appearing at the door.

"Too late," grunted the editor.

"He says it's very particular, sir, and to tell you it's something Mr. Morrison is interested in."

"Morrison, eh? All right. Just step into the inner office, will you, Jones? Leave the door open. There might be something interesting."

Hardly had Average Jones found a chair in the darkened office when the late caller appeared. He was middle-aged, pursy,* and dressed with slap-dash ostentation. His face was bloated and seared with excesses. But it was not intoxication that sweated on his forehead and quivered in his jaw. It was terror. He slumped into the waiting chair and mouthed mutely at the editor.

"Well?" The bullet-like snap of the interrogation stung the man into babbling speech.

"'S like this, Misser Wald'mar. 'S like this. Y-y-yuh see, 's like this. Fer Gavvsake, kill out an ad for me!"

"What? In to-morrow's paper? Nonsense! You're too late, even if I wished to do it."

The visitor stood up and dug both hands into his side

---

* Fat, obese.

pockets. He produced, first a binocular, which, with a snarl, he flung upon the floor. Before it had stopped bumping, there fluttered down upon the seat of his chair a handful of green-backs. Another followed, and another, and another. The bills toppled and spread, and some of them slid to the floor. Still the man delved.

"There!" he panted at last. "Money talks. There's the stuff. Count it. Eighteen hundred if there's a dollar. More likely two thou. If that ain't enough, make your own price. I don't care what it is. Make it, Misser. Put a price on it."

There was something loathsome and obscene in the creature's gibbering flux of words. The editor leaned forward.

"Bribery, eh?" he inquired softly.

The man flinched from the tone. "It ain't bribery, is it, to ast you to rout out jus' one line from an ad an' pay you for the trouble. My own ad, too. If it runs, it's my finish. I was nutty when I wrote it. Fer Gawsake, Misser—"

"Stop it! You say Morrison sent you here?"

"No, sir. Not exac'ly. 'S like this, Misser Wald'mar. I hadda get to you some way. It's important to Misser Morrison, too. But he don't know I come. He don't know nothing about it. Oh, Gaw! If he finds out—"

"Put that money back in your pockets."

With an ashen face of despair, the man obeyed. As he finished, he began to sag at the joints. Slowly he slackened down until he was on his knees, an abject spectacle of disgust.

"Stand up," ordered Waldemar.

"Liss'n; liss'n t' me," moaned the man. "I'll make it three thou-sand. Fi' thou—"

"Stand *up*!"

The editor's hearty grip on his coat collar heaved the crea-ture to his feet. For a moment he struggled, panting, then spun, helpless and headlong from the room, striking heavily against the passage-wall outside. There was a half-choked groan; then his footsteps slumped away into silence.

"Ugh!" grunted Waldemar. "Come back, Jones."

Average Jones reëntered. "Have you no curiosity in your composition?" he asked.

"Not much—having been reared in the newspaper business."

Stooping, Average Jones picked up the glasses which the man had thrown on the floor and examined them carefully. "Rather a fine instrument," he observed. "Marked N. K. I think I'll follow up the owner."

"You'll never find him now. He has too much start."

"Not at all. When a man is in his state of abject funk, it's ten to one he lands at the nearest bar. Wait for me."

In fifteen minutes Average Jones was back. There was a curious expression on his face as he nodded an assent to his friend's inquiring eyebrows.

"Where?" asked Waldemar.

"On the floor of a Park Row saloon."

"Dead drunk, eh?"

"No—er; not—er—drunk. Dead."

Waldemar stiffened in his chair. "Dead!" he repeated.

"Poison, probably. The ad was his finish, as he said. The next thing is to find it."

"The first edition will be down any minute now. But it'll take some finding. Why, counting 'classified,' we're carrying fifteen hundred ads in every issue. With no clue to the character of this one—"

"Plenty of clue," said Average Jones suavely. "You'll find it on the sporting page, I think."

"Judging from the man's appearance? Rather far-fetched, isn't it?"

"Judging from a pair of very fine binoculars, a mention of Carroll Morrison's name, and, principally, some two thousand dollars in a huge heap."

"I don't quite see where that leads."

"No? The bills must have been mostly ones and twos. Those are a book-maker's takings. The binocular is a racing-man's glass. Our late friend used the language of the track. I think we'll find him on page nine."

"Try," said Waldemar, handing him a paper still spicy with the keen odor of printer's ink.

Swiftly the Ad-Visor's practised eye ran over the column. It checked at the "offer" of a notorious firm of tipsters who advertised to sell "inside information" on the races to their patrons. As a special lure, they were, on this day, letting the public in on a few particularly "good things" free.

"There you are," said Average Jones, pointing out the advertisement.

To his astonishment, Waldemar noted that his friend's indicatory finger shook a little. Normally, Average Jones was the coolest and most controlled of men.

"Noble and Gale's form ad," he observed. "I see nothing unusual in that."

"Yet—er—I fancy it's quite important—er—in its way."

The editor stared. "When you talk like a bored Britisher, Average," he remarked, "there's sure to be something in the air. What is it?"

"Look at the last line."

Again Waldemar turned to the paper. "'One Best Bet,'" he read. "'That the Pharisee will never finish.' Well?"

"'That the Pharisee will never finish,'" repeated Average Jones. "If the Pharisee is a horse, the line becomes absurd at once. How could any one know that a horse would fail to finish in a race? But if it—er—referred—er—to a man, an official known—er—as Pharisee Phil—"

"Wait!" Waldemar had jumped to his feet. A thrill, increasing and pulsating through the floor beneath them, shook the building. The editor jumped for the telephone.

"Composing room; quick! Give me the foreman. Hello! That you, Corrigan? Stop the presses…I don't care if we miss every train in the country…Don't answer back. This is Mr. Waldemar. Stop the presses!"

The thrill waned and ceased. At the telephone, Waldemar continued: "Look up the Noble and Gale tip ad, page nine, column six. Kill the last line—the One Best Bet…Don't ask *me* how. Chisel it out. Burn it out. Dynamite it out. But kill it. After that's done, print.…Hello; Dan? Send the sporting editor in here in a hurry."

"Good work," said Average Jones. "They'll never know how near their idea of removing Governor Arthur came to being boasted of in plain print."

Waldemar took his huge head in his hands and rocked it gently. "It's on," he said. "And right-side-before. Yet, it tries to tell me that a man, plotting to murder the governor, advertises the fact in my paper! I'll get a new head."

"Keep that one for a while," advised Average Jones. "It may be better than you think. Anyway, here's the ad. And down yonder is the dead man whom it killed when he failed to kill it. So much is real."

"And here's Bendig," said the other, as the sporting editor entered. "Any such horse as 'The Pharisee,' Bendig?"

"No, sir. I suppose you mean that Noble and Gale ad. I saw it in proof. Some of Nick Karboe's funny work, I expect."

"Nick Karboe; N. K.," murmured Average Jones, laying a hand on the abandoned field glass. "Who is this man Karboe, Mr. Bendig?"

"Junior partner of Noble and Gale. He puts out their advertising."

"Any connection whatever with Mr. Carroll Morrison?"

"Why, yes. Before he went to pieces he used to be Mr. Morrison's confidential man, and lately he's been doing some lobbying for the association. I understood he'd quit it again."

"Quit what?" asked Waldemar. "Drink?"

"Worse. The white stuff. Coke."

Average Jones whistled softly. "That explains it all," he said. "A cocaine fiend on a debauch becomes a mental and moral imbecile. It would be perfectly in character that he should boast of a projected crime."

"Very well," said Waldemar, after the sporting editor had left, "but you don't really connect Morrison with this?"

"Don't I! At least I propose to try. See here, Waldemar; two months ago at a private dinner, Morrison made a speech in which he said that men who interfered with the rights of property, like Governor Arthur, were no better than anarchists and ought to be handled accordingly. Therefore, I don't think that a plan—a safe one, of course—to put 'Pharisee Phil' away would greatly disturb our friend's distorted conscience. You see, the governor has laid impious hands on Morrison's holy of holies, the dividend. By the way, where is Governor Arthur?"

"On the train for this city. He's to review the parade at the Harrisonia Centennial, and unveil the statute to-morrow night; that is, to-night, to be accurate."

"A good opportunity," murmured Average Jones.

"What! In the sight of a hundred thousand people?"

"That might be the very core of the opportunity. And at night."

"If you feel certain, it's a case for the police, isn't it?"

"Hardly! The gambling gang control the police, wholly. They would destroy the trail at once."

"Then why not warn the governor?"

"I don't know him."

"Suppose I make an appointment to take you to see him in the morning?"

This was agreed upon. At ten o'clock Governor Arthur received them at his hotel, greeting Average Jones with flattering warmth.

"You're the amateur detective who scared the Honorable William Linder out of the mayoralty nomination," said he, shaking hands. "What are you going to do to me?"

"Give you some racing news to read, Governor."

The governor took the advertisement proof and read it carefully. Characteristically, he then re-read it throughout.

"You think this is meant for me?" he asked, handing it back.

"I do. You're not exactly what one would call popular with the racing crowd, you know, Governor."

"Mr. Morrison, in the politest manner in the world, has allowed me to surmise as much," said the other, smiling broadly. "A very polished person, Mr. Morrison. He can make threats of extinction—political, of course—more delicately than any other subtle blackmailer I have ever met. And I have met several in my time."

"If this were merely political extinction, which I fancy you can take care of yourself, I shouldn't be taking up your time, sir."

"My dear Jones"—a friendly hand fell on the visitor's shoulder—"I gravely fear that you lack the judicial mind. It's a great thing—to lack—at times." Governor Arthur's eyes twinkled again, and his visitor wondered whence had come his reputation as a dry, unhumorous man. "As to assassination," he pursued, "I'm a sort of Christian Scientist. The best protection is a profound conviction that you're safe. That reacts on the mind of any would-be assassin. To my mind, my best chance of safety lies in never thinking of danger."

"Then," said Waldemar, "any attempt to persuade you against appearing at Harrisonia to-night would be time wasted."

"Absolutely, my dear Waldemar. But don't think that I'm not appreciative of your thoughtfulness and that of Mr. Jones."

"What is the program of the day, Governor?" asked Average Jones.

"Rather a theatrical one. I'm to ride along Harrison Avenue to the reviewing stand, in the old coach-of-state of the Harrison family, a lofty old ark, high as a circus wagon, which has been patched up for the occasion. Just before I reach the reviewing stand, a silk cord is to be handed to me and I am to pull the veil from the great civic statue with that, as I move on."

"Then I think that Mr. Waldemar and I will look the ground over. Could we get you by telephone, sir, if necessary?"

"Any time up to seven o'clock."

"What do you think of the chance of their passing the bill over your veto?" asked Waldemar.

"They are spending money as it has never been spent before," replied Governor Arthur. "I'll admit to you, Waldemar, that if I could find any legitimate method of calling Morrison off, I would not scruple to use it. It is, of course, Morrison's money that we are fighting."

"Possibly—er—that, too—er—might be done," drawled Average Jones.

The governor looked at him sharply. "After the Linder affair, Mr. Jones," said he, "I would follow you far. Call my secretary at any time, if you want me."

"Now to look over the line of parade," said Average Jones as he and Waldemar emerged from the hotel.

Half an hour's ride brought them to the lively suburban city of Harrisonia, gay with flags and bunting. From the railroad station, where the guest of honor was to be met by the old coach, to the spot where the civic statue awaited its unveiling at his hands, was about half a mile along Harrison Avenue, the principal street. The walk along this street developed nothing of interest to Average Jones until they reached the statue. Here he paused to look curiously at a number of square platforms built out from windows in the business blocks.

"For flash-light outfits," explained Waldemar. "One of them is our paper's."

"Flash-lights, eh?" said Average Jones. "And there'll be fireworks and the air will be full of light and noise, under cover of which almost anything might be done. I don't like it! Hello! What's here?"

He turned to the glass front of a prosperous-looking cigar store on the south side of the avenue and pointed to a shattered hole in the window. Behind it a bullet swung on a thread from the ceiling, and this agent of disaster the proprietor had ingeniously turned to account in advertising, by the following placard:

AIM LOWER

If you expect to shoot holes in *our* prices.

WE CHALLENGE COMPETITION.

"Not bad," approved Average Jones. "I feel a great yearning to smoke."

They entered the store and were served by the proprietor. As he was making change, Average Jones asked:

"When was the bombardment?"

"Night before last, some time," replied the man.

"Done by a deflected bullet, wasn't it?"

"Haven't any idea how it was done or why. I got here in the morning and there she was. What makes you think it was a deflected bullet?"

"Because it was whirling end-over. Normally, a bullet bores a pretty clean hole in plate glass."

"That's so, too," agreed the man with some interest.

Average Jones handed a cigar to Waldemar and lighted one himself. Puffing at it as he walked to the door, he gazed casually around and finally centered his attention on a telegraph pole standing on the edge of the sidewalk. He even walked out and around the pole. Returning, he remarked to the tobacconist:

"Very good cigars, these. Ever advertise 'em?"

"Sure." The man displayed a tin square vaunting the virtues of his "Camarados."

"Outside the shop, I meant. Why wouldn't one of those signs look good on that telegraph pole?"

"It would look good to me," said the vendor, "but it wouldn't look good to the telegraph people. They'd have it down."

"Oh, I don't know. Give me one, lend me a ladder, and I'll make the experiment."

The tobacconist stared. "All right," he said. "Go as far as you like." And he got the required articles for his customer.

With silent curiosity Waldemar watched Average Jones place the ladder against the outside of the pole, mount, nail up the sign, drop a plumb-line, improvised from a key and a length of string, to the ground, set a careful knot in the string and return to earth.

"What did you find?" asked the editor.

"Four holes that you could cover with a silver dollar. Some gunnery, that!"

"Then how did the other shot happen to go so far wrong?"

"Do you see that steel work over there?"

Average Jones pointed across to the north side of the street, just opposite, where a number of buildings had been torn down to permit of the erection of a new one. The frame had risen three stories, and through the open spaces in the gaunt skeleton the rear of the houses facing on the street next northward could be seen. Waldemar indicated that he did see the edifice pointed out by Average Jones.

"The bullet came from back of that—perhaps from the next street. They sighted by the telegraph pole. Suppose, now, a man riding in a high coach passes along this avenue between the pole and the gun operator, over yonder to the northward. Every one of the bullets which hit the pole would have gone right through his body. Probably a fixed gun. As for the wide shot, we'll see."

As he spoke, the Ad-Visor was leading the way across the street. With upturned face he carefully studied the steel joists from end to end. Presently he pointed. Following the line of his finger, Waldemar saw a raw scar on the under side of one of the joists.

"There it is," said Average Jones. "The sights were a trifle off at the first shot, and the bullet ticked the steel and deflected."

"So far, so good," approved Waldemar.

"I can approximate the height of the steel beam from the ground, close enough for a trial formula," continued Average Jones. "Now, Waldemar, I call your attention to that restaurant on the opposite corner."

Waldemar conned the designated building with attention. "Well," he said finally, "what of it? I don't see anything wrong with it."

"Precisely my point," returned the Ad-Visor with a grin. "Neither do I. Therefore, suppose you go there and order luncheon for two, while I walk down to the next block and back again. I'll be with you in four minutes."

He was somewhat better than his word. Dropping into the chair opposite his friend, he figured swiftly and briefly on the back of an envelope, which he returned to his pocket.

"I suppose you've done a vast amount of investigating since

you left me," remarked the editor sardonically. "Meanwhile, the plot to murder the governor goes merrily on."

"I've done a fair amount of pacing over distance," retorted Average Jones imperturbably. "As for the governor, they can't kill him till he comes, can they? Besides, there's plenty of time for them to change their minds. As a result of my little constitutional just now, and a simple exercise in mathematics, you and I will call at a house on Spencer Street, the next street north, after luncheon."

"What house?"

"Ah! that I don't know, as yet. We'll see when we get there."

Comfortably fed, the two strolled up to Spencer Street and turned into it, Average Jones eying the upper windows of the houses. He stopped in front of an old-fashioned frame structure, which was built on a different plan of floor level from its smaller neighbors of brick. Up the low steps went Jones, followed by the editor. An aged lady, of the species commonly conjectured as "maiden," opened the door.

"Madam," said Average Jones, "could we rent your third floor rear for this evening?"

"No, sir," said she. "It's rented."

"Perhaps I could buy the renters off," suggested Jones. "Could I see them?"

"Both out," she answered shortly. "And I don't believe you could get the room from them, for they're all fixed up to take photographs of the parade."

"Indee—ee—eed," drawled Average Jones, in accents so prolonged, even for him, that Waldemar's interest flamed within him. "I—er—ra—a—a—ather hoped—er—when do you expect them back?"

"About four o'clock."

"Thank you. Please tell them that—er—Mr. Nick Karboe called."

"For heaven's sake, Average," rumbled Waldemar, as they regained the pavement, "why did you use the dead man's name? It gave me a shiver."

"It'll give them a worse one," replied the Ad-Visor grimly. "I want to prepare their nerves for a subsequent shock. If you'll meet me here this evening at seven, I think I can promise you a queer spectacle."

"And meantime?"

"On that point I want your advice. Shall we make a sure catch of two hired assassins who don't amount to much, or take a chance at the bigger game?"

"Meaning Morrison?"

"Meaning Morrison. Incidentally, if we get him we'll be able to kill the Personal Liberty bill so dead it will never raise its head again."

"Then I'm for that course," decided the editor, after a little consideration, "though I can't yet make myself believe that Carroll Morrison is party to a deliberate murder plot."

"How the normal mind does shrink from connecting crime with good clothes and a social position!" remarked the Ad-Visor. "Just give me a moment's time."

The moment he spent jotting down words on a bit of paper, which, after some emendation, he put away.

"That'll do for a heading," he remarked. "Now, Waldemar, I want you to get the governor on the 'phone and tell him, if he'll follow directions, we'll put the Personal Liberty bill where the wicked cease from troubling. Morrison is to be in the reviewing stand, isn't he?"

"Yes; there's a special place reserved for him, next the press seats."

"Good! By the way, you'd better send for two press seats for you and myself. Now, what I want the governor to do is this: get a copy of the Harrisonia *Evening Bell*, fold it to an advertisement headed 'Offer to Photographers,' and as he passes Carroll Morrison on the stand, hold it up and say to him just this: 'Better luck next time.' For anything further, I'll see you in the reviewing stand. Do you think he'll do it?"

"It sounds as foolish as a college initiation stunt. Still, you heard what Governor Arthur said about his confidence in you. But what is this advertisement?"

"As yet, it isn't. But it will be, as soon as I can get to the office of the *Bell*. You'll meet me on this corner at seven o'clock, then?"

"Yes. Meantime, to be safe, I'll look after the reviewing stand tickets myself."

At the hour named, the editor arrived. Average Jones was already there, accompanied by a messenger boy. The boy wore the cheerful grin of one who has met with an unexpected favor of fortune.

"They've returned, both of 'em," said Average Jones as Waldemar approached. "What about the governor?"

"It took a mighty lot of persuasion, but he'll do it," replied the editor.

"Skip, son," said the Ad-Visor, handing the messenger boy a folded newspaper. "The two gentlemen on the third floor rear. And be sure you say that it's a personal, marked copy."

The boy crossed the street and entered the house. In two minutes he emerged, nodded to Average Jones and walked away. Five minutes passed. Then the front door opened cautiously and a tall, evil-looking man slunk into the vestibule. A second man followed him. They glanced eagerly from left to right. Average Jones stepped out to the curbstone.

"Here's the message from Karboe," he called.

"My God!" gasped the tall man.

For an instant he made as if to turn back. Then, clearing the steps at one jump, he stumbled, sprawled, was up again instantly and speeding up the street, away from Average Jones, turned the corner neck and neck with his companion who, running powerfully, had overtaken him.

The door of the house stood ajar. Before Waldemar had recovered from his surprise, Average Jones was inside the house. Hesitation beset the editor. Should he follow or wait? He paused, one foot on the step. A loud crash within resolved his doubts. Up he started, when the voice of Average Jones in colloquy with the woman who had received them before, checked him. The colloquy seemed excited but peaceful. Presently Average Jones came down the steps.

"They left the ad," said he. "Have you seen it?"

"No; I hadn't time to get a paper," replied Waldemar, taking the copy extended to him and reading, in large display:

OFFER TO PHOTOGRAPHERS

$1,000 Reward for Special Flash-light Photo of Governor Arthur in To-night's Pageant. Must be Taken According to Plans and Specifications Designated by the Late Nick Karboe.

APPLY TO A. JONES, AD-VISOR.
ASTOR COURT TEMPLE, NEW YORK CITY.

"No wonder they ran," said Waldemar with a grin, as he digested this document.

"And so must we if we're to get through the crowd and reach the reviewing stand," warned Average Jones, glancing at his watch.

Their seats, which they attained with some difficulty, were within a few feet of the governor's box. Within reach of them sat Carroll Morrison, his long, pale, black-bearded face set in that immobility to which he had schooled it. But the cold eyes roved restlessly and the little muscles at the corners of the lips twitched.

"Tell me that he isn't in on the game!" whispered Average Jones, and Waldemar nodded.

The sound of music from down the street turned all faces in that direction. A roar of cheering swept toward them and was taken up in the stands. The governor, in his high coach, came in sight. And, at that moment, terror struck into the soul of Waldemar.

"Suppose they came back!" he whispered to Average Jones. "We've left the house unguarded."

"I've fixed that," replied the Ad-Visor in the same tone. "Watch Morrison!"

Governor Arthur approached the civic statue. An official, running out to the coach, handed him a silken cord, which he secured with a turn around the wrist. The coach rolled on. The cord tautened; the swathings sundered and fell from the gleaming splendor of marble, and a blinding flash, followed by another, and a third, blotted out the scene in unbearable radiance.

Involuntarily Morrison, like thousands of others, had screened his sight with his hands after the second flash. Now, as the kindlier light returned, he half rose, rubbing his eyes furiously. A half-groan escaped him. He sank back, staring in amaze. For Governor Arthur was riding on, calm and smiling amid the shouts.

Morrison shrank. Could it be that the governor's eyes were fixed on his? He strove to shake off the delusion. He felt, rather than saw, the guest of honor descend from the coach; felt rather than saw him making straight toward himself; and he winced and quivered at the sound of his own name.

"Mr. Morrison," the governor was saying, at his elbow, "Mr.

Morrison, here is a paper that may interest you. Better luck next time."

Morrison strove to reply. His voice clucked in his throat, and the hand with which he took the folded newspaper was as the hand of a paralytic.

"He's broken," whispered Average Jones.

He went straight to Governor Arthur, speaking in his ear. The governor nodded. Average Jones returned to his seat to watch Carroll Morrison who sat, with hell-fires of fear scorching him, until the last band had blared its way into silence.

Again the governor was speaking to him.

"Mr. Morrison, I want you to visit a house near here. Mr. Jones and Mr. Waldemar will come along; you know them, perhaps. Please don't protest. I positively will not take a refusal. We have a motor-car waiting."

Furious, but not daring to refuse, Morrison found himself whirled swiftly away, and after a few turns to shake off the crowd, into Spencer Street. With his captors, he mounted to the third floor of an old frame house. The rear room door had been broken in. Inside stood a strange instrument, resembling a large camera, which had once stood upright on a steel tripod riveted to the floor. The legs of the tripod were twisted and bent. A half-demolished chair near by suggested the agency of destruction.

"Just to render it harmless," explained Average Jones. "It formerly pointed through that window, so that a bullet from the barrel would strike that pole 'way yonder in Harrison Street, after first passing through any intervening body. Yours, for instance, Governor."

"Do I understand that this is a gun, Mr. Jones?" asked that official.

"Of a sort," replied the Ad-Visor, opening up the camera-box and showing a large barrel superimposed on a smaller one. "This is a sighting-glass," he explained, tapping the larger barrel. "And this," tapping the smaller, "carries a small but efficient bullet. This curious sheath"—he pointed to a cylindrical jacket around part of the rifle barrel—"is a Coulomb silencer,* which reduces a small-arm report almost to a whisper. Here is an electric button which was connected with yonder battery before I operated on it with the chair, and distributed its spark, part to the gun, part to the flash-light powder on this little shelf. Do you see the plan now? The instant that the governor, riding through the street yonder, is sighted through this glass, the operator presses the button, and flash-light and bullet go off instantaneously."

"But why the flash-light?" asked the governor.

"Merely a blind to fool the landlady and avert any possible suspicion. They had told her that they had a new invention to take flash-lights at a distance. Amidst the other flashes, this one wouldn't be noticed particularly. They had covered their trail well."

"Well, indeed," said the governor. "May I congratulate you, Mr. Morrison, on this interesting achievement in ballistics?"

"As there is no way of properly resenting an insult from a man in your position," said Morrison venomously, "I will reserve my answer to that outrageous suggestion."

"Meantime," put in Average Jones, "let me direct your attention to a simple mathematical formula." He drew from his pocket an envelope on which were drawn some angles, subjoined by a formula. Morrison waved it aside.

"Not interested in mathematics?" asked Average Jones solicitously. "Very well, I'll elucidate informally. Given a bullet hole in a telegraph pole at a certain distance, a bullet scar on an iron girder at a certain lesser distance, and the length of a block from

---

* A sound suppressor. The first successful model was invented by Hiram Maxim in 1902. Charles-Augustin de Coulomb (1736–1806) was a French physicist, and many devices using principles of friction that Coulomb discovered bear his name.

here to Harrison Avenue—which I paced off while you were skillfully ordering luncheon, Waldemar—and an easy triangulation brings us direct to this room and to two fugitive gentlemen with whom—I mention the hypothesis with all deference, Mr. Morrison—you are probably acquainted."

"And who may they have been?" retorted Morrison contemptuously.

"I don't know," said Average Jones.

"Then, sir," retorted the racing king, "your hypothesis is as impudent as your company is intolerable. Have you anything further to say to me?"

"Yes. It would greatly please Mr. Waldemar to publish in tomorrow's paper an authorized statement from you to the effect that the Personal Liberty bill will be withdrawn permanently."

"Mr. Waldemar may go to the devil. I have endured all the hectoring I propose to. Men in my position are targets for muckrakers and blackmailers—"

"Wait a moment," Waldemar's heavy voice broke in. "You speak of men in your position. Do you understand just what position you are in at present?"

Morrison rose. "Governor Arthur," he said with stony dignity, "I bid you good evening."

Waldemar set his bulky back against the door. The lips drew back from Morrison's strong teeth with the snarl of an animal in the fury and terror of approaching peril.

"Do you know Nick Karboe?"

Morrison whirled about to face Average Jones. But he did not answer the question. He only stared.

"Carroll Morrison," continued Average Jones in his quiet drawl, "the half-hour before he—er—committed suicide—er—Nick Karboe spent in the office of the—er—*Universal* with Mr. Waldemar and—er—myself. Catch him, Waldemar!"

For Morrison had wilted. They propped him against the wall and he, the man who had insolently defied the laws of a great commonwealth, who had bribed legislatures and bossed judges and browbeaten the public, slobbered, denied and begged. For two disgustful minutes they extracted from him his solemn promise that henceforth he would keep his hands off the laws. Then they turned him out.

"Suppose you enlighten me with the story, gentlemen," suggested the governor.

Average Jones told it, simply and modestly. At the conclusion, Governor Arthur looked from the wrecked camera-gun to the mathematical formula which had fallen to the floor.

"Mr. Jones," he said, "you've done me the service of saving my life; you've done the public the service of killing a vicious bill. I wish I could thank you more publicly than this."

"Thank you, Governor," said Average Jones modestly. "But I owed the public something, you know, on account of my uncle, the late Mayor Van Reypen."

Governor Arthur nodded. "The debt is paid," he said. "That knowledge must be your reward; that and the consciousness of having worked out a remarkable and original problem."

"Original?" said Average Jones, eying the diagram on the envelope's back, with his quaint smile. "Why, Governor, you're giving me too much credit. It was worked out by one of the greatest detectives of all time, some two thousand years ago. His name was Euclid."

CHAPTER XI
THE MILLION-DOLLAR DOG

To this day, Average Jones maintains that he felt a distinct thrill at first sight of the advertisement. Yet Fate might well have chosen a more appropriate ambush in any one of a hundred of the strange clippings which were grist to the Ad-Visor's mill. Out of a bulky pile of the day's paragraphs, however, it was this one that leaped, significant, to his eye.

> WANTED—Ten thousand loathly black beetles, by a leaseholder who contracted to leave a house in the same condition as he found it. ACKROYD, 100 W. Sixteenth St., New York.

"Black beetles, eh?" observed Average Jones. "This Ackroyd person seems to be a merry little jester. Well, I'm feeling rather jocular, myself, this morning. How does one collect black beetles, I wonder? When in doubt, inquire of the resourceful Simpson."

He pressed a button and his confidential clerk entered.

"Good morning, Simpson," said Average Jones. "Are you acquainted with that shy but pervasive animal, the domestic black beetle?"

"Yes, sir; I board," said Simpson simply.

"I suppose there aren't ten thousand black beetles in your boarding-house, though?" inquired Average Jones.

Simpson took it under advisement. "Hardly," he decided.

"I've got to have 'em to fill an order. At least, I've got to have an instalment of 'em, and to-morrow."

Being wholly without imagination, the confidential clerk was impervious to surprise or shock. This was fortunate, for otherwise, his employment as practical aide to Average Jones would probably have driven him into a madhouse. He now ran his long, thin, clerkly hands through his long, thin, clerkly hair.

"Ramson, down on Fulton Street, will have them, if any one has," he said presently. "He does business under the title of the Insect Nemesis, you know. I'll go there at once."

Returning to his routine work, Average Jones found himself unable to dislodge the advertisement from his mind. So presently he gave way to temptation, called up Bertram at the Cosmic Club, and asked him to come to the Astor Court Temple offices at his convenience. Scenting more adventure, Bertram found it convenient to come promptly. Average Jones handed him the clipping. Bertram read it with ascending eyebrows.

"Hoots!" he said. "The man's mad."

"I didn't ask you here to diagnose the advertiser's trouble. That's plain enough—though you've made a bad guess. What I want of you is to tap your flow of information about old New York. What's at One Hundred West Sixteenth Street?"

"One hundred West Sixteenth; let me see. Why, of course; it's the old Feltner mansion. You must know it. It has a walled garden at the side; the only one left in the city, south of Central Park."

"Any one named Ackroyd there?"

"That must be Hawley Ackroyd. I remember, now, hearing

that he had rented it. Judge Ackroyd, you know, better known as 'Oily' Ackroyd. He's a smooth old rascal."

"Indeed? What particular sort?"

"Oh, most sorts, in private. Professionally, he's a legislative crook; head lobbyist of the Consolidated."

"Ever hear of his collecting insects?"

"Never heard of his collecting anything but graft. In fact, he'd have been in jail years ago, but for his family connections. He married a Van Haltern. You remember the famous Van Haltern will case, surely; the million-dollar dog. The papers fairly reeked of it a year ago. Sylvia Graham had to take the dog and leave the country to escape the notoriety. She's back now, I believe."

"I've heard of Miss Graham," remarked Average Jones, "through friends of mine whom she visits."

"Well, if you've only heard of her and not seen her," returned Bertram, with something as nearly resembling enthusiasm as his habitual languor permitted, "you've got something to look forward to. Sylvia Graham is a distinct asset to the Scheme of Creation."

"An asset with assets of her own, I believe," said Average Jones. "The million dollars left by her grandmother, old Mrs. Van Haltern, goes to her eventually, doesn't it?"

"Provided she carries out the terms of the will, keeps the dog in proper luxury and buries him in the grave on the family estate at Schuylkill designated by the testator. If these terms are not rigidly carried out, the fortune is to be divided, most of it going to Mrs. Hawley Ackroyd, which would mean the judge himself. I should say that the dog was as good as sausage meat if 'Oily' ever gets hold of him."

"H'm. What about Mrs. Ackroyd?"

"Poor, sickly, frightened lady! She's very fond of Sylvia Graham, who is her niece. But she's completely dominated by her husband."

"Information is your long suit, Bert. Now, if you only had intelligence to correspond—" Average Jones broke off and grinned mildly, first at his friend, then at the advertisement.

Bertram caught up the paper and studied it. "Well, what *does* it mean?" he demanded.

"It means that Ackroyd, being about to give up his rented house, intends to saddle it with a bad name. Probably he's had a row with the agent or owner, and is getting even by making the place difficult to rent again. Nobody wants to take a house with the reputation of an entomological resort."

"It would be just like Oily Ackroyd," remarked Bertram. "He's a vindictive scoundrel. Only a few days ago, he nearly killed a poor devil of a drug clerk, over some trifling dispute. He managed to keep it out of the newspapers but he had to pay a stiff fine."

"That might be worth looking up, too," ruminated Average Jones thoughtfully.

He turned to his telephone in answer to a ring. "All right, come in, Simpson," he said.

The confidential clerk appeared. "Ramson says that regular black beetles are out of season, sir," he reported. "But he can send to the country and dig up plenty of red-and-black ones."

"That will do," returned the Ad-Visor. "Tell him to have two or three hundred here to-morrow morning."

Bertram bent a severe gaze on his friend. "Meaning that you're going to follow up this freak affair?" he inquired.

"Just that. I can't explain why, but—well, Bert, it's a hunch. At the worst, Ackroyd's face when he sees the beetles should be worth the money."

"When you frivol, Average, I wash my hands of you. But I warn you, look out for Ackroyd. He's as big as he is ugly; a tough customer."

"All right. I'll just put on some old clothes, to dress the part of a beetle-purveyor correctly, and also in case I get 'em torn in my meeting with Judge 'Oily.' I'll see you later and report, if I survive his wrath."

Thus it was that, on the morning after this dialogue, a clean-built young fellow walked along West Sixteenth Street, appreciatively sniffing the sunny crispness of the May air. He was rather shabby-looking, yet his demeanor was by no means shabby. It was confident and easy. On the evidence of the bandbox which he carried, his mission should have been menial; but he bore himself wholly unlike one subdued to petty employments. His steady, gray eyes showed a glint of anticipation as he turned in at the gate of the high, broad, brown house standing back, aloof and indignant, from the roaring encroachments of trade. He set his burden down and pulled the bell.

The door opened promptly to the deep, far-away clangor. A flashing impression of girlish freshness, vigor, and grace was disclosed to the caller against a background of interior gloom. He stared a little more patently than was polite. Whatever his expectation of amusement, this, evidently, was not the manifestation looked for. The girl glanced not at him, but at the box, and spoke a trifle impatiently.

"If it's my hat, it's very late. You should have gone to the basement."

"It isn't, miss," said the young man, in a form of address, the semi-servility of which seemed distinctly out of tone with the quietly clear and assured voice. "It's the insects."

"The *what*?"

"The bugs, miss."

He extracted from his pocket a slip of paper, looked from it to the numbered door, as one verifying an address, and handed it to her.

"From yesterday's copy of the *Banner*, miss. You're not going back on that, surely," he said somewhat reproachfully.

She read, and as she read her eyes widened to lakes of limpid brown. Then they crinkled at the corners, and her laugh rose from the mid-tone contralto, to a high, bird-like trill of joyousness. The infection of it tugged at the young man's throat, but he successfully preserved his mask of flat and respectful dullness.

"It must have been uncle," she gasped finally. "He said he'd be quits with the real estate agent before he left. How perfectly absurd! And are those the creatures in that box?"

"The first couple of hundred of 'em, miss."

"Two hundred!" Again the access of laughter swelled the rounded bosom as the breeze fills a sail. "Where did you get them?"

"Woodpile, ash-heap, garbage-pail," said the young man stolidly. "Any particular kind preferred, Miss Ackroyd?"

The girl looked at him with suspicion, but his face was blankly innocent.

"I'm not Miss Ackroyd," she began with emphasis, when a querulous voice from an inner room called out: "Whom are you talking to, Sylvia?"

"A young man with a boxful of beetles," returned the girl, adding in brisk French: "*Il est très amusant ce farceur. Je ne le comprends pas du tout. C'est une blague, peut-être. Si on l'invitait dans la maison pour un moment?*"*

Through one of the air-holes, considerately punched in the cardboard cover of the box, a sturdy crawler had succeeded in pushing himself. He was, in the main, of a shiny and well-groomed black, but two large patches of crimson gave him the festive appearance of being garbed in a brilliant sash. As he stood rubbing his fore-legs together in self-congratulation over his exploit, his bearer addressed him in French quite as ready as the girl's:

---

* "This joker is very amusing. I don't understand it at all. Maybe it's a joke. How about we invite him into the house for a while?"

"*Permettez-moi, Monsieur le Coléoptère, de vous présenter mes excuses pour cette demoiselle qui s'exprime en langue étrangère chez elle.*"*

"Don't apologize to the beetle on my account," retorted the girl with spirit. "You're here on your own terms, you know, both of you."

Average Jones mutely held up the box in one hand and the advertisement in the other. The adventurer-bug flourished a farewell to the girl with his antennæ, and retired within to advise his fellows of the charms of freedom.

"Very well," said the girl, in demure tones, though lambent mirth still flickered, golden, in the depths of the brown eyes. "If you persist, I can only suggest that you come back when Judge Ackroyd is here. You won't find him particularly amenable to humor, particularly when perpetrated by a practical joker in masquerade."

"Discovered," murmured Average Jones. "I shouldn't have vaunted my poor French. But must I really take my little friends all the way back? You suggested to the mystic voice within that I might be invited inside."

"You seem a decidedly unconventional person," began the other with dawning disfavor.

"Conventionality, like charity, begins at home," he replied quickly. "And one would hardly call this advertisement a pattern of formal etiquette."

"True enough," she admitted, dimpling, and Average Jones was congratulating himself on his diplomacy, when the querulous voice broke in again, this time too low for his ears.

"I don't ask you the real reason for your extraordinary call," pursued the girl with a glint of mischief in her eyes, after she had

---

* "Allow me, Mr. Beetle, to apologize to you for this young lady who speaks a foreign language at home."

responded in an aside, "but auntie thinks you've come to steal my dog. She thinks that of every one lately."

"Auntie? Your dog? Then you're Sylvia Graham. I might have known it."

"I don't know how you might have known it. But I am Sylvia Graham—if you insist on introducing me to yourself."

"Miss Graham," said the visitor promptly and gravely, "let me present A. V. R. E. Jones, a friend—"

"Not the famous Average Jones!" cried the girl. "That is why your face seemed so familiar. I've seen your picture at Edna Hale's. You got her 'blue fires' back for her. But really, that hardly explains your being here, in this way, you know."

"Frankly, Miss Graham, it was just as a lark that I answered the advertisement. But now that I'm here and find you here, it looks—er—as if it might—er—be more serious."

A tinge of pink came into the girl's cheeks, but she answered lightly enough:

"Indeed, it may, for you, if uncle finds you here with those beetles."

"Never mind me or the beetles. I'd like to know about the dog that your aunt is worrying over. Is he here with you?"

The soft curve of Miss Graham's lips straightened a little. "I really think," she said with decision, "that you had better explain further before questioning."

"Nothing simpler. Once upon a time there lived a crack-brained young Don Quixote who wandered through an age of buried romance piously searching for trouble. And, twice upon a time, there dwelt in an enchanted stone castle in West Sixteenth Street an enchanting young damsel in distress—"

"I'm not a damsel in distress," interrupted Miss Graham, passing over the adjective.

The young man leaned to her. The half smile had passed from his lips, and his eyes were very grave.

"Not—er—if your dog were to—er—disappear?" he drawled quietly.

The swift unexpectedness of the counter broke down the girl's guard.

"You mean Uncle Hawley," she said.

"And your suspicions jump with mine."

"They don't!" she denied hotly. "You're very unjust and impertinent."

"I don't mean to be impertinent," he said evenly. "And I have no monopoly of injustice."

"What do you know about Uncle Hawley?"

"Your aunt—"

"I won't hear a word against my aunt."

"Not from me, be assured. Your aunt, so you have just told me, believes that your dog is in danger of being stolen. Why? Because she knows that the person most interested has been scheming against the animal, and yet she is afraid to warn you openly. Doesn't that indicate who it is?"

"Mr. Jones, I've no right even to let you talk like this to me. Have you anything definite against Judge Ackroyd?"

"In this case, only suspicion."

Her head went up. "Then I think there is nothing more to be said."

The young man flushed, but his voice was steady as he returned:

"I disagree with you. And I beg you to cut short your visit here, and return to your home at once."

In spite of herself the girl was shaken by his persistence.

"I can't do that," she said uneasily. And added, with a flash of anger, "I think you had better leave this house."

"If I leave this house now I may never have a chance to see you again."

The girl regarded him with level, non-committal eyes.

"And I have every intention of seeing you again—and again—and again. Give me a chance; a moment."

Average Jones' mind was of the emergency type. It summoned to its aid, without effort of cerebration on the part of its owner, whatever was most needed at the moment. Now it came to his rescue with the memory of Judge Ackroyd's encounter with the drug clerk, as mentioned by Bertram. There was a strangely hopeful suggestion of some link between a drug-store quarrel and the arrival of a million-dollar dog, "better dead" in the hopes of his host.

"Miss Graham, I've gone rather far, I'll admit," said Jones; "but, if you'll give me the benefit of the doubt, I think I can show you some basis to work on. If I can produce something tangible, may I come back here this afternoon? I'll promise not to come unless I have good reason."

"Very well," conceded Miss Graham reluctantly, "it's a most unusual thing. But I'll agree to that."

"*Au revoir*, then," he said, and was gone.

Somewhat to her surprise and uneasiness, Sylvia Graham experienced a distinct satisfaction when, late that afternoon, she beheld her unconventional acquaintance mounting the steps with a buoyant and assured step. Upon being admitted, he went promptly to the point.

"I've got it."

"Your justification for coming back?" she asked.

"Exactly. Have you heard anything of some trouble in which Judge Ackroyd was involved last week?"

"Uncle has a very violent temper," admitted the girl evasively. "But I don't see what—"

"Pardon me. You will see. That row was with a drug clerk."

"Well?"

"In an obscure drug store several blocks from here."

"Yes?"

"The drug clerk insisted—as the law requires—on Judge Ackroyd registering for a certain purchase."

"Perhaps he was impertinent about it."

"Possibly. The point is that the prospective purchase was cyanide of potassium, a deadly and instantaneous poison."

"Are you sure?" asked the girl, in a low voice.

"I've just come from the store. How long have you been here at your uncle's?"

"A week."

"Then just about the time of your coming with the dog, your uncle undertook to obtain a swift and sure poison. Have I gone far enough?"

"I—I don't know."

"Well, am I still ordered out of the house?"

"N-n-no."

"Thank you for your enthusiastic hospitality," said Average Jones so dryly that a smile relaxed the girl's troubled face. "With that encouragement we'll go on. What is your uncle's attitude toward the dog?"

"Almost what you might call ingratiating. But Peter Paul—that's my dog's name, you know—doesn't take to uncle. He's a crotchety old doggie."

"He's a wise old doggie," amended the other, with emphasis. "Has your uncle taken him out, at all?"

"Once he tried to. I met them at the corner. All four of Peter Paul's poor old fat legs were braced, and he was hauling back as hard as he could against the leash."

"And the occurrence didn't strike you as peculiar?"

"Well, not then."

"When does your uncle give up this house?"

"At the end of the week. Uncle and aunt leave for Europe."

"Then let me suggest again that you and Peter Paul go at once."

Miss Graham pondered. "That would mean explanations and a quarrel, and more strain for auntie, who is nervous enough, anyway. No, I can't do that."

"Do you realize that every day Peter Paul remains here is an added opportunity for Judge Ackroyd to make a million dollars, or a big share of it, by some very simple stratagem?"

"I haven't admitted yet that I believe my uncle to be a—a murderer," Miss Graham quietly reminded him.

"A strong word," said Average Jones smiling. "The law would hardly support your view. Now, Miss Graham, would it grieve you very much if Peter Paul were to die?"

"I won't have him put to death," said she quickly. "That would be cheating my grandmother's intentions."

"I supposed you wouldn't. Yet it would be the simplest way. Once dead, and buried in accordance with the terms of the will, the dog would be out of his troubles, and you would be out of yours."

"It would really be a relief. Peter Paul suffers so from asthma, poor old beastie. The vet. says he can live only a month or two longer, anyway. But I've got to do as Grandmother wished, and keep Peter Paul alive as long as possible."

"Admitted." Average Jones fell into a baffled silence, studying the pattern of the rug with restless eyes. When he looked up into Miss Graham's face again it was with a changed expression.

"Miss Graham," he said slowly, "won't you try to forget, for the moment, the circumstances of our meeting, and think of me only as a friend of your friends who is very honestly eager to be a friend to you, when you most need one?"

Now, Average Jones' birth-fairy had endowed him with one priceless gift: the power of inspiring an instinctive confidence in himself. Sylvia Graham felt, suddenly, that a hand, sure and firm, had been outstretched to guide her on a dark path. In one of those rare flashes of companionship which come only when clean and honorable spirits recognize one another, all consciousness of sex was lost between them. The girl's gaze met the man's level, and was held in a long, silent regard.

"Yes," she said simply; and the heart of Average Jones rose and swore a high loyalty.

"Listen, then. I think I see a clear way. Judge Ackroyd will kill the dog if he can, and so effectually conceal the body that no funeral can be held over it, thereby rendering your grandmother's bequest to you void. He has only a few days to do it in, but I don't think that all your watchfulness can restrain him. Now, on the other hand, if the dog should die a natural death and be buried, he can still contest the will. But if he should kill Peter Paul and hide the body where we could discover it, the game would be up for him, as he then wouldn't even dare to come into court with a contest. Do you follow me?"

"Yes. But you wouldn't ask me to be a party to any such thing."

"You're a party, involuntarily, by remaining here. But do your best to save Peter Paul, if you will. And please call me up immediately at the Cosmic Club, if anything in my line turns up."

"What is your line?" asked Miss Graham, the smile returning to her lips. "Creepy, crawly bugs? Or imperiled dogs? Or rescuing prospectively distressed damsels?"

"Technically it's advertising," replied Average Jones, who had been formulating a shrewd little plan of his own. "Let me recommend to you the advertising columns of the daily press. They're often amusing. Moreover, your uncle might break out in print again. Who knows?"

"Who, indeed? I'll read religiously."

"And, by the way, my beetles. I forgot and left them here. Oh, there's the box. I may have a very specific use for them later. *Au revoir*—and may it be soon!"

The two days succeeding seemed to Average Jones, haunted as he was by an importunate craving to look again into Miss Graham's limpid and changeful eyes, a dull and sodden period of probation. The messenger boy who finally brought her expected note, looked to him like a Greek godling. The note enclosed this clipping:

> LOST—Pug dog answering to the name of Peter Paul. Very old and asthmatic. Last seen on West 16th Street. Liberal reward for information to ANXIOUS. Care of *Banner* office.

Dear Mr. Jones (she had written)*:*
Are you a prophet? (Average Jones chuckled, at this point.) *The enclosed seems to be distinctly in our line. Could you come some time this afternoon? I'm puzzled and a little anxious.*

> *Sincerely yours,*
> *Sylvia Graham.*

Average Jones could, and did. He found Miss Graham's piquant face under the stress of excitement, distinctly more alluring than before.

"Isn't it strange?" she said, holding out a hand in welcome. "Why should any one advertise for my Peter Paul? He isn't lost."

"I am glad to hear that," said the caller gravely.

"I've kept my promise, you see," pursued the girl. "Can you do as well, and live up to your profession of aid?"

"Try me."

"Very well, do you know what that advertisement means?"

"Perfectly."

"Then you're a very extraordinary person."

"Not in the least. I wrote it."

"Wrote it! You? Well—really! Why in the world did *you* write it?"

"Because of an unconquerable longing to see"—Average Jones paused, and his quick glance caught the storm signal in her eyes— "your uncle," he concluded calmly.

For one fleeting instant a dimple flickered at the corner of her mouth. It departed. But departing, it swept the storm before it.

"What do you want to see uncle about, if it isn't an impertinent question?"

"It is, rather," returned the young man judicially. "Particularly, as I'm not sure, myself. I may want to quarrel with him."

"You won't have the slightest difficulty in that," the girl assured him.

She rang the bell, despatched a servant, and presently Judge Ackroyd stalked into the room. As Average Jones was being presented, he took comprehensive note and estimate of the broad-cheeked, thin-lipped face; the square shoulders and corded neck, and the lithe and formidable carriage of the man. Judge "Oily" Ackroyd's greeting of the guest within his gates did not bear out the *sobriquet* of his public life. It was curt to the verge of harshness.

"What is the market quotation on beetles, Judge?" asked the young man, tapping the rug with his stick.

"What are you talking about?" demanded the other, drawing down his heavy brows.

"The black beetle; the humble but brisk haunter of household crevices," explained Average Jones. "You advertised for ten thousand specimens. I've got a few thousand I'd like to dispose of, if the inducements are sufficient."

"I'm in no mood for joking, young man," retorted the other, rising.

"You seldom are, I understand," replied Average Jones blandly. "Well, if you won't talk about bugs, let's talk about dogs."

"The topic does not interest me, sir," retorted the other, and the glance of his eye was baleful, but uneasy.

The tapping of the young man's cane ceased. He looked up into his host's glowering face with a seraphic and innocent smile.

"Not even if it—er—touched upon a device for guarding the street corners in case—er—Peter Paul went walking—er—once too often?"

Judge Ackroyd took one step forward. Average Jones was on his feet instantly, and, even in her alarm, Sylvia Graham noticed how swiftly and naturally his whole form "set." But the big man turned away, and abruptly left the room.

"Were you wise to anger him?" asked the girl, as the heavy tread died away on the stairs.

"Sometimes open declaration of war is the soundest strategy."

"War?" she repeated. "You make me feel like a traitor to my own family."

"That's the unfortunate part of it," he said; "but it can't be helped."

"You spoke of having some one guard the corners of the block," continued the girl, after a thoughtful silence. "Do you think I'd better arrange for that?"

"No need. There'll be a hundred people on watch."

"Have you called out the militia?" she asked, twinkling.

"Better than that. I've employed the tools of my trade."

He handed her a galley proof marked with many corrections. She ran through it with growing amazement.

HAVE YOU SEEN THE DOG?

$100—One Hundred Dollars—$100

FOR THE BEST ANSWER IN 500 WORDS

OPEN TO ALL HIGH SCHOOL BOYS

Between now and next Saturday an old Pug Dog will come out of a big House on West 16th Street, between 5th and 6th Avenues. It may be by Day. It may be any hour of the Night. Now, you Boys, get to work.

REMEMBER: $100 IN CASH

HERE ARE THE POINTS TO MIND—

1—Description of Dog.
2—Description of Person with him.
3—Description of House he Comes from.
4—Account of Where they Go.
5—Account of What they Do.

Manuscripts must be written plainly and mailed within twenty-four hours of the discovery of the dog to

A. JONES : AD-VISOR,

ASTOR COURT TEMPLE, NEW YORK

"That will appear in every New York paper to-morrow morning," explained its deviser.

"I see," said the girl. "Any one who attempts to take Peter Paul away will be tracked by a band of boy detectives. A stroke of genius, Mr. Average Jones."

She curtsied low to him. But Average Jones was in no mood for playfulness now.

"That restricts the judge's endeavors to the house and garden," said he, "since, of course he'll see the advertisement."

"I'll see that he does," said Miss Graham maliciously.

"Good! I'll also ask you to watch the garden for any suspicious excavating."

"Very well. But is that all?" Miss Graham's voice was wistful.

"Isn't it enough?"

"You've been so good to me," she said hesitantly. "I don't like to think of you as setting those boys to an impossible task."

"Oh, bless you!" returned the Ad-Visor heartily; "that's all arranged for. One of my men will duly parade with a canine especially obtained for the occasion. I'm not going to swindle the youngsters."

"It didn't seem like you," returned Miss Graham warmly. "But you must let me pay for it, that and the advertising bill."

"As an unauthorized expense—" he began.

She laid a small, persuasive hand on his arm.

"You must let me pay it. Won't you?"

Average Jones was conscious of a strange sensation, starting from the point where the firm, little hand lay. It spread in his veins and thickened his speech.

"Of course," he drawled, uncertainly, "if you—er—put it— er—that way!"

The hand lifted. "Mr. Average Jones," said the owner, "do you know you haven't once disappointed me in speech or action during our short but rather eventful acquaintance?"

"I hope you'll be able to say the same ten years from now," he returned significantly.

She flushed a little at the implication. "What am I to do next?" she asked.

"Do as you would ordinarily do; only don't take Peter Paul into the street, or you'll have a score of high-school boys trailing you. And—this is the most important—if the dog fails to answer your call at any time, and you can't readily find him by searching, telephone me, at once, at my office. Good-by."

"I think you are a very staunch friend to those who need you," she said, gravely and sweetly, giving him her hand.

She clung in his mind like a remembered fragrance, after he had gone back to Astor Court Temple to wait. And though he plunged into an intricate scheme of political advertising which was to launch a new local party, her eyes and her voice haunted him. Nor had he banished them, when, two days later, the telephone brought him her clear accents, a little tremulous now.

"Peter Paul is gone."

"Since when?"

"Since ten this morning. The house is in an uproar."

"I'll be up in half an hour at the latest."

"Do come quickly. I'm—I'm a little frightened."

"Then you must have something to do," said Average Jones decisively. "Have you been keeping an eye on the garden?"

"Yes."

"Go through it again, looking carefully for signs of disarranged earth. I don't think you'll find it, but it's well to be sure. Let me in at the basement door at half-past one. Judge Ackroyd mustn't see me."

It was a strangely misshapen presentation of the normally spick-and-span Average Jones that gently rang the basement bell of the old house at the specified hour. All his pockets bulged with lumpy angles. Immediately, upon being admitted by Miss Graham herself, he proceeded to disemburden himself of box after box, such as elastic bands come in, all exhibiting a homogeneous peculiarity, a hole at one end thinly covered with a gelatinous substance.

"Be very careful not to let that get broken," he instructed the mystified girl. "In the course of an hour or so it will melt away itself. Did you see anything suspicious in the garden?"

"No!" replied the girl. She picked up one of the boxes. "How odd!" she cried. "Why, there's something in it that's alive!"

"Very much so. Your friends, the beetles, in fact."

"What! Again? Aren't you carrying the joke rather far?"

"It's not a joke any more. It's deadly serious. I'm quite sure," he concluded in the manner of one who picks his words carefully, "that it may turn out to be just the most serious matter in the world to me."

"As bad as that?" she queried, but the color that flamed in her cheeks belied the lightness of her tone.

"Quite. However, that must wait. Where is your uncle?"

"Up-stairs in his study."

"Do you think you could take me all through the house some time this afternoon without his seeing me?"

"No, I'm sure I couldn't. He's been wandering like an uneasy spirit since Peter Paul disappeared. And he won't go out, because he is packing."

"So much the worse, either for him or me. Where are your rooms?"

"On the second floor."

"Very well. Now, I want one of these little boxes left in every room in the house, if possible, except on your floor, which is probably out of the reckoning. Do you think you could manage it soon?"

"I think so. I'll try."

"Do most of the rooms open into one another?"

"Yes, all through the house."

"Please see that they're all unlocked, and as far as possible, open. I'll be here at four o'clock, and will call for Judge Ackroyd. You must be sure that he receives me. Tell him it is a matter of great importance. It is."

"You're putting a fearful strain on my feminine curiosity," said Miss Graham, the provocative smile quirking at the corners of her mouth.

"Doubtless," returned the other dryly. "If you strictly follow directions, I'll undertake to satisfy it in time. Four o'clock sharp, I'll be here. Don't be frightened whatever happens. You keep ready, but out of the way, until I call you. Good-by."

With even more than his usual nicety was Average Jones attired, when, at four o'clock, he sent his card to Judge Ackroyd. Small favor, however, did his appearance find, in the scowling eyes of the judge.

"What do *you* want?" he growled.

"I'll take a cigar, thank you very much," said Average Jones innocently.

"You'll take your leave, or state your business."

"It has to do with your niece."

"Then what do you take my time for, damn your impudence?"

"Don't swear." Average Jones was deliberately provoking the older man to an outbreak. "Let's—er—sit down and—er—be chatty."

The drawl, actually an evidence of excitement, had all the effect of studied insolence. Judge Ackroyd's big frame shook.

"I'm going to k-k-kick you out into the street, you young p-p-p-pup," he stuttered in his rage.

His knotted fingers writhed out for a hold on the other's collar. With a sinuous movement, the visitor swerved aside and struck the other man, flat-handed, across the face. There was an answering howl of demoniac fury. Then a strange thing happened. The assailant turned and fled, not to the ready egress of the front door, but down the dark stairway to the basement. The judge thundered after, in maddened, unthinking pursuit. Average Jones ran fleetly and easily. And his running was not for the purpose of flight alone, for as he sped through the basement rooms, he kept casting swift glances from side to side, and up and down the walls. The heavy-weight pursuer could not get nearer than half-a-dozen paces.

From the kitchen Average Jones burst into the hallway, doubled back up the stairs and made a tour of the big drawing-rooms and living-rooms of the first floor. Here, too, his glance swept room after room, from floor to ceiling. The chase then led upward to the second floor, and by direct ascent to the third. Breathing heavily, Judge Ackroyd lumbered after the more active man. In his dogged rage, he never thought to stop and block the hallway; but trailed his quarry like a bloodhound through every room of the third floor, and upward to the fourth. Halfway up this stairway, Average Jones checked his speed and surveyed the hall above. As he started again he stumbled and sprawled. A more competent observer than the infuriated pursuer might have noticed that he fell cunningly. But Judge Ackroyd gave a shout of savage triumph and increased his speed. He stretched his hand to grip the fugitive. It had almost touched him when he leaped to his feet and resumed his flight.

"I'll get you now!" panted the judge.

The fourth floor of the old house was almost bare. In a hall-embrasure hung a full-length mirror. All along the borders of this, Average Jones' quick-ranging vision had discerned small red-banded objects which moved and shifted. As the glass reflected his extended figure, it showed, almost at the same instant, the outstretched, bony hand of "Oily" Ackroyd. With a snarl, half rage, half satisfaction, the pursuer hurled himself forward—and fell, with a plunge that rattled the house's old bones. For, as he reached, Jones, trained on many a foot-ball field, had whirled and dived at his knees. Before the fallen man could gather his shaken wits, he was pinned with the most disabling grip known in the science of combat, a strangle-hold with the assailant's wrist clamped in below and behind the ear. Average Jones lifted his voice and the name that came to his lips was the name that had lurked subconsciously, in his heart, for days.

"Sylvia!" he cried. "The fourth floor! Come!"

There was a stir and a cry from two floors below. Sylvia Graham had broken from the grasp of her terrified aunt, and now came up the sharp ascent like a deer, her eyes blazing with resolve and courage.

"The mirror," said Average Jones. "Push it aside. Pull it down. Get behind it somehow. Lie quiet, Ackroyd or I'll have to choke your worthless head off!"

With an effort of nervous strength, the girl lifted aside the big glass. Behind it a hundred scarlet-banded insects swarmed and scampered.

"It's a panel. Open it."

She tugged at the woodwork with quick, clever fingers. A section loosened and fell outward with a bang. The red-and-black beetles fled in all directions. And now, Judge Ackroyd found his voice.

"Help!" he roared. "Murder!"

The sinewy pressure of Average Jones' wrist smothered further attempts at vocality to a gurgle. He looked up into Sylvia Graham's tense face, and jerked his head toward the opening.

"Unless my little detectives have deceived me," he said, "you'll find the body in there."

She groped, and drew forth a large box. In it was packed the body of Peter Paul. There was a cord about the fat neck.

"Strangled," whispered the girl. "Poor old doggie!" Then she whirled upon the prostrate man. "You murderer!" she said very low.

"It's not murder to put a dying brute out of the way," said the shaken man sullenly.

"But it's fraud, in this case," retorted Average Jones. "A fraud of which you're self-convicted. Get up." He himself rose and stepped back, but his eye was intent, and his muscles were in readiness.

There was no more fight in Judge "Oily" Ackroyd. He slunk to the stairs and limped heavily down to his frightened and sobbing wife. Miss Graham leaned against the wall, white and spent. Average Jones, his heart in his eyes, took a step forward.

"No!" she said peremptorily. "Don't touch me. I shall be all right."

"Do you mind my saying," said he, very low, "that you are the bravest and finest human being I've met in a-a-somewhat varied career."

The girl shuddered. "I could have stood it all," she said, "but for those awful, crawling, red creatures."

"Those?" said Average Jones. "Why, they were my bloodhounds, my little detectives. There's nothing very awful about those, Sylvia. They've done their work as nature gave 'em to do it. I knew that as soon as they got out, they would find the trail."

"And what are they?"

"Carrion beetles," said Average Jones. "Where the vultures of the insect kingdom are gathered together, there the quarry lies."

Sylvia Graham drew a long breath. "I'm all right now," she pronounced. "There's nothing left, I suppose, but to leave this house. And to thank you. How am I ever to thank you?" She lifted her eyes to his.

"Never mind the thanks," said Average Jones unevenly. "It was nothing."

"It was—everything! It was wonderful!" cried the girl, and held out her slender hands to him.

As they clasped warmly upon his, Average Jones' reason lost its balance. He forgot that he was in that house on an equivocal footing; he forgot that he had exposed and disgraced Sylvia Graham's near relative; he forgot that this was but his third meeting with Sylvia Graham herself; he forgot everything except that the sum total of all that was sweetest and finest and most desirable in womanhood stood warm and vivid before him; and, bending over the little, clinging hands, he pressed his lips to them. Only for a moment. The hands slipped from his. There was a quick, frightened gasp, and the girl's face, all aflush with a new, sweet fearfulness and wondering confusion, vanished behind a ponderous swinging door.

The young man's knees shook a little as he walked forward and put his lips close to the lintel.

"Sylvia."

There was a faint rustle from within.

"I'm sorry. I mean, I'm glad. Gladder than of anything I've ever done in my life."

Silence from within.

"If I've frightened you, forgive me. I couldn't help it. It was stronger than I. This isn't the place where I can tell you. Sylvia, I'm going now."

No answer.

"The work is done," he continued. "You won't need me any more. (Did he hear, from within, a faint indrawn breath?) Not for any help that I can give. But I—I shall need you always, and long for you. Listen, there mustn't be any misunderstanding about this, dear. If you send for me, it must be because you want me; knowing that, when I come, I shall come for you. Good-by, dear."

"Good-by." It was the merest whisper from behind the door. But it echoed in the tones of a thousand golden hopes and dismal fears in the whirling brain of Average Jones as he walked, unseeingly, back to his offices.

Two days later he sat at his desk, in a murk of woe. Nor word nor sign had come to him from Miss Sylvia Graham. He frowned heavily as Simpson entered the inner sanctum with the usual packet of clippings.

"Leave them," he ordered.

"Yes, sir." The confidential clerk lingered, looking uncomfortable. "Anything from yesterday's lot, sir?"

"Haven't looked them over yet."

"Or day before's?"

"Haven't taken those up either."

"Pardon me, Mr. Jones, but—are you ill, sir?"

"No," snapped Average Jones.

"Ramson is inquiring whether he shall ship more beetles. I see in the paper that Judge Ackroyd has sailed for Europe on six hours' notice, so I suppose you won't want any more?"

Average Jones mentioned a destination for Ramson's beetles deeper than they had ever digged for prey.

"Yes, sir," assented Simpson. "But if I might suggest, there's a very interesting advertisement in yesterday's paper repeated this morn—"

"I don't want to see it."

"No, sir. But—but still—it—it seems to have a strange reference to the burial of the million-dollar dog, and an invitation that I thought—"

"Where is it? Give it to me!" For once in his life, high pressure of excitement had blotted out Average Jones' drawl. His employee thrust into his hand this announcement from the *Banner* of that morning:

DIED—At 100 West 16th Street, Sept. 14, Peter Paul, a dog, for many years the faithful and fond companion of the late Amelia Van Haltern. Burial in accordance with the wish and will of Mrs. Van Haltern, at the family estate, Schuylkill, Sept. 17, at 3 o'clock. His friend, Don Quixote, is especially bidden to come, if he will.

Average Jones leaped to his feet. "My parable," he cried. "Don Quixote and the damsel in distress. Where's my hat? Where's the time-table? Get a cab! Simpson, you idiot, why didn't you make me read this before, confound you! I mean God bless you. Your salary's doubled from to-day. I'm off."

"Yes, sir," said the bewildered Simpson, "but about Ramson's beetles?"

"Tell him to turn 'em out to pasture and keep 'em as long as they live, at my expense," called back Average Jones as the door slammed behind him.

Miss Sylvia Graham looked down upon a slender finger ornamented with the oddest and the most appropriate of engagement rings, a scarab beetle red-banded with three deep-hued rubies.

"But, Average," she said, and the golden laughter flickered again in the brown depths of her eyes, "not even you could expect a girl to accept a man through a keyhole."

"I suppose not," said Average Jones with a sigh of profoundest content. "Some are for privacy in these matters; others for publicity. But I suppose I'm the first man in history who ever got his heart's answer in an advertisement."

THE END

READING GROUP GUIDE

1. How do you feel about Average Jones as a person? Do you find his attitudes affected or pretentious? If so, do you think that that was Adams's intention?

2. Do you find the stories realistic, in the sense that they could have really happened?

3. How does Adams's use of contemporary social and political issues in his stories compare to current writers of crime fiction? What kinds of cases might Average Jones pursue today?

4. If you've read English "golden age" detective fiction (e.g., Agatha Christie, Dorothy Sayers, Margery Allingham), do you agree that Adams presaged some of the same tropes that those writers would adopt?

5. Do you think that the Average Jones stories are particularly American? Why wouldn't the stories work in, say, England?

6. Which of the stories was your favorite? Why?

FURTHER READING

BY SAMUEL HOPKINS ADAMS:

Selected Fiction

The Mystery (together with Stewart Edward White). New York: McClure, Phillips, 1907.

The Secret of Lonesome Cove. Indianapolis: Bobbs-Merrill, 1912.

Flaming Youth. New York: Boni and Liveright, 1923. Under pseudonym Warner Fabian.

Sailors' Wives. New York: Boni and Liveright, 1924. Under pseudonym Warner Fabian.

The Flagrant Years: A Novel of the Beauty Market. New York: H. Liveright, 1929.

The Men in Her Life. New York: Sears Publishing, 1930. Under pseudonym Warner Fabian.

The Gorgeous Hussy. Boston: Houghton Mifflin, 1934.

It Happened One Night. Akron, OH: Saalfield Publishing, 1935. With Robert Riskin, screenwriter of the 1934 film.

The Harvey Girls. New York: Random House, 1942.

Chingo Smith of the Erie Canal. New York: Random House, 1958. Juvenile.

Tenderloin. New York: Random House, 1959. Published posthumously.

Selected Nonfiction

The Great American Fraud. New York: P. F. Collier and Son, 1905.

The Adams Articles. New York: Trow Press, 1915.

The Pony Express. New York: Random House, 1950. Juvenile.

The Erie Canal. New York: Random House, 1953. Juvenile.

BY OTHER WRITERS:

Chesterton, G. K. *The Innocence of Father Brown*. London: Cassell, 1911.

Futrelle, Jacques. *The Thinking Machine*. New York: Dodd, 1907.

Post, Melville Davisson. *Uncle Abner, Master of Mysteries*. New York: D. Appleton, 1918.

Reeve, Arthur B. *The Silent Bullet*. Naperville, IL: Sourcebooks in association with the Library of Congress, 2021. First published by Dodd (New York) in 1912.

CRITICAL STUDIES:

Kennedy, Samuel V., III. *Samuel Hopkins Adams and the Business of Writing*. Syracuse, NY: Syracuse University Press, 1999.

Weinberg, Arthur and Lila, eds. *The Muckrakers*. New York: Simon & Schuster, 1961.

Wilson, Harold S. McClure's Magazine *and the Muckrakers*. Princeton, NJ: Princeton University Press, 1970.

ABOUT THE AUTHOR

Crime fiction was only a small part of the body of work of Samuel Hopkins Adams (1871–1958). Born on January 26, 1871, in Dunkirk, New York, in the western part of the state, on Lake Erie, Adams was the only child of the Reverend Myron Adams Junior and Hester Rose Hopkins Adams. He proudly traced his ancestry to Henry Adams and the deeply rooted Hopkins family. The Adamses soon moved to Rochester, and Sam began spending summers in Auburn, a smaller industrial city where much of the Adams and Hopkins extended family lived. In the words of his biographer Samuel V. Kennedy, "The independence of his father, the humanness of his grandfather Hopkins who scorned pretension, the love of life of his grandfather Adams, the forcefulness of his mother, and the appreciation for a good story, well told, all left their marks."[*] In 1887, Adams traveled east to Clinton, New York, to attend Hamilton College, the alma mater of many of his family.[†]

While at Hamilton, Adams dreamed of a career as a writer.

---

[*] Samuel V. Kennedy III, *Samuel Hopkins Adams and the Business of Writing* (Syracuse, NY: Syracuse University Press, 1999), 11.

[†] Adams made his creation Average Jones a Hamilton alumnus as well.

He later recalled, "In that bright dream, I strode up and down a spacious and orderly library, rustling richly in a silken robe, whilst dictating without pause or check, page upon page of fluent romance to a fair, scholarly, and awed private secretary."* In reality, he began writing poems, essays, and short stories for campus publications. When he graduated from Hamilton, he moved to New York City and, in August 1891, joined the staff of the New York *Sun*, edited by the legendary Charles A. Dana. There, Adams developed a fondness for both science and realism. He embraced the Progressive movement, but most importantly, he learned the importance of facts. In 1896, he began supplementing his newspaper work with magazine writing, his first piece a nonfiction article for *Scribner's Magazine* about the management of department stores. At the same time, he was covering the sensational trial of Miss Mary Alice Almont Livingston (who called herself Mrs. Fleming), accused of poisoning her mother, for the *Sun*. A year later, he published his first short story. This was a melodramatic tale called "Blinky," about a young newsboy and a girl with tuberculosis. The story is noteworthy, however, for the strain of indignation at the condition of the New York slums. This was Adams's first foray into "muckraking," the new school of writing that had as its goal public exposure of misconduct and corruption.

In 1898, Adams married Elizabeth R. Noyes, and by 1900, they had their first child, a daughter, Hester.† He lost confidence in his future as a newspaperman and began concentrating on magazine writing, joining the staff of *McClure's Magazine*. Here he handled advertising and promotion (especially books), but he found himself watching from the sidelines as *McClure's* plunged

---

* Samuel Hopkins Adams, "How I Write," *The Writer* (April 1936), 107.

† Adams had a second daughter by Beth, Katherine Noyes Adams, later Mrs. Cecil Adell. Hester died in 1991, Katherine in 1992.

into publishing "exposures"—condemnations of corrupt politics and business practices—including Ida Tarbell's history of
Standard Oil, Lincoln Steffens's "The Shame of Minneapolis,"
and Ray Stannard Baker's "Right to Work." Adams soon joined
their ranks, with a piece of investigative journalism into a wrong-
ful conviction, published in 1904. Yearning for his own niche,
he began turning to public health investigations. In 1905, he
delivered the first of a six-part series called "The Great American
Fraud," in which he took on the patent medicine industry. Based
on meticulous research, he gloried in combat with his oppo-
nents. In 1906, with Adams's investigations fueling many of
the debates, Congress at last passed the Pure Food and Drug
Act, which aimed to curtail the sale of nostrums. "Adams was at
the apex of his career as a muckraker," observes his biographer
Samuel Kennedy.[*]

But Adams wanted a broader career path. An adventure-mystery
novel several years in the making, *The Mystery*, cowritten with
his friend Stewart Edward White, appeared serially in *American
Illustrated Magazine*[†] beginning in May 1906. Based on the 1872
abandonment of the ship *Mary Celeste*, it was published as a novel
in 1908. Adams also continued to write extensively about public
health. His marriage broke up,[‡] probably in significant part due
to his extended writing commitments (including covering the
twelve-week Harry Kendall Thaw murder trial), and Adams traveled to Europe to continue researching public health issues. Like
many journalists, he also transitioned into writing more and more
fiction. He wrote his first mystery story, "Forsaken Mountain,"
for *Collier's*, published in 1906, and penned several more before

---

[*] Kennedy, *Samuel Hopkins Adams*, 57.

[†] Renamed *American Magazine* before the serial was complete.

[‡] Adams divorced Beth Noyes in 1907.

beginning work on "The Flying Death," a serial for *McClure's* about a series of murders (later published as a novel in 1908).

The year 1910 found Adams traveling to California to visit his friend White. He continued to write about public health, but at the same time he was weighing the idea of detective fiction. The result was a series of short stories about Average Jones, a wealthy young man with a "hobby" of detection. This was a short-lived creation, however. By 1911, Adams abandoned the character to try his hand at another detective, the scientific sleuth Chester Kent, who appeared in four stories. The most successful was a novel, *The Secret of Lonesome Cove*, published in 1912 by Bobbs-Merrill, the publisher of his *Average Jones* collection. It garnered weak reviews, and although two more stories about Kent would appear, Adams was through with him too. In a 1916 letter to a journalist, Adams confirmed that he had given up on detective fiction, saying that he had run out of plots.[*]

Of course, Adams's writing career was far from over. In the years after 1912, he published almost fifty more books, including novels (with his more risqué material appearing under the pen name of Werner Fabian); nonfiction; biographies of President Warren G. Harding, Daniel Webster, and his friend and fellow writer Alexander Woollcott; nonfiction works aimed at young readers; books of American history and especially New York State; and memoirs of his grandfather. His appearances in periodicals numbered more than 360, including many columns in which he criticized advertising, under the byline "Ad-Visor" (the same description adopted by Average Jones).

In 1915, after a three-year affair, Adams married the stage actress Jane Peyton. Peyton, who had been married three times

---

[*] Letter to an unknown correspondent dated July 10, 1916, in the Samuel Hopkins Adams papers at the Burke Library, Hamilton College, Clinton, New York.

previously, did not obtain an annulment of her third marriage until only a few weeks before she and Adams wed. However, this marriage lasted, ending only when Jane died in 1946, when Adams was seventy-five.*

Later in his career, Adams's books were recognized as fine fodder for films, and twenty films were adapted from them, including the Oscar-winning *It Happened One Night* (1934), *The Gorgeous Hussy* (starring Joan Crawford in 1936), and the popular *The Harvey Girls* (1945). Three were turned into theatrical performances, including the 1961 Broadway musical *Tenderloin*, based on his last book of the same name.

When Adams died on November 16, 1958, of a heart ailment, the Associated Press obituary named him "one of America's great social reform writers [and] author of such best sellers as 'Flaming Youth' and 'Revelry.'"† The United Press International obituary chose to herald him as a novelist, a biographer, and a chronicler of the Erie Canal who "also wrote crusading magazine articles."‡ His friend Louis Jones, director of the New York State Historical Association, commented, "He never pretended that he was a great literary artist but he was surely what he pretended to be, a master storyteller."§ We remember Adams here for a small fraction of his vast repertoire of tales, those of the brilliant Average Jones.

---

* Jane was also seventy-five years old at the time; she was born exactly four months before Adams, on October 26, 1870.

† Associated Press, "Social Writer Samuel Adams Dies at Age 87," *The Capital Journal* (Salem, Oregon), November 17, 1958, 13.

‡ United Press International, "Samuel Hopkins Adams Is Dead; Novelist and Biographer Was 87," *New York Times*, November 17, 1958, 31.

§ Quoted in Kennedy, *Samuel Hopkins Adams*, 306. At his death, Adams was survived by his two daughters by Beth and Jane's adopted daughter.